THE FEDOROVICH FILE

THE FEDOROVICH FILE

A NOVEL BY

ROSS SPENCER

DⅡF

DONALD I. FINE, INC.
New York

Copyright © 1991 by Ross H. Spencer

Library of Congress Cataloging-in-Publication Data
Spencer, Ross H.
The Fedorovich file / by Ross H. Spencer
p. cm.
ISBN 1-55611-249-1
I. Title
PS3569.P454F43   1991
813'.54—dc20   90-56071
CIP

Manufactured in the United States of America

10 9 8 7 6 5 4 3 2 1

Designed by Irving Perkins Associates

S

To the dreams I have lost and will never retrieve,
To the jungle of thought where I hid,
To all of the people who didn't believe,
And to Shirley R. Spencer, who did.

ROSS H. SPENCER

1 LATER, MUCH LATER, when most of the Devereaux matter had soaked in and the rest of it had trickled off, he'd taken to spending his evenings at the tiny four-stool bar in the basement of the modest residence on North Dunlap Avenue, listening to ragtime piano from the tape recorder on the backbar, sipping Martell's cognac, looking back.

If looking back wasn't Lacey Lockington's only vice, it was probably his favorite. He found it dependably comforting, that certain knowledge that the past had *been*, that for better or for worse it was *there*, unalterable, even by God. It provided a substantiality in a world swarming with uncertainties, and Lockington clung to it like a bulldog to a bone, living for the moment at hand, because he was never fully convinced that the future would ever arrive or that he'd be around to see it if it did.

Lockington had spent the biggest piece of his life sitting on the rim of one volcano or another, and he'd developed a severe case of fatalism—if it was going to blow it was going to blow. He couldn't escape it, he was powerless to delay it, and once fully cognizant of these facts, he'd discovered that he didn't much give a damn one way or the other.

At ten-thirty in the evening or thereabouts, his dribble of thought would subside and his faraway gaze would return to focus, shifting to Natasha Gorky curled in her white satin pajamas on their basement couch with a glass of Smirnoff vodka and a bulky book on American government and its processes, her tight little buttocks canted saucily in his direction, their division line curling into that dark infinity between her legs.

Natasha wasn't a United States citizen and she hadn't filed application for that status. Some four months earlier she'd walked out on the Chicago Polish Consulate and the KGB, but she'd made no move toward requesting political asylum. She wasn't prepared to accept United States citizenship yet, but she *would* be, she'd assured him. She was working on it.

Lockington had ventured the observation that a few dozen more volumes would probably qualify her for political office, at *least* the Ohio State Legislature, and she'd winked at him, remarking that when she was ready, she'd be on the ballot. And because she was so unusually gifted, and because she was so damned beautiful, and because he was head over heels in love with her, he'd volunteered to become her campaign manager.

Natasha Gorky was all he had, more than he'd ever *hoped* to have. She'd probably saved his life in late May and he'd thanked her for that. In early June, she'd certainly used him shamelessly, and she'd offered her apologies. They'd called the account square as lovers are wont to do, particularly when they're early in love, which they'd been at that time, and still were.

At eleven o'clock, Lockington would turn on the television set on a wall shelf and watch the local news, or as much of it as he could stand. He'd cap his bottle of Martell's cognac, leaving his barstool to walk to the couch and extend his hand to Natasha. She'd nod, take it, closing her book, and they'd climb the stairs in anticipatory silence.

It'd become a nightly ritual, unvarying until they stepped through their bedroom doorway into unpredictability. From that moment through their next hour or so, there'd been no telling what the hell was likely to happen in there. Never had it been twice the same. Lockington had taken no credit for this—at forty-nine years he was humbly grateful for Natasha's favors. She'd managed to convince him that he was far more accomplished than he'd thought he was, he'd experienced soaring sensations, his successes had built on successes in the fashion of compound interest, and all of this had been due to the fact that Natasha Gorky was very good in bed.

Although never a womanizer as defined by Webster, Lacey Lockington had known women—their hills and valleys, their warm nooks and moist crannies were not strange to him— but never, *ever*, had he encountered anything that could have gotten to within miles of Natasha Gorky. Natasha had been a KGB agent and a damned good one. Sex is a highly effective tool in the espionage game, Lockington was aware of that— it'd been that way since Delilah had introduced the crewcut, and it followed that a female operative's sexual proficiency would bear strong influence on her chances of discovering where the bear had burped in the buckwheat—but what had always puzzled Lockington was how the CIA, the KGB, the SSD, MI.6, the Mossad, and other world-class cloak and dagger organizations managed to come upon ladies eager to shed and spread for God and country. He'd pondered the subject, and one night before they'd drifted off to sleep, he'd put the question to Natasha. How had she been recruited?

Around a yawn, Natasha had informed Lockington that she *hadn't* been *recruited*, she'd *volunteered*.

For *sex*?

Oh, no, no, *no*—for the *KGB*! Her numerous qualifications and her strong backing notwithstanding, it'd taken her nearly two years to gain admission to the KGB Academy— background security checks and that sort of thing—the sex business had come quite a long time following her acceptance.

Uh-huh. And what had 'quite a long time' amounted to?

Well, let's see—it'd happened a bit over a year into her training period. They'd called her in and they'd laid it on the line—could she go to bed with a man for Mother Russia? She'd said of course.

Just like *that*?

Natasha had said certainly, just like that.

Lockington had said oh.

Natasha had said that there'd been an instruction period of several months.

Uhh-h-h, just what *kind* of instruction?

What *kind* of instruction? *Sexual* instruction, what *else*?

This had been on a purely voluntary basis?

Purely voluntary, yes.

Sexual instruction? Sexual instruction by *whom*?

Skilled personnel, obviously. People who knew the answers. Female instructors, naturally.

Both sexes.

Both at the same goddam *time*?

Well, now, *really*, there'd be no other way it'd *work*, would there?

This had happened with the *lights* on?

Yes, how else could they possibly have graded her performance?

Had she received good grades?

She'd been second in a class of forty-six.

Lockington had whistled, low and long.

She'd have been first if Katerina Kruska hadn't cheated— Ilya had faked orgasms.

Well, didn't *all* women fake a few orgasms?

Natasha had propped herself on an elbow to stare at him. It'd been a withering stare. She'd said that when she had to fake orgasms, she'd stop *doing* it. She'd never faked an orgasm in her *life*.

But, Jesus Christ, hadn't it been difficult with others *watching*?

Just a trifle at the beginning, perhaps, but she'd gotten over that. It'd been for her country, you see.

Lockington had said, "I see." But he hadn't, not even a little bit.

She'd fallen asleep then, her head on his chest, breathing slowly, deeply, and Lockington had stroked her auburn pixie hairdo, staring at the ceiling, thinking that he'd gotten out of sync with reality somewhere back there, probably in the vicinity of the same place he'd fallen in love with Natasha Gorky.

2 HE WAS A LONG WAY from Chicago, Illinois—four hundred and twenty-five miles, give or take a few axe handles. He'd turned against the giant gray city on the lake, or, more accurately, *it* had turned against *him*. There'd been a time when Lacey Lockington had cared deeply for Chicago, regarding it with that same understanding affection one tends to accord a drunken uncle in the family. *This* drunken uncle had turned vicious, not merely violent on occasion—most drunken uncles have their violent streaks, these are acceptable to a point—but Chicago had become a *jungle*, its Union Station a dark, dank refuge for vagrants and panhandlers, its Grant Park a dispatching center for muggers and rapists. Chicago's neighborhoods were deteriorating in the track of the storm. The South Side, always an excellent place to stay the hell away from, was downright life-threatening, its North and West Sides weren't a great deal better. There were the suburbs, of course, Wilmette and Elmwood Park and LaGrange and Blue Island—they hadn't gone down yet, but they'd get there. Lockington had never been a suburbanite in fact or in fancy, he'd been a Chicagoan, born and bred, and if you can't be an honest-to-God Chicagoan, why lollygag around on the fringes? It'd boiled down to a matter of staying in or getting out, and Lockington had gotten out. He'd packed it in midway through the first week in June and, thus far, he hadn't experienced the slightest urge to return, even for a brief visit.

He sat on his office bench in the heat of the Mahoning Valley October afternoon, paging disinterestedly through the month-old sports magazine he'd paged disinterestedly through four or five times during the previous week, smoking one of the few cigarettes remaining in the crumpled pack he'd popped that morning, waiting for the door to open, or the telephone to ring, or the roof to cave in. *Some*thing, *any*thing.

LACEY LOCKINGTON WAS a big man, not big by professional sports standards, but big enough, heavy-shouldered, narrow-hipped, dark-haired with touches of silver at the temples. He had steely-gray eyes, a slightly hawkish nose that'd been busted three times, maybe four, he wasn't sure. He had a tight, thin-lipped mouth, a cleft, resolute chin, and capable looking hands with upturned thumbs—upturned thumbs being a sign of self-confidence, he'd been told, but he doubted that.

He was nearly one full day into his second week of occupancy of the 12′ × 20′ enclosure at the northwestern tip of the Mahoning Avenue Shopping Plaza. It'd been a candy shop—it still reeked of cheap chocolate—and the sign on its north window had cost him one hundred and thirty-five dollars. It said CONFIDENTIAL INVESTIGATIONS in large, red-shadowed white block lettering. They'd visited a second hand office furniture store in Austintown. Natasha had selected the desk and the swivel chair and the wooden bench that stood by the west window. Lockington had chosen the two pictures that hung on the wall behind the desk, one a reproduction of Gabby Hartnett's Wrigley Field homer in the gloaming, the other a blowup of a photograph of the first triple dead heat in American thoroughbred racing history—Bossuet, Wait-A-Bit, and Brownie, all right there, noses on the wire. Then Natasha had hung the drapes, and the room had been tastefully enough done, he supposed, but he'd grown increasingly weary in it because there's probably nothing quite so exhausting as inactivity, and Lockington had run into a surplus of it. There'd been a couple of highlights—a tousle-headed blonde girl had opened the door a crack, tossing in a pizza circular, and a fat man wearing a Cleveland Indians cap had come in to ask Lockington to sign a petition, and Lockington had signed the damned thing, having not the remotest idea of what it objected to, and not caring enough to find out.

Occasionally, along about noon, Natasha would break the monotony by stopping by in the 1978 white Buick Regal she'd purchased in Lockington's name. It had cost seventeen hundred dollars and it was a sharp little automobile with less than 60,000 on the clock. Natasha had insisted that Lockington drive her black Mercedes—she wanted him to look prestigious, she'd told him. Lockington would hang his BACK AT 1:00 sign on the door, and they'd go to lunch, usually at Dickey's on North Meridian Road, because the barmaid at Dickey's made excellent vodka martinis. They'd have a few of those and ribeye sandwiches, then Natasha would drive him back to the office and he'd take down his BACK AT 1:00 sign, probably at 1:45, and Natasha would go home and Lockington would page disinterestedly through that same goddamned sports magazine.

When they'd returned to Youngstown, Ohio, in early June, they'd known each other less than a week, and they'd spent fewer than seventy-two hours in each other's company. Theirs had been a spontaneous matchup, the kind that flares with searing intensity before guttering out in the swamp of reality, but it was worth a shot, they'd figured. Natasha had bought the little white and brown house on North Dunlap Avenue, and despite the fact that four months' close association fails to constitute an acid test, it'd been, so far, so wonderful.

Lacey Lockington was forty-nine, Natasha Gorky was working on thirty-one. The age gap had been intimidating, but they were both adults possessing balance and their quotas of sound judgment, they'd shared burnout, and in the lull of fatigue harmony can be found, because disagreement requires a certain amount of energy.

It'd been a honeymoon for unmarrieds. They'd unpacked, hired a neighborhood kid to mow the lawn, switched on the air conditioner, had a few drinks, and then gone to bed for sixteen hours, learning that they liked each other and this was important, because while both viewed sex as a great convenience, neither regarded it as being the end and all of everything.

LOCKINGTON YAWNED and closed the sports magazine, realizing that he'd learned the damned thing word-for-word and that he hadn't read a blessed page of it, that he'd been looking back again.

He wondered just how much of his life had been frittered away on the musing process, which didn't really amount to a *process*, not in Lockington's case. In Lockington's case, it was a trancelike condition that descended unpredictably, departing just as unpredictably, never helping, never hurting, bringing no laughter, leaving no tears, and when it'd gone away, he found himself hard pressed to remember just what the hell he'd been musing about, because it rarely concerned anything of consequence, the period having been a kaleidoscopic span devoid of focus and substance.

It was five o'clock and Lockington secured the office before walking to the florist's shop at the east end of the plaza. He bought the usual single red rose and the elderly lady behind the counter tied the usual silver bow on its stem. He tooled the Mercedes two blocks east, then three blocks north, pulling into the blacktopped drive of the house on the cul-de-sac. Natasha met him at the door, kissing him ferociously as usual. She took the rose, tucking it into her hair, just above her left ear. She slipped a long, covered casserole dish into the oven, prepared frosty vodka martinis with twists of lime, and they sat in the living room, Lockington on the couch, Natasha in the overstuffed chair, nipping at their drinks, smoking, chatting, also as usual. The timer went off and Natasha served up beef stroganoff and a crisp green salad and strawberry shortcake, and when they'd finished eating, she'd worked on straightening up the kitchen. Back in July he'd offered to help her, but she'd shooed him away, remarking that men in kitchens were like dinosaurs in art galleries, so he spent that time of evening watching her.

Natasha Gorky stood five-six, weighed one hundred and eighteen pounds, had large pale blue eyes, an absolutely perfect nose, a full-lipped off-center smile—she was constructed as women should be but hardly ever are, and she moved lightly with the fluid grace of a kitten, alertly intent, quickly, deftly, quietly, her facial expression never changing, efficiency epitomized. Lockington figured that she'd been born that way, because efficiency is a gift that can be polished, but it can't be taught. Natasha didn't make mistakes in the kitchen, or in bed, and she certainly hadn't made any four months earlier when she'd worked with him and against him during the Devereaux affair.

She put away the last of the dinner dishes, folded her towel, and they went down to the basement where Natasha pored over another book on United States government and Lockington listened to ragtime piano music. Following the news, they climbed the stairs and went to bed. It was an excellent life, carefree, relaxed, even idyllic, and it was driving Lacey Lockington bonkers because it was so filled with usualities, if there was such a word, and there probably wasn't, but, what the hell, it worked, so he let it stand.

He hadn't told Natasha that he was bored because he wasn't bored with Natasha, just with the usualities, and he hadn't mentioned the usualities because he knew that boredom invariably precedes change, usually for the worse. Tangling with boredom is like going a couple of rounds with a washed-up heavyweight, Lockington thought—he'll shuffle and he'll grab and he'll hold, but watch out for that old bastard's left hook. It can put your lights out.

3 OCTOBER 9, 1988 / COMMLINK LANGLEY–CHICAGO / CODE 3 UNSCRAMBLED

LINE OPENED LANGLEY 0900 EDT

LANGLEY–CHICAGO / ATTN CARRUTHERS / 0901 EDT
BEGIN TEXT: PER YOUR REQUEST SEATTLE OFFICE
HAS DISPATCHED CHECKMATE YOUNGSTOWN OHIO
/ WORD ON CHECKMATE? / END TEXT / MASSEY

CHICAGO–LANGLEY / ATTN MASSEY / 0803 CDT
BEGIN TEXT: AFFIRMATIVE / CHECKMATE IN
YOUNGSTOWN AWAITING DEVELOPMENTS IF ANY /
END TEXT / CARRUTHERS

LANGLEY–CHICAGO / ATTN CARRUTHERS / 0904 EDT
BEGIN TEXT: DEVELOPMENTS CERTAIN /
CHECKMATE HAS CONTACTED FOXFIRE? / END TEXT
/ MASSEY

CHICAGO–LANGLEY / ATTN MASSEY / 0805 CDT
BEGIN TEXT: NO MENTION BUT ASSUME CONTACT
SOON / END TEXT / CARRUTHERS

LANGLEY–CHICAGO / ATTN CARRUTHERS / 0906 EDT
BEGIN TEXT: HOT ITEM / GLUE TO IT / END TEXT /
MASSEY

CHICAGO–LANGLEY / ATTN MASSEY / 0806 CDT
BEGIN TEXT: WILCO / END TEXT / CARRUTHERS

LINE CLEARED LANGLEY 0907 EDT

4 MONDAY, OCTOBER 10, 1988, dawned chilly and wispy gray. By nine o'clock that morning the sun had burned through the Mahoning Valley mists, the temperature had clambered into the mid-sixties, the skies were cloudless blue, the heavily wooded slopes were yellow, rust, and scarlet, and Lacey Lockington's scowl was blacker than the ace of spades. He parked Natasha's Mercedes, unlocked his office door, ambled into the stuffy little room, and hung his hat on a nail. He flopped into his swivel chair, leaning back, placing his feet squarely in the middle of his desk top. He put a match to a cigarette and began the disconsolate three hour wait for lunchtime. Silence closed in on the big fellow in the tiny room, and his thoughts drifted.

HE'D SPENT what had been left of June and all of July tinkering in the basement, building a closet, installing shelves, paneling a wall. Then he'd done some yard work and he'd painted the garage. Natasha had watched him, saying nothing, until she'd suggested that he get back into harness before he went stark staring insane. He'd argued the point just long enough and in August he'd applied for a Class B license—investigative work only. The required four thousand hours of supervised detection employment had been verified by the Chicago Police Department and Natasha had driven with him to Columbus where he'd taken the State of Ohio examination—five hundred bucks, whether he passed it or not, and he'd romped through it like a dose of salts. Natasha had shelled out five thousand dollars for the required million dollar liability insurance policy, this in the event that Lockington shot a wrong party in the excercise of his office, which had struck him as being a bit on the extravagant side because he'd shot a few people in his time,

11

but never a wrong party. However, the precaution was justified, because in the light of current affairs, you could shoot a man who's holding up a service station with a Browning automatic rifle and find yourself in court the next morning on a charge of disturbing the peace.

Following the exam, they'd stopped for beer and ribs, taken a motel room fifty miles north of Columbus, and gone to bed at eight o'clock in the evening—by ten-thirty Lockington had learned why there are so many Russians.

HE'D BEEN HALF-DROWSING, looking back again, when the unimaginable occurred—the office door swung open and a man came in. He wore a lightweight gray hat, an ill-fitting dark green leisure suit, and a rumpled, open-at-the-collar white shirt. His thick-lensed tortoise-shell spectacles rode the bridge of an aquiline nose, his deep-set eyes were the color of horseshoe-court clay, his lips were tightly pursed in about-to-pass-judgment fashion. Lockington put the visitor's age at forty or so. He was a lean, leathery man, probably six-one, slight of build, he carried a black cane, and his deliberate, halting approach was that of a crippled daddy-longlegs. He pulled up halfway to the desk, eyeing Lockington myopically and said, "I noticed your sign yesterday evening. This *is* a private detective agency, is it not?" His voice was soft and deep, the kind readily associated with the reading of bedtime stories to cantankerous children.

Lockington stifled a yawn. He said, "Today, yes—tomorrow it may be a tortilla joint."

The man nodded, making his way through the gathering morning heat to the straight-backed wooden chair on Lockington's right, seating himself with a groan and a grimace. Lockington said, "Bum back?"

The spidery man shook his head. "Damaged hip—football-connected injury—had it for years."

"College ball?"

"No, professional—Pittsburgh Steelers—I was trampled during half time at a beer counter in Three Rivers Stadium."

Lockington grinned, liking him for that. He could just as easily have claimed to be a wide receiver. He shoved out his hand. "I'm Lacey Lockington. What can I do for you?"

The newcomer's handshake was a limp-wristed perfunctory thing. He said, "The name is Kilbuck—Gordon Kilbuck. Tell me, Mr. Lockington, do you, err-r-r, *trace* people?"

Lockington said, "I've tried. Some are, some aren't."

Gordon Kilbuck repursed his lips. "Some are and some aren't *what?*"

"Traceable."

"Yes, of course—well, I suppose that figures. Mr. Lockington, I'm a writer." While he waited for the statement to soak in, Kilbuck produced a battered briar pipe, stuffing it with evil-looking black shag tobacco, firing it up.

Lockington was nodding. He said, "Well, don't sweat it, Gordon—we've all made mistakes."

With an obvious effort, Kilbuck swung his left leg over his right, leaning his cane against the desk, shifting on the chair to face Lockington directly. He said, "I do biographies. I've completed one book—it was a three-year project—a biography of Rylon Jennings."

"Oh, yeah, the country singer."

Kilbuck was shaking his head. "*Rylon* Jennings—British general—Second World War."

Lockington said, "Oh." The name was meaningless to him.

Kilbuck said, "I'm a military buff. Rylon Jennings was a devotee of Clausewitz."

Lockington winced. "Sorry to hear that. Was it fatal?"

Kilbuck cracked a patient half-smile. "To his army career, indeed it was. Karl von Clausewitz was a Prussian officer, a military genius—late eighteenth century, early nineteenth. He served both Prussia *and* Russia."

"A mercenary?"

"In a sense, yes."

Lockington nodded. The name Clausewitz was ringing no bells.

Kilbuck was saying, "You're familiar with the military, Mr. Lockington?"

"As familiar as I intend to get."

"You've served?"

"After a fashion."

"Well, Karl von Clausewitz was the first to refine combat to equation status—his formula, numbers times variables times quality, has withstood the test of a thousand battles—ninety-five percent accurate!"

"Did fear figure into Clausewitz's equation?"

"Only as a generality—Clausewitz didn't dwell on it. Fear is a virus, a contagious thing."

"And it's chronic—I've come down with it on numerous occasions." Lockington didn't have the slightest notion what Kilbuck was doing in his office, but he'd fractured the monotony and Lockington was grateful for that.

Kilbuck was saying, "Currently, I'm working on my second book, a biography of Alexi Fedorovich. Fedorovich is a contemporary figure—to the best of my knowledge, he hasn't been done before."

Lockington squinted. "Fedorovich...Notre Dame?"

Kilbuck's pipe had gone out and he tamped it with a forefinger, relighting it. He said, "That's the trouble with pipes—can't keep the damned things going." He puffed furiously and blue smoke billowed. "No, second-in-command, Soviet Military Planning Division."

Lockington peered through the smoke. He said, "Uh-huh," stopping there.

Kilbuck sucked in a deep breath. "You see, years back, at the crescendo of the cold war, Russia had amassed armored forces sufficient to the overrunning of Western Europe within weeks. NATO countered that buildup with nuclear missiles locked in on those Warsaw Pact nations harboring Soviet armor. It was NATO's only logical move, and it nullified the

Russian advantage. That was where Gen. Alexi Fedorovich stepped in."

Lockington didn't say anything, a habit of his when he didn't have anything to say.

Kilbuck's muddy eyes were lighting up, he was getting into his subject. "A stalemate existed, and to break it, Fedorovich offered a two-stage plan, immediately accepted and implemented by the Russian high command. The first Soviet step was to install vast numbers of nuclear missile launchers in Eastern Bloc countries—East Germany, Poland, Czechoslovakia, Yugoslavia, Hungary, Romania—thereby neutralizing NATO's move, and converting the whole of Europe into a sea of launching platforms. NATO countries began to get edgy—the missiles they'd welcomed were suddenly perceived as liabilities, possible catalysts—Western Europe could be taken off the map in a matter of hours, and *this* was the precise reaction anticipated by General Fedorovich!"

Lockington said, "You've mentioned a second stage." He'd made the statement, hoping to keep the show on the road. The subject matter was of no great concern to him, but Kilbuck was someone to *talk* to. Prior to his entrance, Lockington had been marooned, and he'd seen Kilbuck much as Robinson Crusoe must have seen Friday. Like Crusoe, Lockington didn't speak his visitor's language, but what the hell, human companionship is human companionship.

Gordon Kilbuck was nodding, sucking on his vile-smelling briar pipe. "The second stage is blossoming now—the Soviets are offering to pull their missiles out of Eastern Europe if NATO will eliminate its own. That way, the Russians insists, *every*body will be able to get a good night's sleep."

"And if NATO bites, the situation returns to Square One."

Kilbuck slapped his knee. "*Exactly*! If NATO scraps its nuclear defenses, Western Europe will be right back where it started, confronted once more by overwhelming Soviet armor that can roll over the continent like a grass fire! The Russian conventional combat potential is awesome, it possesses approximately two-and-one-half-to-one superiority in *every* facet—foot soldiers, tanks, artillery, aircraft, and *no* military defense can entertain the slightest hope for survival if it doesn't have at *least* two-thirds of the numbers thrown against it. Alexi Fedorovich *knew* this—Fedorovich has studied *Clausewitz!* NATO would be extremely fortunate to muster *one*-third!"

Lockington nodded. "In short, NATO is about to fuck itself."

"*Royally*, with the expert assistance of Gen. Alexi Fedorovich—he foresaw NATO's response to nuclear proliferation. The Soviet move was bluff, pure and simple, but Fedorovich knew damned well that the West would knuckle under! Westerners are poor chess players, and he was aware of it, more so because he spent the first fifteen years of his life in America. When his mother died of diphtheria, his father, an immigrant steelworker, took young Alexi back to the Ukraine. That would have been fifty years ago—in 1938."

"Just in time for the big shootout. Fedorovich is sixty-five now?"

"Yes, he was barely twenty when he distinguished himself during the siege of Stalingrad. He received a battlefield commission, and at the close of the war he was the Soviet Army's youngest colonel. Fedorovich was valuable—he spoke perfect English, he'd learned Russian from his parents, he was courageous, intelligent, innovative. He spent the early postwar years at the Soviet Military Institute in Minsk and he became a general in 1955! Can you *imagine* that? A Soviet general at thirty-two? Absolutely *unheard* of in the Russian military!"

"How interesting." It wasn't, but Lockington felt that he should say *some*thing.

Kilbuck said, "Fedorovich was a great man, a *great* man."

Lockington said, "You keep referring to him in the past tense. Is Fedorovich dead?"

"Not yet." Kilbuck cleared his throat, a dead giveaway—here came the commercial. "In late May of this year, Alexi

Fedorovich defected to the United States. He was in East Germany on an inspection tour and he went sightseeing in West Berlin. He entered a nightclub, left by a side entrance, hailed a cab, and went to the United States Embassy where he asked for political asylum."

"Quite a catch."

"Tremendous! He was flown to Washington, questioned for three months, then was granted United States citizenship under a new identity."

Lockington found a cigarette and lit it. He said, "Uhh-h-h, Gordon, tell me, how have you managed to acquire such information?"

Kilbuck shifted his gaze to the floor of Lockington's office. "I research thoroughly, Mr. Lockington—and I have certain sources."

"Tell me about your sources."

"I can't do that—I'd be placing people at risk."

"Physical risk?"

"Not necessarily, but I'd certainly be jeopardizing their careers."

"Why did Fedorovich defect—what were the motivating factors?" Lockington was genuinely interested now.

Gordon Kilbuck spread his hands, palms up. "Who can say? Ostensibly, he has come to regard Russia as an unstable explosive capable of destroying the civilized world—when he was masterminding Soviet strategy, he felt that he was doing the patriotic thing, helping the land of his father's birth. Now he claims to foresee disaster, *global* disaster on a scale that would curl your hair."

"That's *ostensibly*."

"Yes. What you see isn't necessarily what you get."

"Fedorovich is shooting it sharp?"

"The CIA doesn't think so."

"He's in the United States?"

"I'm certain of it, but the CIA has lost track of the man."

"The KGB wants his ass, probably."

"The KGB wants his ass, *certainly!*"

"Pardon me if I'm wrong, but I'm beginning to get the impression that you want me to find the sonofabitch."

"Yes! I simply *must* interview Alexi Fedorovich!"

"Forget it!"

Kilbuck hunched forward on the wooden chair. "Mr. Lockington, what are your rates?"

"Three hundred a day plus expenses, I make no guarantees, and I'm not interested."

"I'll pay *five* plus expenses, and I'll *require* no guarantees. Just an honest effort."

Lockington scratched his jowl. He grated, "Now, look, Kilbuck—you expect me to believe that you just happened to notice the sign on my window, and you dropped in to offer five hundred dollars a day to a nickel-and-dime private detective that you know nothing about for a case that has world-class political ramifications? You'll have to come up with a better yarn."

Kilbuck's smile was sheepish. "Frankly, I didn't really believe that one would fly. Mr. Lockington, I've heard of you."

"Why, *sure*, you have! I've lived in Youngstown for four months, and I've been in business for a week. You *must* have heard of me!"

"You're from Chicago—you handled the Devereaux business, didn't you?"

"What about the Devereaux business?"

"Why go into that? Lets just say that I know people in the Central Intelligence Agency. Will that suffice?"

Lockington shrugged. "Probably. It might also explain your knowledge of Fedorovich."

"Yes, it might. Will you accept the job?"

Lockington brought his feet from the desk top to the floor with a resounding thump. He placed an elbow on the arm of the swivel chair and rested his chin in the palm of his hand. He stared unblinkingly at Gordon Kilbuck. "All right, let's see if I've got this straight—*you* are going to pay *me* five hundred dollars per day to go stomping around a country of two hundred and fifty million people, looking for a man I don't *know*, who is on the lam from the Central Intelligence Agency, with the fucking *KGB* snapping at his ass. Is *that* how it plays, Kilbuck?"

Kilbuck's smile was of the infinitely superior variety. People who smile infinitely superior smiles usually know more than you do, or they *think* they do. Kilbuck said, "It might not be as difficult as it appears. I have excellent cause to believe that Gen. Alexi Fedorovich is here in Youngstown, Ohio."

"I'd have to hear your excellent cause."

"Fedorovich was *born* in Youngstown, he lived here for fifteen years—all of us have that homing pigeon instinct—he knows this area, he probably has childhood friends here!"

"You have leads to that effect?"

"Certainly."

"How strong—how many?"

"Just one, and it's strong, but I can't run it down."

"Why not?"

"I don't possess the expertise for that sort of job. It begs for a professional."

"If I find Fedorovich, then what?"

"Then I'll interview him—the success of my book may hinge on that, but I'll have to get to him ahead of the KGB!"

Lockington said, "Yes, Lord, I'd *think* so!" He stood up, feeling a dryness in his mouth. A rush of adrenalin always gave Lockington a dry mouth. "Care for a drink?"

Kilbuck grabbed his cane, heaving himself to his feet. His smile was the smile of a kodiak bear for a twenty pound salmon. He said, "I'll drive—I know just the place."

5 GORDON KILBUCK OWNED a sparkling dark blue '87 Cadillac Coupe de Ville with Indiana plates. It was upholstered in leather and it was computerized to the nuts. Lockington said, "Your Rylon Jennings book must be doing well."

Kilbuck's snort was derisive. "Less than three thousand copies in eighteen months. If I didn't have an inheritance, I'd be getting around on a bicycle."

"No market for military stuff?"

"Nothing to brag about. America's few male readers are into science fiction—people with three heads, that sort of thing. Women are slopping up historical romances faster than they're printed. My work comes under the heading of reference material—it's bought by libraries. That's gratifying, of course, but it doesn't buy good whisky."

Lockington said, "You can probably blame television for people not reading these days."

Kilbuck nodded. "Pap for imbeciles." There'd been no bitterness in the remark, it'd come more as a flat statement of fact. They'd rolled east to Steel Street, turning north for three-quarters of a mile before Kilbuck wheeled the Caddy into the parking lot of a low gray frame building. The big red neon sign on the roof said POLLY'S PLACE. Kilbuck said, "I've gravitated to this joint—it's down-to-earth."

They went in. Polly's was a clean establishment, a combination restaurant and bar with neatly lettered specials signs on the walls. Monday's offer was pork shanks and sauerkraut $3.95.

"In New York pork shanks and sauerkraut would cost you twenty-five dollars." Lockington said.

"Yeah, and that'd be without the pork shanks."

They sat in a booth lighted by an Old Washensachs Beer

lamp. A waitress drifted to their table. Kilbuck ordered a bottle of Budweiser, Lockington a double Martell's cognac. She was back in a flash, a perky, peroxide blonde bit of fluff with saucerlike dark brown eyes, a pug nose, and a bee-stung lower lip, wearing a too-tight sheer white blouse, too-tight black satin shorts, and spike heeled red pumps. The plastic badge on her blouse said NANETTE. Lockington raised his glass to Kilbuck. He said, "Been in Youngstown long?"

Nanette said, "Long enough to know better. What did you have in mind?" She had a voice like Minnie Mouse.

"I was speaking to Mr. Kilbuck."

Nanette said, "'Scuse me." She went away, her bulging little buttocks rolling as she walked.

Kilbuck said, "I'll be here a week come tomorrow—drove in from New York City. I'm from Indiana—Muncie."

"Good town?"

"Good as any, better than most. Do you like Youngstown?"

"After Chicago, I'd like Beirut. So, in a week you haven't turned up much on Fedorovich?"

"Naw— I've prowled around—been through his childhood haunts, Upper South Side, rotten area. It all went to hell after the war, they told me."

"'They'?"

"People in the neighborhood taverns—I've sat at every bar in that neck of the woods. Nobody remembers the Fedorovich family. Alexi was just a kid when his old man decided to go back to Russia."

"Maybe you should sound out people in his age bracket—sixty-five or so."

"Most of the old-timers have moved to the West Side or to the suburbs—Boardman, Poland, Canfield, Hubbard—the South Side is *rough*."

Lockington watched Kilbuck load his pipe and light it. He said, "You mentioned having a lead."

"Yes, well, to get into that, I should tell you that Alexi Fedorovich has written a book, and it's just hit the stands—

The Wheels of Treachery—Millard and Cummings, New York. It's going for $23.95."

"It's selling?"

"Too early to say—far as I know, it hasn't even been reviewed."

Lockington was frowning. "Fedorovich hits the bricks in late May, he's questioned for three months—that takes us to the front end of September. He knocks out a book and gets it published in that amount of time? Unlikely, wouldn't you say?"

"Next to impossible—the book had to be written before he defected."

"What's it about?"

"What you'd expect—East-West relations, crystal ball stuff—predictions, mostly. Fedorovich claims that glasnost-perestroika will wear thin in the Soviet Union, that the hard-liners will oust Gorbachev or shoot him, and that they'll attack Western Europe without provocation or warning, possibly as early as 1991."

"Pearl Harbor style?"

"Not exactly. The war with Japan was predictable enough— we'd embargoed its oil and steel—Japan *had* to fight. The Soviet Union doesn't."

"Then why fight?"

"According to Fedorovich, it'll be a reunification war— Communism is crumbling, Warsaw Pact countries are restless, there's clamoring for democracy, even in Moscow. A good old-fashioned war would shoo all the chickens back into the coop."

"Anything concrete in that?"

Kilbuck gnawed on his lower lip, considering the question. "I don't know—it's possible, of course. Fedorovich gives it as the reason for his defection—he says that he wanted no part of it."

"He goes into detail?"

"Hell, yes—timetable, early targets, overall Soviet strategy, the whole ball of wax. I have a couple of copies in the car—one is yours." He motioned to Nanette for another round.

Nanette delivered it, bending over their table, rounding up the old glasses, putting down the new. Three buttons at the top of her white sheer blouse were undone and she wore a low-cut brassiere. There was a black and blue splotch above the nipple of her right breast. She hadn't been nibbled on, she'd been *bitten*, Lockington figured. She said, "Something else I can do for you boys?"

Kilbuck winked at her. "Probably, but you couldn't do it *here*."

Nanette squealed, "Oh, naughty, *naughty!*" She popped Kilbuck playfully on the top of his head with her fist, smiling at Lockington. Lockington shrugged and Nanette faded into the gloom of the bar area, her buttocks swaying, her black satin shorts shimmering in the half-light. Kilbuck continued.

"Fedorovich predicts a dual-pronged Soviet attack—to the south it'll swing out of Czechoslovakia's Bohemian Forest into Bavaria, driving toward Munich, throwing nine divisions with eight thousand armored vehicles against five or six NATO divisions, half of these only partially mobilized. To the north, he sees the Russians blasting through the Fulda Gap, making a run to reach the Danube within thirty-six hours, and that'd be the only possible hitch in the operation—Fedorovich regards NATO's Danube defenses as being tough to breach, but once Soviet forces are across the river, he says that Western Europe will be Russia's oyster."

Lockington said, "Well, there really isn't much that I can do about *that*, is there?"

"Not a great deal."

Lockington said, "All right, tell me about your Fedorovich lead."

Kilbuck glanced around, leaning toward Lockington, lowering his voice to a confidential level. "I was in New York last week, and I dropped in at Millard and Cummings on 43rd Street. I talked to Fedorovich's editor, a Patti Walton. Patti clammed up instantly, but I managed to get acquainted with the Millard and Cummings receptionist, a heavyweight from Queens. I met her at a 42nd Street lounge when she got off work and I bought her a drink—*several* drinks, in fact." Kilbuck smiled. "Women seem to see something romantic in a guy with a cane."

Lockington said, "Yeah, especially when he smokes a pipe."

"Well, we ended up in bed and she promised to do everything she could."

"And did she?"

"My God, you'd better believe it—she damned near *killed* me! She weighed about two-fifty and was one of those women who likes to be on top—some sort of female-dominant complex, you know?"

"No, I didn't know. I meant, did she come up with information on Fedorovich?"

"Sure did. I met her for lunch the next day, and she'd spent the morning digging into files. There was minor stuff—for instance, Fedorovich insisted on designing his own dust jacket. More interesting, I thought, was the fact that he's never been to the Millard and Cummings offices. They have no address for him—contact is maintained through a Youngstown woman, an Olga Karelinko—she has a postal box, number 11, West Side Post Office at the corner of Millet and Mahoning Avenues."

Lockington said, "That could be a start."

"I've been to the West Side Post Office. It's a cramped one-horse affair. The boxes are in the vestibule. I'd intended to hang around, keeping an eye on Box 11, but the place is so small, I'd have stuck out like a sore thumb. If Olga Karelinko is playing it cool, she'd have spotted me."

"Anything else?"

"Yeah—*The Wheels of Treachery* is *dedicated* to Olga Karelinko!"

"She's in the telephone book?"

Kilbuck shook his head. "No Karelinkos at all. Apparently she's an older lady."

"Why so?"

"Because the dedication reads, 'To Olga Karelinko for the old days on West Dewey Avenue.' You see, as a boy, Fedorovich lived at 326 West Dewey—the house isn't there now."

"Torn down recently?"

"No, I talked to a couple of black youngsters—they were maybe ten or twelve years old, and they couldn't recall a house ever having *been* there, so it's been gone a while."

"Anybody around there remember an Olga Karelinko?"

"No one that I questioned. Do you think you can help me?"

"I think I can try."

Kilbuck leaned back in the booth, sighing, "Oh, *excellent!*" He dug into a pocket of his green leisure suit, producing a white business envelope, leaning it against Lockington's cognac glass. "You have five thousand there. Do you think it'll take more than ten days?"

Lockington said, "If I can't find him in ten days, I can't *find* him."

"When will you start?"

"Tomorrow—I'll need today to kick it around."

"All right, you're the doctor. I'll be in touch, and if anything pops, I'm staying at the Howard Johnson Motor Inn on Belmont Avenue."

Lockington shoved the envelope into his jacket pocket, glancing at his wristwatch. He said, "I'd better get back to the office—luncheon appointment."

Kilbuck nodded, lurching to his feet. Nanette was approaching their booth with the tab. She said, "Seven dollars." Kilbuck handed her a ten dollar bill, waving away the change. Nanette curtsied. Kilbuck turned to Lockington. "You're married?"

Nanette said, "Three times—does it matter?"

"I was talking to Mr. Lockington."

Nanette squeaked, "Oops!" and busied herself with clearing the table.

Lockington said, "No, not married." He wished he was. He'd have married Natasha Gorky in a minute. One of these days he'd ask her, he thought.

6 AT THE DOOR of Lockington's office Gordon Kilbuck had opened the Cadillac's trunk, reaching into a small cardboard box and coming out with a copy of *The Wheels of Treachery*. "My compliments," he'd said. Now Lockington slouched in his swivel chair, paging idly through the book while waiting for Natasha. *The Wheels of Treachery* was a hefty volume, nearly eight hundred pages in length. It had an intriguing dust jacket, the front of which sported an excellent charcoal sketch of a group of loose-robed men wheeling a gigantic wooden horse through the gates of a high-walled fortified area. The horse was mounted on a six-wheeled platform and its inference was perfectly clear—the men in the picture would represent the NATO nations, and the horse would be fabled Trojan Horse. According to Lockington's vague recollection of the old story, the Greeks had come to Troy in hope of conquering it, but the Trojans had been nobody's pushovers so the Greeks had built a horse, leaving it at the gates of Troy before sailing away—apparently in search of greener pastures—and the Trojans had hauled the horse into Troy. That night the Greeks had returned, the Greek soldiers hidden inside the horse had slipped out to open the gates, and Troy had been overrun. Moral: Beware of Greeks bearing gifts. And Russians waving olive branches.

The Wheels of Treachery would be laborious reading. It was packed with statistics, numerous references to the theories of Karl von Clausewitz, hundreds of footnotes, and there were dire predictions by the carload—it'd probably be a smashing success because nothing sells like bad news. Lockington's smile was wry—write something with a sunny outlook and you couldn't give it away, but adopt a pessimistic view and you had a worldbeater. There was a touch of the masochist in American readers, Lockington thought, but he didn't concern himself with it, reasoning that most Americans didn't read anymore, possibly because they wouldn't, probably because they *couldn't*. He'd heard that there'd be a gigantic 14.5 mill property tax on Youngstown's November ballot. The money was required by the schools, it'd been said—more student counselors were needed, more courses should be offered, Peruvian Pottery for one, Indian Basketweaving for another. Lockington dropped *The Wheels of Treachery* into a desk drawer, lighting a cigarette, marveling at the progress of American education. Nowadays, when a kid got his high school diploma he could weave an Indian basket, but the poor bastard didn't know how to read or write, and if you took away his pocket calculator, he couldn't add three and three to save his educated soul.

Natasha came in at 12:05, prim in a tailored gray suit, blue blouse, and blue pumps, a bulky package under her arm. She smiled her wonderfully lopsided smile. "Sorry I'm late, but I was buying something for you." She unwrapped the package, opened an oblong box, and placed a plastic radio on the desk. She said, "This is to keep you from going off the deep end, sitting here all by yourself." She plugged the radio in, turned it on, and a flood of discordant guitar noises crashed into the office, rattling the windows. A couple of hoarse-voiced guys were screaming, "Yeah, yeah, yeah—Yeah, yeah, yeah!" Lockington said, "The London Philharmonic, no doubt."

Natasha was doubled up with silent laughter. "Don't you just *love* the lyrics?"

Lockington nodded. "Pure genius."

Natasha killed the radio, rumpling his hair. "Come on, bright eyes, let's go to lunch."

The noonday weather was ideal and they walked the two blocks to Dickey's through the sweet sad scents of autumn, the sun warm on their backs. Natasha squeezed Lockington's hand.

"Lacey, I'm so glad I've found you!" It wasn't a considered pronouncement—she just blurted it out.

Lockington said, "And vice versa, lady."

They turned right on Meridian Road, walking north. A reddish leaf tumbled, catching in Natasha's pixie hairdo. Lockington reached for it, noting that it was the exact color of her hair. It was an excellent day for being alive, he thought.

7 HE HADN'T MENTIONED Gordon Kilbuck's visit to Natasha—he'd save that and the five thousand dollar jackpot for their predinner martini hour, he figured, wondering just how she'd respond to his attempting to track down a former top-flight Soviet military man. He'd turned his attention to the radio she'd brought, sitting at his desk, experimenting with its rod antenna, prowling the FM band, crossing three classical music frequencies, encountering no fewer than fifteen rock stations. For the most part, classical music went over Lockington's head like a bullet, and rock music—if it *was* music—brought on severe diarrheic spasms. He'd heard a couple of holy-rolling preachers spewing fire and brimstone and pleading for "love offerings." There'd been quite a few country stations, but country wasn't country anymore—it'd sold out to the influence of rock.

He'd switched to the AM dial, hitting a phone-in talk show, then another, then a half-dozen more rock stations and a black gospel program. He'd been close to exhausting the AM band when he'd come to 1390—WHOT, Youngstown—where his scalded eardrums had been soothed by the sounds of music from the thirties and forties, and he'd stopped there, settling back in the swivel chair, listening to "Smoke Rings" and "Maria Elena" and "Deep Purple." There'd been a short commercial break, then "Stardust," and Lockington had basked in the soft glow of melody from a better day when the plague of heroin hadn't swept the country and abortion clinics hadn't been founded and funded by the United States Government. "Back in Your Own Backyard" was playing when his office door flew open, nearly departing its hinges. A man came careening into the office like an off-the-rails steam locomotive, a huge, belligerent-looking creature, probably six-five, not an ounce under two-forty. Lockington figured his age was in the ball park of fifty years. A wilted Pittsburgh Pirates baseball cap topped an unruly shock of silver-streaked brown hair. He wore a faded blue cotton work shirt, his baggy jeans were oil-splotched and threadbare at the knees, his black brogans were scarred and run over at the heels, his prominent nose was bent into an S-shape, he was missing at least three front teeth, he had icy bluish green eyes, and he looked like he could have started at middle linebacker for the Roman Empire. The behemoth lumbered toward Lockington's desk, growling, "So, okay, I wanta speak to the chief motherfucker." His voice possessed the gentle tonal qualities of a Nantucket foghorn.

Lockington managed to force a yawn. He said, "You just did."

The visitor said, "So, okay, what's your handle?"

Lockington frowned. He said, "Sit down, you're blocking the light." It was his way of gaining a splinter of the initiative.

The big man shrugged a ho-hum shrug, seating himself. The straight-backed wooden chair creaked, protesting the sudden stress. Lockington gazed at the newcomer.

"My name's Lockington—Lacey Lockington."

"So, okay, Lockington, I'm Vic Kozlowski." He extended a greasy paw, grabbing Lockington's hand, pumping it vigorously. Vic Kozlowski's palm had the texture of a hunting boot and his grip was that of a seventeen hundred dollar hydraulic vise. He said, "I happened to notice the sign on your window—you gotta be brand-new in the neighborhood."

"No, not brand-new—just recent."

"I was here earlier. The joint was locked, so you was prob'ly out."

Lockington nodded. "If it was locked, I probably was. What can I do for you, Mr. Kozlowski?"

"For starters you can call me 'Vic.' Just about everybody calls me 'Vic'."

Lockington said, "'Vic,' it is." He'd have called him 'Exalted Majesty,' if Kozlowski had insisted.

Kozlowski was prying a Parodi cigar from a shirt pocket. He said, "Hey, look, Lockington, how many assistants you employ here?"

"As many as it takes to do nothing."

Kozlowski was putting a match to his cigar, speaking from a corner of his mouth through bluish haze. "Business slow?"

"You're understating an understatement."

"So, okay, what the hell, don't sweat it—things'll shape up."

"I simply can't tell you just how glad I am to hear that."

Kozlowski said, "Hey, look, Lockington, when the mills went bust ten years back, I was up the creek without a paddle—forty-one years old and no job! So, you know what I went and done?"

"No, what did you went and done?"

"So, okay, I opened a transmission repair shop down on Steel Street. Damn near starved to death for six months, and now I can't handle all the work!"

Lockington said, "Great idea, but I can't repair transmissions."

"Hey, look, same principle applies, don't it? You just gotta hang in there! How many kids you got, Lockington?"

"Probably none."

Kozlowski nodded, hunching forward on the wooden chair, elbows on his knees, grizzled chin cupped in his hands. He said, "Well, Lockington, you don't got the slightest idea what you've missed."

"The hell I don't," Lockington said. "That's why I missed it."

Kozlowski said, "So, okay, I got one kid—raised him from a pup all by my lonesome. Eighteen years ago my wife hauled ass with a used car salesman. Nice Catholic Polish girl. Can you imagine *that*?"

"Oh, sure—most Polish girls are."

"What—nice?"

"Catholic. What's on your mind, Vic?"

"So, okay, it's this kid of mine—name's Barney—*Bernard*,

if you wanta get technical. Y'know, Lockington, today's kids are funny."

"Uh-huh—well, if they're so funny, how come you ain't laughing?"

"I didn't mean *that* kind of funny—I should of probly said 'different'."

"From what?"

"From every damn thing I ever run into. Now you take Barney—he's been a real good kid, as kids go—made it through high school okay, got fair-to-middling grades, played all-City nose tackle at Chaney High, got half a dozen college scholarship offers—Pitt, Purdue, Michigan State, Syracuse— and he turned 'em down, every one. No great shakes, but Barney ain't never been in no trouble. He ain't running around with his cock in his hand, no drugs, and, hell, he don't even smoke or *drink!*"

"That makes him different, all right. How old is he?" Lockington didn't give a damn how old Barney was, but he had a hunch that Vic Kozlowski was going to tell him whether he gave a damn or not.

"He turned twenty-one just last month, and he ain't never had a job in his whole life." Kozlowski blew a blue shaft of Parodi smoke into the sunlight streaming through the west window. "Y'know, I'd take him into the business, but he don't got no mechanical aptitude. He got a car, a beat-up 1981 Mustang I bought for him, but Barney don't know a screwdriver from a fucking driveshaft."

"Yeah, well, I've had considerable difficulty with that myself. Uhh-h-h, look, Vic, it's getting late."

"So, okay, what I been trying to get around to is Barney's been reading private detective and spy stories since he was fifteen years old—you know, Marlowe and McGee and all that KGB and CIA stuff, secret agents and snipers and assassinations. You ever get hung up on that kind of crap?"

"With me it was Tom Sawyer."

"Sawyer—was he a spy or a private detective?"

"Not when I knew him."

"Hey, look, that ain't all. Barney never misses them sort of shows on TV. He ain't like most boys his age—he don't wanta be no big-time athlete, or no railroad engineer, or no airplane pilot—all Barney wants to be is a spy or a private detective. Only Barney never says 'private detective,' he always says 'P.I.'—'P.I.' stands for 'private investigator,' he tells me. Anybody ever call you a 'P.I.'?"

"Among other things, yes."

"So, okay, Lockington, reason I'm here is, you couldn't maybe use an apprentice, could you? I mean for *free*. Y'see, I been thinking that if Barney ever gets around to finding out that this racket ain't all cocktails and big money and fast cars and sex orgies, then he just might come down to earth—like if he could maybe hang around with you for a while and go out on a few cases till he gets the drift. Whaddaya think about that, Lockington?"

Lockington said, "Well, Vic, at the moment the problem is that I'm not exactly overburdened by cases."

Kozlowski hadn't heard him, he'd had a full head of steam and he'd widened on the throttle. He said, "There's a couple other investigations outfits in Youngstown, but they wasn't interested—wouldn't even *listen* to me! Hell, all I was asking was a few weeks, it wouldn't of cost them a damn *penny*, and I might even of thrown in a free transmission job. *Shit!*"

Pathos hung in the office air like swamp fog and Lockington's Chicago-hardened heart went out to Vic Kozlowski. He said, "That's a real good offer, Vic, and I'll tell you what—I'm gonna keep Barney in mind, and the very minute something worthwhile pops, I'll give you a call—how's that?" He probably wouldn't, Lockington knew, but he wanted to let the big fellow down easy.

A grin sliced Kozlowski's melon-shaped face. He got to his feet, towering over Lockington's desk like the Colossus of Rhodes, stooping to offer a smudged houndeared business card. Lockington accepted the card, glancing at it—

KOZLOWSKI'S TRANSMISSION SERVICE, 84 North Steel Street, Youngstown, Ohio. SATISFACTION GUARANTEED. JUST TRY TO BEAT OUR PRICE. 10% DISCOUNT TO SENIOR CITIZENS. There was a telephone number. Lockington tucked the card into a shirt pocket. Kozlowski was saying, "You're a square guy, Lockington, I can tell!" He cuffed Lockington on the shoulder, they shook hands, and Kozlowski went out, easing the door shut behind him. Lockington watched him climb into a battered black Ford pickup truck and drive through the plaza parking lot to Mahoning Avenue. He checked his watch. Five-ten. He'd be closing late and he still had to pick up a rose for Natasha. Well, he didn't really *have* to, he *wanted* to. Bringing a rose gave Lockington a glow.

8 WHEN SHE MET HIM at the door, Natasha took her
rose, kissing him, then stepping back, her pale blue eyes
searching his face.

"Something wrong?" she asked. Lockington shook
his head, smiling. Her radar was amazingly sensitive—she
could read the fine print in him.

"No."

"Then what *is* it?"

"Nothing to become alarmed about."

Natasha went into the kitchen, worked on the vodka
martinis, placed his on the coffee table in front of the sofa,
hers on the end table by the overstuffed chair. She seated
herself, crossing her legs, and Lockington caught a brief flash
of black half-slip and tawny thigh. She said, "I'm listening."

He told her of Vic Kozlowski's appeal and Natasha laughed.
She said, "Well, there's an old American adage—'Never look
a gift horse in the mouth'."

Lockington said, "And there's another—'Leave well enough
alone'."

Natasha was studying him. "There's something else, isn't
there?"

"Yes—tell me, have you ever heard of a man named Alexi
Fedorovich?"

She nipped at her martini, licking her lips with what
Lockington assumed was the most educated tongue in the
Northern Hemisphere. She said, "Yes, I've heard of a man
named Alexi Fedorovich—have you ever heard of a man
named Douglas MacArthur?"

"Certainly. Douglas MacArthur was an egomaniac."

"Alexi Fedorovich *isn't*—he's a master military strategist, a
great man, highly respected in the Soviet Union."

Lockington said, "Uh-huh—well, for your information,

36

Alexi Fedorovich ain't *in* the Soviet Union anymore."

Natasha's eyebrows arched puzzledly. "He *isn't*? *Why* isn't he in the Soviet Union?"

"Because he's in Youngstown, Ohio, that's why."

Natasha returned her martini glass to the end table, fishing a cigarette from the pack in her blouse pocket, lighting it. "You'll have to explain that. Is he on some sort of goodwill tour?"

Lockington shook his head. "Fedorovich defected from the Soviet Union in May."

"*Impossible!*"

"Maybe so, but today a man paid me five thousand dollars to locate him. Fedorovich was *born* in Youngstown."

"I've heard that he was American-born, but Alexi Fedorovich is a Russian *hero!*"

"Benedict Arnold was an *American* hero—until he sold out to the British."

"You're *sure* of this?"

"*I'm* not, but a guy by the name of Gordon Kilbuck *is*—five thousand dollars worth."

Natasha picked up her glass, sipped, peered over its rim with unbelieving eyes. "I—I just can't *comprehend* this! It isn't that I *care*, you understand—I'm through with Russia—but General Fedorovich was a public figure, and—and, well, I'm as shocked as *you'd* be if—well, if an American Supreme Court justice turned out to be a Communist agent."

"If you're talking about Earl Warren, he probably *was*. Did you know that Fedorovich has written a book?"

Natasha was grinding her cigarette into the ashtray at her elbow, lighting another, chain-smoking, obviously disturbed. "A *book*?"

"Yeah, it's called *The Wheels of Treachery*, and it has to do with Soviet Union plans to dominate Western Europe."

Natasha got up to mix more martinis. From the kitchen she said, "Well, there's nothing new about *that*, is there? *Both* sides are ambitious—the West wants to restructure middle-Europe to its own liking, the East wants the whole damned continent—it's a tug of war that's been going on for *decades*—economic pressures, propaganda barrages, the art of—"

Lockington cut her off. "Natasha, I'm not talking about economics or propaganda or the art of *anything*—I'm talking about a surprise attack out of Czechoslovakia and East Germany, an all-out armored assault, and relatively *soon!*" Lockington hadn't read Fedorovich's book, so Gordon Kilbuck's synopsis would have to do.

She came back from the kitchen with the martinis, reseating herself, not crossing her legs this time to Lockington's disappointment. She said, "That manure is in the book?"

"It is."

"And under what circumstances is this supposed to occur?"

"Eastern Europe breaking free of Moscow, Gorbachev out of office, the old guard back in power, looking for a war that will restore Russia to what she *used* to be."

"Lacey, that won't happen—*any* of it."

"It won't?"

"No, and I suspect that if General Fedorovich has defected to the West, he's learned a Western trick—write a sensational book and make a fast buck. You see, both sides suffer from paranoia, sharing a pronounced tendency to subscribe to the worst imaginable scenario. The West believes the Soviet Union's strategic aims to be as clearly defined as its tactical goals. The truth of the matter is that the KGB is a tactical organization, powerful, efficient, ruthless, but the KGB does *not* dictate Kremlin policy!"

"No, but the Kremlin dictates KGB policy."

"Of course, but only in the broadest sense. I doubt that Moscow is more than twenty-five percent aware of KGB activity, just as every CIA move isn't necessarily ordered by the White House, possibly not even *condoned*. There are zealots at every level of government, here and in the Soviet Union, and there are alarmists, but that doesn't place us on the brink of a third world war."

Lockington worked on his martini, making no response.

Natasha said, "America's CIA is probably much like Russia's KGB in the respect that both are bedeviled by splinter groups, some radical, even fanatical, surviving by keeping low profiles—the same way that the Nazi element has managed to survive in a common sense democratic West Germany."

Lockington said, "Low profiles or no low profiles, they're *there*."

"Yes, and in a touch-and-go situation they could prove dangerous."

Lockington said, "Okay, class dismissed."

"The Fedorovich book—it's on the American market—you've *seen* it?"

"Kilbuck gave me a copy—it's in a desk drawer at the office."

"Lacey, would you go over this for me—from the beginning?"

Lockington took it from the top—Kilbuck's visit, his desire to interview Fedorovich, his information, his five thousand dollar advance. He tossed Kilbuck's envelope into Natasha's lap. "Count it."

She placed the envelope unopened on the end table, leaning toward Lockington, her face taut, her speech terse. "The KGB will want Fedorovich, you know that, don't you?"

"On Kremlin orders?"

"No, probably on its own initiative. Leave it alone, Lacey—return Kilbuck's money and stay *out* of it!"

Lockington spread his hands helplessly. "I can't *do* that—what the hell, it's a *job*! I've been living on your money since June."

"Correction: *we've* been living on *KGB* money since June."

"Whatever. I have a habit of paying my own way."

"There'll be other cases, nice quiet divorce matters, things of that nature. This one could get you *killed*!"

"I'm not going to get *involved* enough to get killed. All I have to do is find Fedorovich, then stand clear."

"Lacey, you won't be *able* to stand clear! I'm ex-KGB, I

know how the KGB works—it leaves no tracks."

"I know that. I saw it in operation last summer." He winked at her. "Hell, I even knew the lady in charge. By the way, she was damned good in bed."

Natasha frowned. "Was? *Was?*"

Lockington said, "Sorry about that."

"Not half as sorry as you're going to be."

Lockington grinned a good-natured grin. He didn't know what she meant by that, but he found out. At eleven-fifteen that night he sprawled panting on a bed that looked like it'd gone through an 8.5 earthquake. He'd never been so thoroughly pussy-whipped, even by Natasha Gorky. She'd destroyed him, and he'd never gotten off of his back. She was straddling him, leaning over him, whispering into his open mouth. She was saying, "*Was?*"

Lockington said, "My error—is."

"Say it again, damn you!"

"*Is*, for Christ's sake, *is!*"

"That's better, Lacey, much better."

Lockington said, "Tell me—this business of the woman being on top—that's a female-dominant complex quirk, isn't it?"

Natasha slipped to her side of the bed, lighting two cigarettes, passing one to him, snuggling beside him. She said, "Who*ever* told you *that?*"

"Gordon Kilbuck."

"Well, you tell Gordon Kilbuck that he's full of purple balloons!"

"All right, I'll tell him."

They finished their cigarettes, putting them out before dozing, Natasha's head on his shoulder, her knee tucked comfortably into Lockington's aching groin area. After a while she murmured, "Did you know that you'd be good for three?"

"Three—my God, was it three?"

"Trust me, it was."

They slept. Natasha hadn't mentioned the Fedorovich matter since their second martini.

9 IN THE MORNING they had toast and coffee, not saying much, yawning, looking out at a gray 8:30 and the light rain that'd come with it. At the doorway, Natasha gave him a light peck on the cheek and he patted her exquisite buttocks. She said, "Lunch?"

Lockington nodded and went out to the Mercedes, shoulders hunched against the rain, waving to Natasha before driving south to Oakwood Avenue, east to Millet, then south again to Mahoning Avenue. The Youngstown West Side Post Office was on the northeast corner of the junction, set back from Mahoning, sharing the location with a delicatessen. The parking lot was a beehive of frustrated activity. Cars whipped in and out, people walked in front of moving automobiles, outraged drivers tooted their horns, and Lockington had difficulty finding a parking place for the Mercedes.

As Gordon Kilbuck had told him, the facility was much too small to accommodate its traffic. Through the glass doors separating the vestibule from the desk Lockington saw a dozen or more people standing in a crooked line, awaiting such counter service as a frazzled-looking bespectacled lady in a blue smock was capable of providing. He didn't go in, just paused briefly in the lobby, noting the position of Post Office Box #11, then departed to drive west on Mahoning Avenue. He swung north on Meridian Road to Youngstown Office Supply where he bought a large padded manila mailing envelope and a packet of address stickers. He returned to Mahoning Avenue, wheeling west to the Austintown Shopping Plaza. He went into Stambaugh-Thompson's Hardware Store, purchasing a large roll of vinyl adhesive tape and a spray can of fast-drying bright red enamel. He left Stambaugh-Thompson's, crossing to the Austintown Post Office where he picked up three twenty-five cent stamps. He bought a Cleveland *Plain Dealer*

41

at a Rite-Aid Pharmacy, and it was 9:25 when he unlocked his office door. After what'd seemed like eons of battling Chicago's impossible morning traffic, getting around in Youngstown was a snap.

He turned on his new radio and WHOT's civilized music flooded the office. He pulled the sports section from the Cleveland *Plain Dealer*, tossing it onto his desk, spreading the remainder of the newspaper on the floor. He sealed the big manila envelope with tape, wrapping it around and around and around, lengthwise and widthwise, smiling a slightly fiendish smile during the process. It wasn't about to be easily opened.

He placed the envelope in the middle of the fanned-out newspaper, spraying it red, two coats. He waited half an hour, sitting on a corner of his desk, dangling his feet, listening to WHOT, whistling to the oldies, smoking. Then he flipped the envelope and sprayed its other side. At 10:30 he affixed an address label, scrawling OLGA KARELINKO, P.O. BOX 11, WEST SIDE POST OFFICE, YOUNGSTOWN, OHIO across it. He glued the postage stamps to the upper right-hand corner of the envelope, holding it up, admiring his handiwork. It could easily be seen for a city block. He tucked the gaudy thing into his top desk drawer, turned off his radio, found *The Wheels of Treachery*, and settled into his swivel chair to further peruse the book.

The Wheels of Treachery contained seven hundred and eighty-eight pages. It had a nineteen-page glossary identifying Soviet military units and armor—the BMP-2 Yozh, the T-80, the T-72MI, the 2SI. The glossary touched on self-propelled artillery, missile vehicles, helicopters, and fighter craft. It was a sturdy book, done on good quality paper. There were fifty-nine chapters, each headed by an eight-spoked wheel with the chapter number on its hub. Apparently Gen. Alexi Fedorovich had a thing for wheels.

The telephone jingled and Lockington grabbed it. Gordon

Kilbuck said, "You aren't in the Goddamned telephone directory."

Lockington said, "That's because I haven't been in business long enough to get *into* the Goddamned telephone directory."

"I got the Confidential Investigations number from the information operator."

"Excellent thinking, Gordon—downright *excellent*."

Kilbuck chuckled. "Just thought I'd call and see if there's anything new."

"I'm working an angle but I won't have anything on it until tomorrow."

"Okay, I'll call you late tomorrow afternoon. If you run into something that won't keep, you can reach me at Howard Johnson's Motor Inn on Belmont Avenue—remember?"

"I remember."

"If a woman answers, don't hang up—it'll be Nanette. Remember Nanette?"

"I remember."

"Say, Lockington, do you recall what I was telling you about women who like to be on top?"

"The female-dominant complex?"

"That's it!"

"Yeah, I remember—what about it?"

"Well, Nanette has a female-dominant complex."

"So did the receptionist from Queens."

Gordon Kilbuck said, "Jesus, Lockington, you have one helluva memory!"

Lockington said, "Thank you for your call, Mr. Murphy."

10 AT 11:50 LOCKINGTON LOCKED the door and sauntered to the east end of the plaza to toss the bright red envelope into a mailbox. He got back to his office in a dead heat with Natasha. The drizzle hadn't let up, so she drove them to Dickey's. They took their favorite table in a corner of the room. Natasha said, "I'm not hungry—are you?"

Lockington said, "No, it must be contagious."

The waitress came by. She said, "Vodka martinis, isn't it?"

Lockington nodded.

Natasha waited for the waitress to leave before she said, "I put Kilbuck's money in the bank this morning."

"Now I'll try to earn it," Lockington said.

"Nothing so far?"

Lockington shook his head.

Natasha said, "You seem out of sorts today."

"No, I'm out of get up and go. Baby, when you throw a party, you throw a *party*! Does Russia have an Olympics sex team?"

"No—such a pity."

Their martinis came and they sipped them slowly. Lockington said, "Maybe it's my biorhythms, or something."

"Do you believe in biorhythms?" Natasha asked.

"Hell, no."

"What *do* you believe in?"

"I've never made a list."

"Would it be a long list?"

"I don't think so."

"Would I be on it?"

"You'd head it."

She squeezed his hand. "You'd head mine." She was smiling her lopsided smile. It was a faraway lopsided smile, like she

44

was recalling something from better days. Lockington couldn't imagine days better than these. Or nights, for that matter. Natasha said, "It's nice to have something to believe in."

Lockington said, "It's *stopping* the believing that hurts."

"You've done that?"

"Yes."

"How many times?"

"I don't know. Several, I guess."

"I haven't—not *several* times—just a few. Perhaps you believe more quickly than I—perhaps you *want* to believe. *Do you?*"

"I suppose so. Doesn't everybody?"

"No, not everybody—at least *I* don't."

"Why not?"

Natasha was silent for a few moments. Then she said, "It isn't so much that I object to believing in something as it is that I've never been determined to find something to believe *in.*"

"I may not understand that."

"I may not either, but wouldn't it seem that unwavering belief can't be sought out, that it comes not *because* of anything, but in *spite* of everything?"

"I don't know—*would* it?"

"Why, of course! Take us, for instance."

"What about us?"

"Well, you see, you've believed in *me* because you've *wanted* to and it might be temporary, but I've believed in *you* without *wanting* to or *not* wanting to, and *that*, Mr. Lockington, is *permanent!*"

"And, if we carry this further, I won't know *what* the hell I believe—it's like messing around with infinity."

Natasha was nodding, staring into her martini glass. She glanced up. She said, "Do you believe in infinity—that it exists without end?"

"There's an end to all things."

"To all *things*, yes, but infinity isn't a *thing.*"

"Then what *is* it?"

"It isn't something you see, it's something you *sense*."

Lockington growled, "Hey, if I can't see it, I don't believe in it."

Natasha's lopsided smile was back. "Not true—you believe in love."

"Oh, sure, but that's different."

Natasha leaned back in her chair, winking at him. It was a triumphant wink. She said, "Oh, Lacey, *isn't* it though?"

They finished their martinis and she drove him back to Mahoning Plaza, blowing him a kiss as she pulled away. Lockington went into his office feeling like he'd just climbed out of a pinball machine, uncertain of why the conversation had taken that tack, knowing that it'd been manipulated throughout, but not knowing how. And not giving two whoops in hell. Forty-nine-year-old ex-Chicago police detectives crazy in love with thirty-one-year-old ex-KGB agents hardly ever give two whoops in hell.

11

HE RIFFLED THROUGH his telephone book and called the Youngstown Board of Education. A man answered. He said, "Yeah?"

Lockington wasn't sure that he'd dialed the right number—he heard a great deal of commotion in the background, scuffling sounds, slamming and banging. He said, "Youngstown Board of Education?"

"Yeah." The man sounded impatient.

Lockington said, "I have a question, sir."

"Okay, shoot, but make it fast." The wail of sirens was drifting through the receiver.

"If a kid lived at 326 West Dewey Avenue in Youngstown, what school would he attend?"

"How old is the kid?"

"Oh, fourteen or so."

"That'd put him in the eighth grade, right?"

"Probably."

"*Probably?*"

"Yeah, make it eighth grade."

"He'd go to Princeton Junior High School."

Lockington could hear more sirens on the line. He said, "Where is Princeton Junior High School?"

"Just a couple blocks south of 326 West Dewey."

"What street's it on?"

"It's on Hillman Street."

"Good! Now where is Hillman Street? I'm new in town."

"Man, you *must* be—I wouldn't *take* a kid into that neighborhood!"

"This is a suppositional kid."

"Hey, his nationality don't matter—what matters is how *big* is he? That's a rough area!"

"About Hillman Street, please."

47

"Oh, yeah, Hillman. Hillman runs north and south between Oakhill and Edwards."

"That might help if I knew the locations of Oakhill and Edwards."

"Oakhill's just west of Market Street—Edwards is a couple blocks east of Glenwood."

Lockington thought about it. He said, "Glenwood—that's the street that runs into Mahoning Avenue from the west, sort of."

"Glenwood runs north and south."

Lockington could hear splintering sounds. He said, "It doesn't run north and south at the foot of the Mahoning Avenue Bridge. At the foot of the Mahoning Avenue Bridge it's headed damned near due west."

"Uh-huh, well, yes, I guess you could say that, but Glenwood goes north and south mostly."

Lockington could hear bells ringing, and rumbling sounds, and the tinkle of breaking glass. He said, "Can I turn right onto Glenwood off of Mahoning Avenue?"

"I wouldn't try it."

"But if I can't turn *right* onto Glenwood, how the hell can I get *onto* Glenwood?"

"You're coming from Mahoning Avenue?"

"That's right."

"Okay, if I was you, I'd cut through Mill Creek Park—you get into Mill Creek Park by going south on Belle Vista a little bit beyond the cemetery, then you swing east down to the lake, turn right, go around the lake and start bearing left. You'll run right into Glenwood."

"And Glenwood is just a few blocks west of Hillman Street?"

"You got it. Look, mister, I gotta get offa this telephone—there's things to be *done* here!"

"Sorry to have held you. To whom have I been speaking, sir?"

"My name's Kevin O'Malley."

Over the line came the sounds of men shouting hoarsely

and women screaming. Lockington said, "Well, thanks, Kevin, you've been extremely helpful. What's your capacity at the Board of Education?"

"I'm not with the Board of Education, I'm with Engine Company Five—somebody phoned in an alarm, only we ain't found the fire yet."

Lockington hung up. Youngstown people were an accommodating bunch, he thought.

12

HE PARKED THE MERCEDES at Princeton Junior High School, knowing how Columbus must have felt when he'd sighted the New World. Mill Creek Park's roads are winding, bordered by trees, and in the rain Lockington had managed to get lost, driving for twenty minutes without seeing a living soul. Eventually he'd found himself on Meridian Road, heading north to Mahoning Avenue, where he'd started. He'd stopped at a Sohio gas station where a bearded attendant had listened to the tale of Lockington's odyssey. He'd said, "You must have turned right at the south end of Lake Glacier—did you cross a bridge?"

"Yeah, a couple dozen, only maybe they were all the same bridge."

"This time," The attendant had said, "turn *left* at the end of the lake, cross a bridge, turn left again, and you'll go up a long hill to Glenwood Avenue. Turn right on Glenwood and you have it made."

It'd worked.

Princeton Junior High School was a large white brick building, probably erected in the thirties, Lockington figured. Old, but well-maintained. Its walls had been freshly painted, its floors gleamed. It was located in an area of South Side Youngstown that had known palmier days, but not recently. Decay had gripped the neighborhood and it was spreading like wood rot. Lockington had seen it all before—the identical irresistible plague was devouring Chicago at the rate of a block a week.

James T. Loftus was Principal of Princeton Junior High School—from the secretary's office Lockington could read the oblong bronze plate on Loftus's desk. It said JAMES T. LOFTUS, PRINCIPAL, but it didn't say PRINCETON JUNIOR HIGH SCHOOL. Good thinking. That way, James T. Loftus could

50

become principal of another school and he wouldn't have to buy a new oblong bronze plate. James T. Loftus wasn't at his desk, but his secretary, Maria Garcia, was at hers. Maria Garcia had her own oblong bronze plate and Lockington sensed that she wasn't going to be easy to get around. She was a shaggy-thatched, hard-eyed, granite-jawed Gibraltar of a woman and she radiated self-importance. She weighed in the vicinity of two seventy-five and it was obvious that she was in no mood for tomfoolery.

"Insurance?" She glared at Lockington. "We don't need no stinking insurance!" Her voice was as mellifluous as a heavy-duty chain saw.

Lockington said, "I'm not *selling* insurance, ma'am—I'm trying to locate the recipient of a policy payoff." He smiled his most disarming smile. Maria Garcia was not disarmed.

"Mutual of Slippery Rock? Never heard of it."

Lockington said, "Life, fire, casualty, industrial, group hospitalization, comprehensive—that sort of thing. We're big, ma'am, *very* big—forty million in policies annually."

Maria Garcia's eyes were boring holes in the bridge of Lockington's nose. "What's the location of Slippery Rock's offices?"

"Chicago, ma'am— downtown Chicago—southwest corner of State and Monroe."

"How very odd— Slippery Rock's in Pennsylvania."

"Yes, ma'am. I've wondered about that myself from time to time."

"And just what do you do with Mutual of Slippery Rock, Mr. . . . ?"

"Lockington, ma'am. Investigation usually, but in this instance I've been assigned to trace the beneficiary of a quarter-million dollar life insurance policy." Lockington was beginning to get a feeling closely akin to that experienced by those confronted by irate water buffalo. "His name is Alexi Fedorovich, ma'am—he may have attended Princeton Junior High."

"Well, obviously, you'd have to speak to Mr. Loftus," Maria Garcia said, "and Mr. Loftus isn't here at the moment."

"I can see that, ma'am—I'd be willing to wait."

A big black man had sauntered into the office, a sheaf of papers under his arm. He was about 40, impeccably attired in sharply pressed gray flannel, his oxblood patent leather oxfords sparkled, he wore a gold wristwatch, three gold rings, and he had a gold front tooth. His voice was soft, low-pitched like distant August thunder. He said, "I'm James Loftus—you wished to see me?"

Lockington said, "Yes, sir, if you can spare a few minutes."

"Certainly, step into my office." Lockington knew him now—Jim Loftus, fullback, Cleveland Browns, three touchdowns against the Chicago Bears, November 1974.

Maria Garcia cut in. "Mr. Loftus, there's been another fire alarm at the Board of Education."

Loftus said, "A phony, I'll bet."

"Yes, no fire, but the firemen did considerable damage trying to find one."

Loftus said, "*Damn*! That makes three this month, doesn't it?"

"Four."

Loftus shook his head concernedly, ushered Lockington into his office, motioning to a chair, seating himself at his desk in a brown leather swivel chair the size of King Tut's throne. Lockington sat, looking around. It was a fine, gleaming room, its floor carpeted in earth tones, its bookshelves holding the *Encyclopedia Britannica*, the Great Books, *Webster's Biographical Dictionary*, *Bartlett's Familiar Quotations*, *Roget's Thesaurus*, the *Complete Works* of William Shakespeare, and countless reference volumes. Loftus was saying, "Miss Garcia has her good days and her bad days."

Lockington said, "And this is one of her bad days."

Loftus grinned, his gold tooth flashing. "No, this is one of her good days. Now, what can I do for you, Mr.—Lockington, is it?"

"Yes, sir—Mutual of Slippery Rock. Mr. Loftus, I'm trying to find a gentleman named Alexi Fedorovich—there's a sizable insurance settlement involved. My information indicates that Mr. Fedorovich attended Princeton Junior High School."

"I see. Do you have Fedorovich's old address?"

"Yes, at the time the policy was written, he lived at 326 West Dewey Avenue."

"That's Princeton district. What were his years of attendance here?"

"Probably late thirties—he'd be sixty-five or better now. I thought that one of your faculty might—"

"No, Mr. Lockington, our records don't go back that far— Princeton's oldest current faculty member came here after the war." He sat frowning, big hands on his chest, neatly manicured fingertips placed together. Then he leaned forward abruptly, stabbing a button on his intercom. "Miss Garcia, do any of Princeton's late thirties' faculty still reside in the Youngstown area?"

There was no immediate response and Loftus waited, smiling a long-suffering smile. Then Maria Garcia's voice ripped from the intercom speaker. "Just one—an Abigail Fleugelham—she taught eighth grade English from '33 to '74. She's on the Princeton newspaper mailing list—she's seventy-seven—lives at the Canterbury Arms retirement home, Tippecanoe Road, Cornersburg."

"Well done, Miss Garcia." Loftus turned to Lockington. "Well, there it is, the best we can do."

Lockington nodded his thanks, leaving Loftus's office, passing Maria Garcia's desk. Maria watched him as she'd have watched an escapee from Death Row. He left the building, stepping into the charcoal gray of the Mahoning Valley afternoon. The rain persisted. He plodded in the direction of the Mercedes, head down, hat tilted over his eyes, getting wet. Behind him a bell was ringing. He checked his watch. 3:30— the hour of liberation—school was out. Lockington frowned in the rain. It'd been a rare day when he'd gotten out of school at 3:30. There'd been all those detention periods—for getting to school late, for not getting to school at all, for not showing up for detention periods—but today Lacey Lockington was out of school at 3:30, just like the kids who abided by the rules. That knowledge was accompanied by a strangely giddy sensation, terminated when he stepped into an ankle-deep rain puddle. He got into the Mercedes, wondering how he was going to find Tippecanoe Road in Cornersburg.

13

HE DROVE WEST on Indianola Avenue back to Glenwood, stopping at Paddy's Bar and Grill, a run-down, grease-soaked eatery that reeked of onions, Lockington's favorite kind of restaurant. He found a pay phone and tried to call Natasha to tell her that he'd probably be late. When there was no answer he remembered that Tuesday was Natasha's shopping day. Come rain, come shine, come hell or high water, Natasha shopped on *Tuesday*, it was her inviolable custom. He had a double cheeseburger and a bottle of beer at the bar, then got involved in a baseball discussion with a truck driver from Ashtabula that carried through another forty-five minutes and two bottles of beer. It was after five o'clock when Lockington left Paddy's Bar and Grill in the continuing rain, armed with explicit Cornersburg directions from the bartender.

Tippecanoe Road picked up where Meridian Road left off, at the point where Route 62 ran through Cornersburg. From there Tippecanoe wound southward, and a mile or so out of Cornersburg Lockington spotted the Canterbury Arms retirement home sign on his left, a blue neon thing done in script, sputtering on a low block of concrete. He swung east to traverse a long rutted gravel trail that twisted through dense stands of pin oak and white birch. Halloween gimmicks had been placed on the grounds—jack-o'-lanterns dotted its leaf-strewn green, old bed sheets cut to resemble ghosts hung limply in the rain, Lockington saw a large wooden black cat with red reflectors for eyes, its back arched, fangs bared. There was a soggy straw-stuffed witch straddling a broom and a cardboard skeleton dangled by its neck from a birch branch.

The Canterbury Arms retirement home was set on a hilltop, a low, sprawling gray rectangular building that covered an area of half an acre or more. Lockington left the gravel drive

55

to pull onto the blacktop of the parking lot, departing the Mercedes with a touch of trepidation, possibly because of the atmosphere surrounding the place—the isolation, the Halloween trappings, the cold rain, the gathering darkness, the melancholy—but more than likely because he was trying to track an old man who was undoubtedly on the hit list of the most vicious secret service organization on the face of planet earth.

The interior of the Canterbury Arms was tastefully done, its white stucco walls were crisscrossed by walnut-stained two-by-fours, it was carpeted in beige, there were a dozen or so comfortable-looking overstuffed brown leather chairs, several tables with brown-shaded bronze lamps, an enormous bookcase jammed with bright-jacketed volumes, a white-stone fireplace in which a couple of logs popped and crackled. A miniature replica of Big Ben stood on the mantel and it was bonging out six o'clock when Lockington approached the desk. A southbound wheelchair whistled in front of him, a northbound wheelchair zipped behind him, ticking a trouser leg. Both vehicles were manned by white-haired men, one wearing goggles, the other a crash helmet with a skull and crossbones decal on its front.

The doe-eyed, dark-haired, pudgy woman at the desk wore a starchy white uniform, a maroon cardigan over her shoulders, and a discreet blue tag indentifying her as THELMA. She was shaking her head exasperatedly. She said, "It happens every damned evening—O'Rourke and Houlihan playing 'chicken.' Fortunately for all concerned, O'Rourke always chickens out."

Lockington said, "Indianapolis East."

Thelma said, "Precisely! Did you wish to see someone, sir?"

"Yes, if possible, I'd like to speak to Abigail Fleugelham."

Thelma's doe eyes widened perceptibly. "My God, are you *sure*?"

Lockington said, "I *shouldn't* be?"

Thelma sighed resignedly. "Oh, well, so be it. I'll tell Miss Fleugelham that you're here." She scooted from behind the desk, walking rapidly down a hallway to her right, then turning left and out of sight. She was back in a matter of moments. "Take a seat, sir—she'll be with you shortly."

Lockington thanked her, finding a chair near the fireplace. The staccato snap of the burning logs and the leap of the flames proved to be hypnotic and Lockington dozed, awakening to a light touch on his shoulder. A woman stood beside his chair, a black cabretta leather coat over her arm, a bulky matching handbag slung over her shoulder. She said, "It'll be cool enough for a coat, don't you think?"

Lockington nodded.

The woman stooped to smooth an imaginary wrinkle at the knee of her gold lamé dress. She said, "Then I'm ready."

Lockington blinked. "For what?"

Her smile was mysterious. "That would depend, I suppose. Perhaps we should hoist a few on Route 224—after that, who can say?"

"Route 224?"

"The highway just south of here." She handed her coat and bag to him. He held the coat as she slipped into it. She took her bag, walking in the direction of the exit, Lockington toddling bewilderedly in her wake. Abigail Fleugelham was probably seventy-seven, all right. She'd *have* to be if she'd taught school in 1933, but she'd have passed for a sprightly sixty. Her hair was shoulder-length, blonde and wavy, her hazel eyes were clear, her face was lined but not withered— face-lifts and skillful makeup application had all but obliterated the deep creases. Her nose was uptilted and unveined, her smile was chipper, her voice light without the gruff texture of age. She was tall, slender, had excellent legs, and walked like a show horse on parade, her gait gracefully mincing.

He helped her into the Mercedes and she smiled her thanks. When they turned south on Tippecanoe Road, she said, "You surprised me—I didn't know that you'd be dropping by. I mean, we'd set up nothing definite."

Lockington said, "Sorry—I should have called."

Abigail turned to stare at him. Her perfume was expensive, vaguely provocative. She said, "You *didn't?*"

Lockington returned her stare. "No."

"You aren't Mr. Mawson?"

Lockington scowled. "No, and probably neither is Mr. Mawson."

"What do you mean—then who called?"

"I don't know—when was the call?"

"Perhaps an hour ago. He told me that his name was Mawson—he was inquiring about one of my former students."

"Alexi Fedorovich?"

"Yes—how did you know?"

"Just a guess."

Abigail Fleugelham said, "Just a guess, my ass!"

Lockington shrugged. In the darkness of the car he could feel her inquisitive hazel gaze. After a while she said, "Well, I'll be diddledy-damned—what's going on?"

"Your guess is as good as mine." It wasn't, but Abigail didn't know that.

She was lighting a cigarette. "Is Alexi in some kind of trouble?"

"Not with me."

They'd come to Route 224 and she motioned for him to turn left. She said, "He was such a good boy—mischievous, but a *good* boy."

Lockington said, "Where are we going?"

"Let's start at Fritzi's."

"Let's *start* at Fritzi's?"

"The night is young—what's your name?"

"Lacey Lockington—I'm an insurance investigator from Chicago."

"Chicago—I've been there—it's a swinging town." Lockington nodded. "Of course, Youngstown isn't all that bad—you can swing in Youngstown." She placed a hand on his knee. It was a warm hand. "If this is an insurance matter,

then Mr. Mawson is probably an investigator from another company. What's the name of yours?"

Lockington said, "Mutual of Slippery Rock."

Her hand tightened on his knee. She said, "Anything I can do for you—anything at all."

Lockington was to wonder about that, but not for long.

14

ROUTE 224 WAS A FAST-TRAFFIC four-lane highway skirting the southern rim of Youngstown, and Fritzi's was no more than a quarter-mile from Tippecanoe Road. Fritzi's was a snappy little cove, all red leatherette and chrome, dimly lighted with frosted blue mirrors and a subdued jukebox. They took a booth to the rear and when the waitress showed up Lockington ordered a double Martell's cognac, no wash. The waitress made a note of Lockington's choice before glancing quizzically at Abigail Fleugelham. Abigail was giving the matter some thought. After a while she said, "Do you have tall glasses—I mean *tall* glasses?"

The waitress said, "Yes, ma'am."

"Then I'll have vodka, blackberry brandy, sloe gin, light rum, and a triple tequila over ice—easy on the ice."

The waitress scribbled furiously on her pad. She said, "Stirred or blended, ma'am?"

Lockington said, "Stir it, *gently*, for God's sake—you could level the joint!"

The waitress said, "Is there a name for this drink, ma'am?"

"Why certainly," Abigail said. "It's a Moon Rocket."

The waitress said, "I don't believe I've ever heard of a Moon Rocket."

Abigail said, "Of course, you haven't—until now, neither have I."

The waitress retreated to the bar, conferring with the white-jacketed bartender, going over the mixture's ingredients with him. Lockington said, "Miss Fleugelham, tell me about Alexi Fedorovich."

"'Abby'—call me 'Abby'."

"All right, Abby—now, about Alexi Fedorovich."

"What about him?"

"Have you seen him recently?"

"Alexi—*recently*? Oh, heavens, *no*! Alexi went to Russia when he was about fifteen—his mother died—his father was originally from Russia."

"Did you know any of his junior high school associates, the kids he hung around with—those with whom he might have maintained contact?"

Their drinks came. Lockington watched Abby lift her Moon Rocket, killing half of the fearsome concoction in two gulps. The remaining half went in two more. She said, "*Delicious*! I believe I'll have another!" She waved to the waitress, pointing to her glass. The waitress's mouth dropped open, but she nodded.

Lockington said, "We were talking about Alexi Fedorovich, I believe."

"Yes, he was a clean-cut youngster, well-behaved, respectful, highly intelligent, mature for his years—excellent student."

"His close friends?"

"Male or female?"

"Either."

Abigail's hazel eyes were slightly blurred. She said, "Well, there was Olga Karelinko—Olga got his cherry, I'm certain of it."

"Olga Karelinko?"

"Yes, but if I'd been ten years younger, I'd have given her a run for it!"

"Uhh-h-h, what can you tell me of Olga Karelinko?"

"Pretty little thing, blonde, heavy-chested—Alexi walked her to school and back every day—I believe that they lived on the same street, West Dewey Avenue, possibly. Olga had the hots for Alexi, that was obvious. I caught them in the cloakroom once—Alexi had a finger in her—I looked the other way—what the hell, boys will be boys, that's what I always say. What do *you* always say, Mr. Lockingwrench?"

Lockington said, "The wrong thing at the wrong time. Olga Karelinko was of Russian descent?"

"That's right—she was the lusty, busty type."

"Have you seen Olga since her junior high school days?"

"Yes, a couple of times—once at Southern Park Mall, once on West Federal Street downtown. This was a few years back and I don't believe she recognized me. Olga left Princeton Junior High shortly after Alexi's father took him to Russia."

"She quit school?"

"No, Olga was a good student. The Karelinko family moved to another district, I'd imagine."

Abby's second Moon Rocket was on their table and Lockington watched transfixed as it disappeared as rapidly as her first. Abby signaled for another. She did this by standing on the seat of the booth and waving both arms in the fashion of an Alamo sentry who has just detected the approach of forty thousand Mexicans.

Lockington assisted in returning her to a sitting position. He said, "Any others come to mind?"

"Any other *whats*?" The blur was gone from Abby's eyes, replaced by a crystalline glaze.

Lockington said, "School pals—he must have had a few buddies."

Abby peered at him through the gloom of the booth. "How come you ash these quesshuns, Mr. Lockingburg?"

"It's Locking*ton*, ma'am. There's an insurance settlement on the line—Alexi Fedorovich is the benificiary. If he's in the United States, I have to find him."

"But he not in Unite Stays—he in *Russia*."

"He *was* in Russia, but isn't it possible that he returned to this country?"

"Also possbul went to Tibet." The Moon Rocket arrived and Abby took a slurp. "Well, there wash Nicholas Corpulungo—Nicholas Corpulungo eighth grade stud—shoot, I could have screw Nicholas Corpulungo into grounn."

"And others?"

"An' *others*? Hell, took on five football coaches, teachers' seminar Clevelunn, 1940!"

"I meant, did Alexi have other male friends?"

"Howard Kramer—Howard Kramer killed in war."

"Whatever happened to Corpulungo?"

"Had automobile aguncy Minneapolis or someplace."

"What kind of agency?"

"*Automobile*—you doan hear well, Missur Lockingstrap?"

"Ford agency, Chevy, Dodge—what make of car?"

"No idea, but Missur Wilmer nailed me in backseat Packard Clipper."

"Mr. Wilmer?"

"Taught algebra South High. Three times, by golly!"

"Three times—where was Mr. Wilmer between jobs?"

"Well, once he had to piss—other time we juss sit arounn till he ready. Mill Creek Park, 1941—full moon, hot pants." Abby gargled another slug of her Moon Rocket. "Like you always say, 'boys will be boys'."

"*I* don't always say that, *you* always say that."

Abby tilted her Moon Rocket glass, draining it. She said, "Looky, Lockingcock, there motel east of here—The Belfry—X-rated movies, water bed, whole nine yards. Whatcha shay, kid?"

Lockington said, "I'd better get you back to the Canterbury—I have an important nine o'clock appointment."

Abby leered at him. "Hey, Lockingfish, I not sevenny-seven years ole for *nothing*—I know my way arounn a *mattress*!"

Lockington stood, helping Abby to her feet. The waitress came to the booth. She said, "That'll be twenty-four dollars." Lockington handed her a twenty and a ten. He muttered, "Keep the change, and for Christ's sake help me get her out of here!"

Abby was saying, "Lissen, Lockingdick, I'll ride you till you're *crosseyed*!" The waitress was holding the door for Lockington and he dragged Abigail Fleugelham into the parking lot, stuffing her into the Mercedes. As they turned west on 224 she said, "Hey, Lockingcrotch, I'm got forty feet clothes line in bag—how you like be tied spread-eagle? Wow, you think you died an' gone *Heaven!*"

Lockington said, "Just take it easy, Abby—you'll be home shortly."

There was no sound from the passenger's side of the Mercedes, Abby was sleeping. Lockington pulled up just short of the Canterbury Arms entrance, allowing an ambulance to roll onto Tippecanoe Road. It turned north, fading into the distance at high speed, lights flashing, siren screaming. He parked close to the Canterbury entrance, going in. Thelma was at the desk. He said, "I have a basket case in my car."

Thelma said, "Blessed *Jesus*, what the hell *next?*"

Lockington said, "I saw an ambulance."

"O'Rourke didn't chicken-out—they must have heard the crash in Cincinnati! Houlihan has a concussion and O'Rourke busted his upper plate—they think he swallowed most of it!" She left the desk. "All right, bring her in."

Lockington went out, returning with Abigail Fleugelham over his shoulder. Thelma led the way to a room and Lockington deposited Abby on a bed. Thelma threw a blanket over her, exhaling audibly. She said, "What a helluva night *this* has been!"

"Thelma, you don't know the *half* of it."

"I didn't catch your name, but if it isn't Attila the Hun, I live alone and I get off at midnight, providing the joint doesn't go up in flames *before* then."

Lockington said, "I have to meet a guy." That was a lie. "But I'll try to get back by midnight." So was that.

15 HE DIDN'T GET BACK to the house on Dunlap Avenue until well after eight o'clock and he didn't have a rose when he arrived, but Natasha hung a kiss on him anyway, a real bellringer. Then she stepped back, holding him at arm's length, looking him over. She said, "Busy afternoon, wasn't it?"

Lockington said, "Sure was—I spent it running in circles."

"*Big* circles?"

"*Little* circles—the kind that never get you there."

"Anything on General Fedorovich?"

"Nothing current—I just nibbled at his past. I might have something tomorrow. Then again I might not." He told her of his visit to Princeton Junior High School and of Abigail Fleugelham.

Natasha's silvery laugh rippled through the living room. "A flattering offer, I must say."

Lockington said, "At seventy-seven, sex is wishful thinking."

"Lacey, don't you *believe* it! At the Academy one of our best sex technique teachers was a woman of seventy-five. She simply *loved* to give demonstrations!"

"With a younger man, of course."

"Well-l-l, yes,—he was seventy-three."

"At seventy-three he was an *instructor*?"

Natasha nodded. "Sergei Gasparov. Sergei Gasparov was *excellent*!"

Lockington said, "*Sure*, he was."

Natasha winked at him. "Don't laugh, Lacey—don't *laugh*!"

Lockington didn't laugh. He didn't so much as smile. He said, "I think the Russians must know something that the Americans haven't found out."

Natasha changed the subject. "Something to eat?"

Lockington shook his head. "I had a sandwich—I'd prefer a drink."

They went down to the basement, Natasha ignoring the couch and her open volume on American Government, choosing to sit close beside him at their bar, sipping a glass of vodka. During their second drink she said, "I called every public library and every book store in the city of Youngstown and not *one* of them has a copy of General Fedorovich's book. You said that this Gordon Kilbuck gave you a copy?"

"Yeah, but it's at the office. Want to look at it?"

"If you wouldn't mind."

"I'll bring it home tomorrow evening."

"Why can't I pick it up during lunch?"

"I doubt that I'll be around for lunch—I may be out of the office most of the day."

"All right, tomorrow night then."

Lockington caught a faint flicker of disappointment in her voice, and he said, "Well, look, I can run down to the office now, if it's important to you."

"It isn't that it's so earth-rattlingly important—it's just that General Fedorovich was a countryman of mine, I've *seen* him in Moscow, I've known *of* him since I was child! Alexi Fedorovich was a big man in the Soviet Union! Imagine how it'd strike you if one of America's Joint Chiefs-of-Staff would defect to Russia, then write a book. You'd be interested, wouldn't you—particularly if *you'd* defected shortly before *he* did?"

Lockington nodded, seeing the parallel.

They had another drink and another before he turned on the 11:00 local news. There was nothing of consequence happening in Youngstown, but Lockington was amused by the report that there'd been another in an irritating chain of false fire alarms at the Youngstown Board of Education. Television crews had arrived on the scene and a portion of the pandemonium had been filmed. Firemen were shown hacking through doors with axes, breaking into storage bins, turning the place upside down, finding neither smoke nor fire. He wondered which of the fireman was Kevin O'Malley, the guy who'd answered the Board of Education telephone that afternoon.

On their way up the stairs Natasha stopped, turning to face Lockington. "General Fedorovich's book—what does it look like?"

"It's just a book—fatter than most—damned near eight hundred pages."

"I mean the dust jacket—is there a picture?"

"Well, yeah, there's a drawing of a bunch of people pushing a platform that has a big hairy-assed horse mounted on it. Kilbuck told me that Fedorovich insisted on designing the dust jacket."

"This platform—it's on wheels?"

"Sure—how the hell could they push it if it *wasn't*? This is one helluva horse!"

"What kind of wheels?"

"Round, I believe."

"*Seriously*, Lacey—what do the wheels *look* like?"

"They're made of wood, apparently—it's a sketch, not a photograph."

"All right, go on."

"That's all—they're wooden wheels."

"*Solid* wooden wheels?"

"No, they have spokes."

"How many spokes per wheel?"

Lockington tried to visualize the wheels on the dust jacket of Fedorovich's book. He said, "Eight, probably. What's the big interest in wheels?"

She nudged him, setting him in motion up the stairs. "Nothing—just curious." They turned toward the bedroom and she gripped his hand, her nails digging into his palm. They were undressing when she placed her hands on the bed, leaning in Lockington's direction, her pale blue eyes wide. She said, "Lacey, do me a favor?"

"Name it."

"Be rough with me tonight."

"I can't be rough with you—I don't *feel* that way about you."

She nodded, standing erect, stripping quickly. "All right, then *I'll* be rough with *you*!"

She was. Her gloss was gone, she snarled, she bit, she kicked and clawed—she was a tigress, a creamy ball of sexual ferocity, and her orgasms were great, grinding, groaning things. Just before he fell asleep he held her in the darkness, stroking her buttocks, feeling the steady throb of her heart, realizing that a man can't possibly know a woman until he's lived with her, and that when he's lived with her he can't possibly know her half as well as he did *before* he lived with her. It was a highly confusing state of affairs.

16 THE RAIN HAD MOVED EAST overnight and if it wasn't the most beautiful October morning in history, it was certainly in the top ten. And if Lacey Lockington wasn't in the world's smallest parking lot, he was probably in the busiest. At 7:45 he'd backed the Mercedes against a parking block on the south side of the cramped blacktopped area, smackdab in front of Youngstown's West Side Post Office. He'd taken out a small notebook and he'd sat there, windows open, soaking up his share of what he knew might be the last decent weather of 1988. In October you never can tell.

The notebook was for the license plate numbers of post-office visitors, a precaution taken against the possibility of losing his quarry in traffic.

John Sebulsky, the bartender at the Flamingo Lounge on Mahoning Avenue, had a brother on the Mahoning County police force. Back in May, during the Devereaux goings-on, John had been of considerable assistance in the matter of linking license plates to their owners. For fifty bucks, of course—twenty-five for John, twenty-five for his brother on the county force. It'd been a bargain.

Nearly two hours had crawled by and the lot had been hyperactive, never a dull moment. Now it was 9:40 and Lockington was working on his second page of license plate numbers, jotting them down as the vehicles arrived, crossing them out if his bright red envelope wasn't in evidence when they departed. It was a task that'd kept him busy because it appeared that Youngstown's West Side Post Office was patronized by every female in the state of Ohio. Then, at 9:48, an old blue Chevette whisked into the parking lot, stopping in front of the delicatessen that shared the post office location. The Chevette was driven by a sturdily built woman wearing a floppy white gardening hat, large-lensed sunglasses, blue sweatshirt, blue slacks, and white jogging shoes. She left her car to head for the post office and Lockington entered the Chevette's license number in his notebook, his eyes narrowing. Olga Karelinko would be an older woman, somewhere in her mid-sixties, and this one was getting up in years, although the broad brim of her hat and her oversize sunglasses made her features difficult to make out. She entered the post office and within a minute she came out, carrying a large bright red mailing envelope. Lockington jammed his notebook into his jacket pocket. Tallyho!

He kicked the Mercedes to life, watching the woman climb into the blue Chevette and back out of her parking slot. A rusty white Dodge van came barreling into the lot, screeching to a halt directly in front of the Mercedes. Lockington hit the horn, indicating with frantic motions that he wanted to leave. The driver of the van, a formidable-looking bushy-faced man, thumbed his nose. Lockington piled out of the Mercedes, watching the blue Chevette roll out of the parking lot onto Millet Avenue, then west on Mahoning. The bushy-faced man had departed his van but with prompt action there'd still be a chance of catching the Chevette. Lockington hollered, "Hey, buddy, would you move 'er up just a few feet? It's *urgent*!"

The bushy-faced man spat tobacco juice, growling, "Urgent, schmurgent." He turned his back, starting for the post office.

Lockington kicked the left front tire of the Mercedes. He said, "Asshole!"

The bushy-faced fellow stopped in his tracks, wheeling to make for Lockington, waving to somebody in the rear of the van. The van door banged open and a man got out. So did another. Both of them were bigger than the bushy-faced character. They advanced on Lockington and to make bad matters worse, one more monster had bailed out of a sagging green Mustang parked on Millet Avenue, sprinting to bring up the rear of the procession. He was half the size of a Diesel locomotive, he wore a gray cardigan, determination was etched on his bulldog face, and he moved like a mountain cat. If Lockington had been in worse jams he couldn't remember them.

The bushy-faced man led the way to Lockington, grabbing the lapel of his jacket, cocking a fist. Interpreting this as a possibly hostile move, Lockington busted him flush on his beard, sending him reeling across the Mahoning Avenue sidewalk and onto the parkway where his knees gave out. Lockington spun to face the remaining three. One was on his feet, two weren't—they were flat on their faces, unconscious. The man in the gray cardigan got into the white van, then backed it into the middle of Millet Avenue, leaving it there parked sideways. He returned at a dogtrot, carrying the van's keys, dropping them through a parking lot grating, waiting for the splash. When it came, he grinned. It was the grin of a Siberian tiger in a bratwurst shop. He threw back his head, studying the cloudless blue October sky. He said, "One helluva morning, ain't it, Mr. Lockington?"

Lockington nodded. "Now that you mention it, it's had its moments."

The man in the gray cardigan put out his hand. "I'm Barney Kozlowski—my old man spoke to you the other day about you maybe teaching me the ropes of the P.I. business."

Lockington sized him up as they shook hands. Barney was bigger that his father, something like six-seven, probably two-sixty. He was a good-looking youngster with a blond crew cut, alert blue eyes, and a resolute jaw. Lockington said, "Yes, I remember."

"Dad told me that you thought you might be able to use me if something came up, so I've been tailing you now and then, just practicing."

Lockington nodded. He said, "Uh-huh."

"You see, I want to stay sharp because you'll probably want me to follow a bunch of people."

Lockington said, "Yeah, well, looky, kid, why don't you swing around by the office tomorrow morning, say nine-thirty or so. We'll see what can be worked out."

17 AT TEN O'CLOCK THAT MORNING the Flamingo Lounge door was wide open, and but for John Sebulsky, the place was deserted. Lockington followed a stray sunbeam to the bar where Sebulsky sat on a stool, elbows on his knees, chin cupped in his hands, studying a Racing Form. Lockington said, "Late scratch."

Sebulsky looked up, his eyes widening. He said, "Well, Jesus Christ!"

Lockington slid onto a barstool. "Mistaken identity—the name's Lockington."

"Lacey, where the hell you *been*?"

"I went back to Chicago for a time." He didn't add that it'd been a very short time—approximately thirty-six hours—just long enough to learn about his former partner Moose Katzenbach and former girlfriend Edna Garson.

"You still working that Pecos Peggy insurance case?"

Lockington shook his head. He didn't care to rehash old business and Sebulsky didn't pursue the subject. He popped a double shot glass onto the bar, splashing Martell's cognac into it, slapping the bar with flat of his hand, the universal signal that the house is buying.

Lockington said, "Much obliged—say, John, is your brother still with the county cops?"

Sebulsky said, "Yeah, he'll die there. Do we have something?"

"Yeah—this." Lockington grabbed a cardboard beer coaster, writing the blue Chevette's license number on its border, sliding it across the bar along with five ten dollar bills.

Sebulsky glanced at it, nodding, stuffing the tens into a shirt pocket. He said, "Should be easy—he's off today so I'll call him at his poker game."

"Little bit early for poker."

"Little bit late—they've been playing since nine o'clock last night." He went to the phone, punched numbers, spoke briefly, and returned. "Ten minutes, maybe less." He poured more cognac, opened a bottle of Michelob Dry for himself, and they sat in the sunlight streaming through the open door, making small talk, Sebulsky remarking that the Chicago Cubs had improved in '88. He said, "I give 'em a shot next year."

Lockington shook his head. "Not in '89—maybe '90 or '91."

"They got good kids on the farm, Walton and Smith, plus this guy Grace figures to mature next season." The phone rang. Sebulsky picked up a pad and pencil, answered it, making rapid notes. He said, "Thanks," hung up, ripping the page from the pad and passing it to Lockington. "Woman by the name of Candice Hoffman, 24 North Brockway."

Lockington said, "Okay, but where the hell is North Brockway?"

"East, six, seven blocks—big red-brick Methodist church on the corner."

The phone rang again and Sebulsky took the call. He said, "Hang on, I'll see." He arched his eyebrows, pointing to Lockington.

Lockington nodded, shrugging.

Sebulsky handed the phone to Lockington, stretching the cord to its limit. Lockington said, "Yes?"

A male voice said, "Mr. Lockington?"

"That would depend on what you're selling."

"Mr. Lockington, this is Barney Kozlowski."

"All right, what's up?"

"I thought you should know that a brown '87 Ford Escort followed you when you left the post office."

"Still practicing, Barney?"

"Well, yeah, just a little bit."

"Did you get a squint at the driver?"

"Oh, sure, from up close—guy in a black Stetson hat, black suit, cowboy shirt, shoestring tie. When you went into the

Flamingo, he parked headed north, just south of the Flamingo lot where he could keep an eye on your car."

"He's there now?"

"No, he's been gone for a few minutes."

"Where did he go—any idea?"

"No, but he was in one helluva hurry to get there."

"Okay, thanks, kid." Lockington returned the phone to Sebulsky. Sebulsky said, "Bad news?"

Lockington said, "Did you ever get *good* news at ten-fucking-fifteen in the morning?"

Sebulsky scratched his head, taking the question under consideration. After a while he said, "Yeah—*once*. My car wouldn't start and the garage called and told me I needed a new ignition switch."

"That's good news?"

Sebulsky said, "Why, hell, yes—it could have been the *timing-chain!*"

18 HE DROVE EAST on Mahoning Avenue, immersed in thought, his eyes flicking from the traffic ahead of him to his rear-view mirror, back and forth. The coffee wasn't perking but the water was beginning to bubble around the edges. Another party, supposedly a Mr. Mawson, was looking for Gen. Alexi Fedorovich, and if Mawson wasn't thinking along Lockington's lines and employing Lockington's methods, then he was permitting Lockington to act as his coon hound, leading the way to Fedorovich.

Mawson couldn't have located Abigail Fleugelham by following Lockington because he'd phoned Abby before Lockington had reached the Canterbury Arms retirement home. If he'd *preceded* Lockington to Princeton Junior High School, asking essentially the same questions asked by Lockington, certainly Maria Garcia or James Lofton would have made mention of the fact. But he *might* have arrived at Princeton shortly following Lockington's departure, receiving the identical information given to Lockington, calling Abby when Lockington was discussing baseball at Paddy's Bar and Grill. Well, no matter how he'd found her, he hadn't learned anything from Abby, but he'd learn a few things if he took her out for an evening. Lockington grinned at the thought.

So, had Mawson followed him to the West Side Post Office, and had Barney Kozlowski spotted him when Lockington had pulled away? If that was the case, he *still* hadn't gained valuable information, *providing* he hadn't known about the red envelope—and he hadn't, obviously, because if he'd known about it, he'd have followed the woman in the blue Chevette, *not* Lockington. At Hazelwood Avenue Lockington tensed at the wheel. His rear-view mirror showed a brown Ford Escort, buzzing out of trailing traffic, slipping behind the Mercedes, then dropping back a quarter-block or so, hanging there.

Lockington passed North Brockway Avenue and the big red-brick Methodist church mentioned by John Sebulsky a few minutes earlier. He continued east, past the post office to Belle Vista Avenue and turned left. The Escort stayed with him. He spun left on Connecticut Avenue, left again on Richview, right on Mahoning. The brown Escort was still on his trail.

He drove west to Schenley Avenue, wheeling the Mercedes north on Schenley, then into a lumpy little parking lot on his right. He left the car, locked it, and went into the Valencia Café through the rear door, sauntering as nonchalantly as he knew how. He waved to the barmaid, an elderly lady he'd never seen before who watched bewilderedly as he hiked along the long row of barstools to exit onto Mahoning Avenue through the front door.

He turned the corner onto Schenley Avenue, heading north. The brown Ford Escort was parked ahead of him on the east side of the street. Lockington stepped from the sidewalk, rapidly skirting the trunk of the little car, jerking open the door, inserting the muzzle of his .38 police special in the driver's ear. He said, "Hi, there—would you care for a drink?" The hammer of the .38 clicked back.

The man in the black Stetson hat said, "I was beginning to think you'd never ask."

Lockington said, "You'd better leave your howitzer in the car."

The man said, "Why, sure—what the hell, there ain't nobody here but us chickens." He slipped a Colt .45 automatic pistol from his shoulder holster, sliding it barrel-first under the front seat of the Escort, and Lockington sheathed his .38, stepping back, watching him get out of the car. He was a gray-haired, hooknosed, stockily built fellow, probably in his mid-fifties. A lapel had been ripped from his Western-cut black suit jacket, and the front of his brown cowboy shirt was missing. Lockington gestured toward Mahoning Avenue and they moved in that direction, Lockington walking to the left, slightly to the rear. Lockington said, "Mr. Mawson, I presume."

The man shook his head. "Bresnahan—Cayuse Bresnahan—Mineral Springs, Montana."

"There ain't been too many songs about Montana."

"Enrico Caruso had one—my grandmother wrote it and sent it to him."

"I haven't heard it."

"No, he died three years later—never got a chance to sing it."

"Your grandmother was probably disappointed."

"She was never the same."

They were at the front door of the Valencia Café when Lockington said, "This is a lousy way to make a living."

Bresnahan said, "I should have mentioned that."

19 THEY MADE THEIR WAY to a rickety table near the Valencia Café's stockroom. It was shadowy back in that area, well removed from a raucous football argument at the south end of the bar. The old lady who was running the Valencia came by, eyeing Lockington suspiciously, recognizing him as the man who'd swished nonstop through the place. She didn't say a word, just stood at their table, arms folded, staring at them, waiting. Lockington went with his customary double Martell's, Bresnahan requested a shot of Corby's and a bottle of Stroh's. The old lady said, "We don't got no Corby's."

"Make it V.O."

"We don't got no Stroh's."

"Make it Budweiser."

"And that ain't all." The old lady glared at Lockington. "We don't got no Martell's.

Lockington said, "Make it brandy."

"What kind of brandy? We don't got no Christian Brothers."

"Okay, what other kinds don't you got?"

"Wait a minute—I'll go see."

Lockington said, "Don't bother, ma'am—just grab a bottle and pour."

She returned to the bar and Cayuse Bresnahan said, "The check is mine."

Lockington said, "I'm glad to hear that." He was waiting for Bresnahan to get down to brass tacks or whatever he was going to get down to.

When their drinks were on the table Bresnahan said, "All right, who's your gorilla?"

Lockington said, "I don't own a gorilla."

"I'm talking about that walking catastrophe who coldcocked two guys in the post office parking lot—the one who dragged me out of my car when you were in the Flamingo Lounge."

"He dragged you out of your car?"

"Yes, and the sonofabitch didn't even open the door—he just reached in and jerked me through the fucking window! Then he hoisted me about six feet off the ground and he shook me like I was a bag of popcorn!"

"Oh, you must mean Barney. What did he say?"

"He didn't say anything. He didn't *have* to—I got the message."

"Apparently you *didn't*—you stayed on my trail."

"Yeah, but that wasn't easy. I had to watch your car from three blocks away—damned good thing I happened to have binoculars!"

"Uh-huh, well, Barney's just a shade on the exuberant side."

"So was Genghis Khan." He offered Lockington a cigarette and Lockington took it because it wasn't a filter-tip. Lockington detested filter-tips. Bresnahan held a match for them and they sat there, looking at each other until Lockington said, "Okay, Bresnahan, let's get at it."

Bresnahan said, "All right, to kick it off, I'm out of Chicago."

"So am I—for keeps."

"You didn't like Chicago?"

"I liked it, but that was before I stopped liking it."

"Well, she ain't what she used to be, that's for certain." He downed his shot of V.O., turning his attention to his bottle of Budweiser. He said, "I'm with the United States government."

"I keep running into you people."

"Yes—you were of considerable assistance during the Devereaux matter."

Lockington concentrated on the coal of his cigarette. At the end of the bar the football argument was heating up. Bresnahan nipped at his beer, organizing his plan of approach, Lockington figured. Following a few silent moments Bresnahan said, "I suppose the best place to begin would be at the beginning."

Lockington said, "Well, if it'll help any, I was born in '39."

"To Kelly and Peggy Lockington."

Lockington nodded. "Fine people."

Bresnahan said, "The best! They got drunk together on Saturday nights, but they made it to church on Sunday mornings."

"Well, not *always*—Sunday mornings were ordeals for Kelly."

"They were good Catholics. How come you turned out to be a fucking agnostic?"

"I'm not a fucking agnostic—I believe in God, but the God I believe in has no religious connections and He doesn't meddle in the affairs of men—that's the only way He makes sense to me. Where's the importance?"

Bresnahan shrugged. "There probably isn't any."

"Then why are we talking about it?"

"Just charge it to curiosity. You were a Chicago cop."

"For a time."

"For *quite* a time. You were a good one as Chicago cops go, not a glowing compliment by any means, but you were reasonably straight-up. You gave second and third chances to a few Clark Street hookers, you bent some rules out of shape, but by and large you came right down the middle of the road. Then you shot a drug pusher, a child molester and a couple of muggers, and the Chicago *Morning Sentinel* hung a trigger-happy tag on you. That got you drummed out of service."

Lockington polished off his double cognac. "What are you looking for, Bresnahan—a psychological portrait?"

"Nothing like that—just getting to know you."

"Why?"

"Later on that, if you don't mind. Any leftovers from your Chicago days?"

"Bad memories, mostly. My badge and handcuffs are in my bedroom bureau drawer."

"And you still have your .38. Tell me, Lockington, why

would you pull a gun on a man who was driving behind you—
are you working on something?"

"Nothing that would concern you."

Bresnahan shrugged it off. He said, "You hired out at Classic
Investigations on West Randolph Street, you got involved in
the Denny-Elwood mess, and when Denny got blown away
by Elwood and vice versa, you took over Classic Investigations.
You hired your old buddy from the Chicago force—a guy
named Katzenjammer."

"Katzen*bach*—Moose Katzen*bach*."

"Yeah, Katzen*bach*. Then you started digging into that
Devereaux business and that was how you met a woman from
the Chicago Polish Consulate, a humdinger by the name of
Natasha Gorky. You handled the Devereaux matter like a
champion—Devereaux was in a position to damage the agency
but you set him up for the axe."

"I set him up to be taken alive by the CIA—the KGB was
a jump ahead of me. It killed him."

"Well, however it worked, it came out just dandy for Uncle
Sam."

"And probably for Devereaux—the poor bastard was dying
of cancer."

Bresnahan said, "Back to you and Natasha Gorky—she was
KGB, but you fell in love with her."

"To put it mildly, yes."

"And *she* went bonkers over *you*."

"I can't speak for Natasha Gorky."

"Aw, come on, Lockington, the woman went out on a *limb*
for you! She blackmailed the KGB for a hundred grand plus
that Mercedes you're driving! She used the threat of an exposé
that Devereaux never *wrote*—she claimed that he'd done one,
she inferred that she might arrange for the manuscript to reach
a publisher, and the KGB let her walk!"

"*Did* it?"

"We've seen nothing to the contrary." Bresnahan shook his
head in disbelief. "Talk about bearding the lion in his den!

She had the guts of a drunken Apache—she was working without a *net*!"

"You're talking ancient history, Bresnahan. That was then and this is now."

"I'm bringing us up to date. You two came to Youngstown. Why Youngstown?"

"Because it has trees."

"That's good enough. Natasha Gorky bought a furnished house from a chickie named Pecos Peggy Smith, a country singer at a joint called Club Crossroads in Austintown, and you're living happily ever after."

"And *you* are spinning your wheels."

"Be patient, we're closing in on it."

"Maybe we'd better grab it before it dries up and blows away."

Bresnahan was waving to the old lady behind the bar. She waved back, arriving shortly with a new round of drinks, peering at the gaping hole in the front of Bresnahan's shirt. She said, "Moths?"

Bresnahan said, "Right."

The old lady said, "Some *moths*!"

Bresnahan said, "We grow 'em big in Montana."

20

CAYUSE BRESNAHAN WAS STUDYING Lockington, nodding. He said, "You'll do."

Lockington said, "That's what the cannibals
told the missionary."

"Look, Lockington, you don't have a clearance of any
priority, but I'm authorized to open the books to you—we
think you can be of help."

"The CIA thought that I could be of help last May—it
thought I could be of help by staying the hell out of the
Devereaux case."

Bresnahan smiled a tolerant smile. "That wasn't exactly how
it worked. The CIA asked you stay out because it wanted you
to get in."

"And now you're going to ask me to get *in* because you
want me to stay *out*. Why don't you bastards ever mean what
you say?"

"Normally, we do, but there are occasions when a touch of
reverse psychology works wonders—you see, the best way to
get a bulldog to hang onto a bone is to try to take it away
from him. You were interested in the Devereaux affair. The
Agency wanted you to *stay* interested."

Lockington yawned. "I'm due back at the office shortly."

Bresnahan leaned forward. "Lockington, a top-flight Soviet
defector has given us the slip."

A tiny bell was jingling insistently in the recesses of
Lockington's mind and he hoped that Bresnahan couldn't hear
it. He cranked up his very best jaded expression. "And that's
why you've been following me around like I'm giving away
doughnuts?"

"Hear me out, please. I got in from Chicago last night. I
rented a car and I tagged you from your residence this
morning. I wanted to discuss this matter, but you didn't go

84

directly to your office—you went to the West Side Post Office and that wasn't the appropriate place. I got the impression that you were waiting for someone."

"Yeah, I was supposed to meet the Youngstown City Council for coffee."

"Then, after you and Paul Bunyan kicked the stuffings out of the hooligans at the post office, I followed you to the Flamingo Lounge, but before I could come in, that man-mountain closed in on me. Since then, I've been waiting for you to light somewhere."

Lockington permitted himself to display a casual interest in Bresnahan's earlier statement. "This Russian defector—what about him?"

"His name's Alexi Fedorovich—*General* Alexi Fedorovich—ever hear of him?"

Lockington managed another yawn. "I'm not acquainted with the Russian Army—I've had enough difficulty with the United States Marines."

"Well, Fedorovich was a biggie—second-in-command of the Soviet Military Planning Division. He was in East Germany on behalf of the Soviet Government. He went over to West Berlin, apparently to pick up a few trinkets and he ducked out on his entourage. He showed up at the United States Embassy, requesting political asylum and he got the red carpet treatment. He was flown to Washington and he handed us a ton of information. He was given a new identity and he was established in a quiet suburb of Rochester, New York—nice house, new Cadillac, fat pension, highly cooperative twenty-five-year-old housekeeper—the whole shot."

"Highly cooperative—*how* highly cooperative?"

"As highly cooperative as it took."

"She was CIA?"

"Of course, but he gave her the slip, he kissed it off, all of it, and the sonofabitch hasn't been seen since! He left no tracks, and here's the punch line—it turned out that he'd written a book on Soviet battle plans *before* he defected—something called *The Wheels of Treachery*. Are you familiar with it?"

Lockington said, "No, I never got much beyond *Robin Hood*."

"Fedorovich peddled it to a New York City publishing house—prominent outfit—Millard and Cummings. He probably got a bundle for it. Then he flew the fucking coop."

"Millard and Cummings can't help you regarding his whereabouts?"

"Can't or *won't*, whichever it is. Fedorovich really blew the whistle, and I'm here to tell you that the KGB takes a mighty dim view of that kind of carrying on!"

Lockington was listening, trying not to look bored—he'd heard most of it from Gordon Kilbuck. Bresnahan was saying, "I suppose you know what happens if the KGB gets to him before we do."

"Instant goulash, I'd imagine. And what happens if *you* get to him first?"

"Well, we're gonna have to take him into protective custody, that's certain. We'll have to point out the error of his ways—we'll probably have to relocate him and watch him to cut down the possibilities of an encore."

"He has money now—that could make him difficult to deal with."

"I doubt it—he's a reasonable man. He probably grew weary of Rochester. We have a hunch that he's in Youngstown to touch a few old bases—that's the kicker—he was born in Youngstown."

"You don't *mean* it!"

"Yep! His old man hauled him back to Russia when he was just a kid. It's probably a sentimental journey—no doubt he has connections somewhere in the Mahoning Valley."

"All right, where do I come in?" Lockington knew exactly where he came in, or exactly where Bresnahan would *want* him to come in.

Bresnahan said, "Let me put it this way—if by some curious twist of fate you should happen to come across General Alexi

Fedorovich, there'll be ten thousand dollars in it for you."

Lockington snorted. "And just how am I supposed to go about coming across him?"

Cayuse Bresnahan's smile was of the type that establishes the smiler as wise beyond the ken of ordinary men. "Well, Lockington, you're never gotten around to walking on water, but your track record shows you to be tough, talented and resourceful—and you should remember that Natasha Gorky's KGB money isn't going to last *forever*."

"Uh-huh—which is why I can't afford to get mixed up in any *maybe* cases. You've given me next to nothing to go on, and after I've spent a month going door-to-door, looking for Ivan the Terrible, I could wind up in the nearest soup line."

Bresnahan threw his hands high in mock horror and the old lady behind the bar hollered, "We don't got no more Budweiser."

Lockington yelled, "That's okay—I think he was drunk when he got here."

Bresnahan was saying, "My God, Lockington, we've had no intentions of letting you starve to death!" He reached into a jacket pocket and popped a roll of currency onto the table top, pushing it to Lockington. It was secured by a rubber band. "There's twenty-five hundred on account—it should get you around the next corner."

Lockington wondered about the guy who'd said that money doesn't grow on trees getting paid twice for one job struck him as being an excellent idea. The football seminar had waxed furious, bordering now on fisticuffs, drowning out a portion of Bresnahan's wrap-up on the subject of Gen. Alexi Fedorovich, but Lockington caught no mention of West Dewey Avenue, or of Princeton Junior High School, or of Abigail Fleugelham, or of Olga Karelinko, or of any number of subjects. He doubted that he was ahead of Mr. Mawson, but he was ahead of *some*body—an unusuality. He liked that one. Unusuality—too bad it wasn't in the dictionary.

Bresnahan was peering quizzically at Lockington, his half-smile not quite a half-smile—Lockington rated it a quarter-smile. Bresnahan said, "One other thing."

"Ah, yes, there's always one other thing."

"Could you tell me if you've been contacted by others expressing an interest in Fedorovich?"

"I could, but I wouldn't."

Bresnahan said, "Client privacy?"

Lockington said, "*What* client?"

Bresnahan nodded, getting to his feet. "I'll be getting back to you."

Lockington said, "Where can I reach you?"

Bresnahan said, "You can't—I'm a very busy man."

21 LEAVING THE VALENCIA CAFÉ, he'd driven past the 24 North Brockway address—an older two-story white-frame building, its garage open and empty, no blue Chevette in sight. Back at his Mahoning Plaza office, Lockington shuffled through the mail that'd been shoved through the door-slot, all of it addressed to OCCUPANT. He learned that he should vote for Bruno F. Bosworth for Judge because Bruno F. Bosworth possessed twenty-five years of experience—twenty-five years of experience in *what* wasn't mentioned. He learned that Rev. Joshua Hammerschmidt was going to build a City of God in the Ozarks and that if Lockington wanted his name etched into the cornerstone he'd better send three thousand dollars pronto. He also learned that Eastwood Mall's Women's Ready-to-Wear was running one helluva sale on pink 36-B brassieres, limit eight to a customer. This knowledge digested, Lockington consigned the whole kit and kaboodle to his wastebasket, relaxing in his swivel chair with a cigarette and the music of WHOT, attempting to get a handle on recent events.

Within a space of less than forty-eight hours he'd been contacted by an author of scholarly military tomes, he'd been propositioned by a seventy-seven-year-old sex maniac who'd offered to tie him to a bed with forty feet of clothesline, he'd gotten involved in a Pier 6 brawl in a post office parking lot and he'd been saved from probable extinction by a young brontosaurus who wanted to become a private detective or a spy, he didn't give a damn which. He'd been followed from the Flamingo Lounge to the Valencia Café by a government man, and he'd garnered seven thousand five hundred dollars for services as yet unrendered.

Somewhere in or near the city of Youngstown, he'd been

89

told, there just might be a Soviet defector, an aging Russian general who'd written a book concerning the dastardly plans of the Soviet Union. Said Russian general was in eager demand by (A): the writer of scholarly military tomes, who wanted to interview him—by (B): the Central Intelligence Agency, who wanted to get him off the streets and out of harm's way—and by (C): the *Komitet Gosudarstvennoye Bezopastnosti*, better known as the KGB, who wanted to blow his ass off.

It amounted to a rather bewildering kettle of fish and Lacey Lockington was in it up to his rapidly receding hairline, but he'd made no firm guarantees, and the money was certainly welcome. What the hell, at the rate of seventy-five hundred dollars every other day, a man could become a millionaire in short order, providing he didn't get killed on his way to the bank.

Late in the afternoon the telephone jangled its way into his musings. Gordon Kilbuck was on the line. "You told me that you might have something today."

Lockington said, "I'm still working on it."

"On what?"

"It'd be difficult to explain on the telephone."

"Could you give me a clue?"

"I could if I had one."

"But you *do* have prospects?"

"Several, probably—I just can't locate the little bastards."

There was a long silence before Kilbuck said, "Well, hang in there."

Lockington said, "Sure." He hung up. Not the best way to inspire client confidence, he thought, but facts are facts. He took Alexi Fedorovich's book from its desk drawer, tucked it under his arm and walked the length of the plaza to the flower shop. He bought two roses.

The elderly lady behind the counter was tying silver ribbons on the stems when she winked at him. "You have *two* girl friends now?"

Lockington said, "Sometimes three or four."

She placed the roses on the counter top. "And you don't understand any of them."

"Hardly ever."

"And they all wear the same dress."

"Right. You're familiar with that problem?"

"Oh, yes—my husband had it for years, but he got over it last spring."

"How did he manage to accomplish that?"

"He got run over by a Greyhound bus."

Lockington nodded. "Well, that's *one* way."

The flower lady said, "Works every damn time. That'll be three dollars and fifteen cents."

Lockington paid her and went out, walking back to the Mercedes, driving to the little brown-trimmed white house on North Dunlap Avenue, looking forward to a quiet evening with Natasha. She met him at the door, giving him an abbreviated kiss, snatching *The Wheels of Treachery* from under his arm, flopping into the overstuffed chair, paging eagerly through the book.

Lockington poked the roses into her pixie hairdo, adjusting them as best he could. Natasha said, "Thank you" absent-mindedly. She added, "The martinis are mixed—second refrigerator shelf." Also absent-mindedly.

He poured their martinis over ice, garnishing them with twists of lime. Natasha accepted hers without looking up, nipping at it, her attention focused on the book. Lockington said, "Maybe we should send out for a pizza."

Natasha didn't respond immediately—she was buried in *The Wheels of Treachery*, her big pale blue eyes flicking hungrily back and forth across its pages. After a while she muttered, "That'd be nice."

Lockington said, "What'd be nice?"

Natasha flipped a page, glancing up. "No anchovies, please."

"Who said anything about anchovies?"

Natasha was silent.

Lockington sat on the couch, cradling his martini, studying

her. He said, "By God, I think *I* should write a book."

Natasha turned another page. "About what?"

"Understanding women—I'm a bona fide expert on the subject."

Natasha sighed, leaving the overstuffed chair, a forefinger marking her place in *The Wheels of Treachery*. She sat beside him on the couch, smiling her wonderfully lopsided smile. She leaned to kiss him on the cheek. "Yes, you are—you really *are*."

Lockington said, "Hey, you better *believe* it!"

Natasha said, "You see, Lacey, the very first thing a man should understand about a woman is that a man cannot possibly understand a woman, and you're aware of that."

"Which makes me an expert—right?"

Natasha had returned to the overstuffed chair and *The Wheels of Treachery*. She murmured, "Right." Absent-mindedly.

22

HE WAS SITTING at their basement bar, drinking cognac, listening to ragtime piano from the tape player, missing Natasha. She was upstairs, reading *The Wheels of Treachery*, no more than fifteen seconds from his barstool but he missed her anyway—he liked Natasha to be where he could *see* her, she was a pleasure to look at. She came downstairs shortly before eleven o'clock, during "World's Fair Rag" done by a ragtime pianist named Zimmerman. Lockington couldn't remember Zimmerman's first name, but he was the best in the business, first name or no first name. Natasha perched on the barstool next to Lockington's. She said, "You didn't order a pizza."

"No, you were intent on your reading—I didn't want to disturb you."

She pinched his cheek. "That was considerate of you."

"Did you finish the book?"

"Yes, I read rapidly. It was interesting, I thought—how thoroughly did you read it?"

"Not very."

"It has an intriguing premise, but it's only a *premise*."

"Fill me in."

"Well, General Fedorovich predicts nothing as a certainty—he doesn't even get into probabilities, he considers *possibilities* and the possibilities stemming from possibilities, nothing more than that."

"And the possibilities are rotten."

"Not particularly good, as seen through Fedorovich's eyes. He considers the likelihood of mid-European Communism coming apart at the seams within the next couple of years."

"He sees it as a *likelihood*?"

"Not exactly, but he says it *could* happen—which it could, of course—he writes from a hypothetical point of view, seeing the potential of the Soviet Union losing its grip on Central Europe. He thinks that Mikhail Gorbachev could be ousted from power as a result, replaced by hard-liners, who might fabricate a cause for invasion of NATO territories, thereby reclaiming those areas lost to Russia."

"And kicking off a third world war."

Natasha said, "If it reaches that point, *certainly*—it would be all or nothing for Moscow."

"Could Fedorovich be right?"

Natasha shrugged. "He knows the factors involved."

Lockington killed the tape player, snapping on Youngstown's eleven o'clock news. Local school authorities were making dire predictions regarding consequences should its 14.5 mill tax levy fail at the polls in November—a hundred assistant-assistant student counselors would be laid off and Chinese gong-bonging would have to be eliminated from the curriculum. Youngstown had an outside chance of becoming a regular stop on Amtrak's New York to Chicago run. Mayor Patrick Ungaro would speak at a Crime Watch meeting at the Italian-American Veterans' Hall on South Meridian Road. An elderly woman, one Abigail Fleugelham, had just been found dead in a room of the Belfry Motel on Route 224, strangled with a forty-foot length of plastic clothesline. The weather for Thursday would be clear with temperatures ranging from the upper sixties to the lower seventies.

Lockington left his barstool to turn off the news and reactivate the tape player. Zimmerman was playing "Teddy in the Jungle" and Lockington still couldn't remember Zimmerman's first name. Natasha was peering at him. She said, "Abigail Fleugelham—wasn't that the name of the woman you met at the Canterbury Arms retirement home?"

Lockington nodded. Zimmerman had finished playing "Teddy in the Jungle," lighting into "Sleepy Hollow Rag." Natasha said, "Are you hungry?"

"For pizza, no—are you?"

"Yes, but not for pizza."

"For what, then?"

"What do you have in mind?"

Lockington spun her barstool, undoing the buttons at the back of her white blouse. He said, "It ain't pizza." He unsnapped the clasp of her brassiere.

She turned the barstool, facing him, shrugging free of her blouse and brassiere, tucking them into her lap. Her nipples were taut. "To hell with pizza."

They went upstairs. *The Wheels of Treachery* lay on the kitchen table. Natasha hadn't spent all of her time reading. He saw several sheets of unlined paper on which a great many eight-spoked wheels had been drawn. Numerals had been jotted around the rims of the wheels, letters in the gaps between the spokes. Lockington paused to study these and Natasha pushed him into the living room, turning out the lamp on the table. She took his hand, turning toward the bedroom. Lockington said, "What's up?"

"My slacks. They should be *down*."

"I might be of assistance on that score."

They were in the bedroom. Natasha said, "I don't believe that I'll require assistance." Lockington heard faint rustling sounds. "See?"

Lockington said, "Not particularly well—it's dark in here."

Natasha Gorky came swiftly around the foot of the bed, naked as a jay-bird, gluing herself to him, her arms encircling his neck. Her scent of spice wafted into Lockington's adoration-befogged brain. She whispered, "Lacey, if you can't see, try Braille— try *Braille!*"

Over breakfast coffee he told her about the woman in the blue Chevette, the altercation at the post office, Barney Kozlowski and Cayuse Bresnahan. He'd intended to do that earlier but circumstances alter cases—there'd been the book.

And the Braille.

23 THURSDAY MORNING WAS WARM and blue, studded with little fleecy-white clouds. Lockington reached the Mahoning Plaza office at exactly nine o'clock. So did Barney Kozlowski. He was a clean-cut, pugnaciously handsome youngster, every bit as large as Lockington had thought him to be, which was very large indeed. He was neatly dressed—dark blue cardigan, powder blue shirt, gray trousers, black loafers. They shook hands and Barney sat in the straight-backed wooden chair to Lockington's right. He said, "Mr. Lockington, I'm afraid I have an apology to make—I ain't got no gun."

Lockington said, "That's all right—you probably won't be needing a gun today. Come to think of it, you probably won't be needing a gun tomorrow."

"Well, maybe not, but I was hoping that you might have something dangerous for starters."

"Such as?"

Barney thought it over briefly. "Oh, like maybe a big cocaine bust."

"That stuff doesn't concern us—coke busts are for local law enforcement and the feds."

"Okay, but what're the chances of recovering some stolen jewels?"

"Not real good—insurance gumshoes work that side of the alley—they usually operate on a percentage of recovery basis."

"Well, what about serial killers—any of them running around loose?"

"Who knows? These days you can't tell a serial killer from your postman."

"Hey, I'll bet you read *Span of Terror* by Ralph Collingsworth!"

96

"Can't say that I did. What about *Span of Terror* by Ralph Collingsworth?"

"There was this serial killer down in Montgomery, Alabama. He murdered over a dozen baldheaded women—busted 'em with a four-pound sledgehammer. It had something to do with his grandmother being bald."

"Uh-huh."

"Yeah, a Montgomery P.I. nailed him and, just like you said, it was a postman! He could tell they were bald because he could see through their windows when he delivered the morning mail—they hadn't gotten around to putting their wigs on, you see."

"Not exactly."

"He carried the sledgehammer in his mailbag, just in case he ran into a baldheaded woman. When he spotted one, he'd ring her doorbell. She'd run and put her wig on before she answered the door, of course, but he already knew she was bald, and he'd tell her that he had a registered letter for her, could he step in for a moment, and when she let him in, *zonko*, he'd let her have it! The Montgomery cops couldn't do anything with it, but this P.I. got him. Wanta know how?"

"Uhh-h-h, not just yet, Barney—it's a bit early in the morning."

Barney studied Lockington. "You're working on something big, I can tell! I know the signs!"

"You *do*?"

"Sure! Yesterday morning those three guys ganged up on you at the post office because they were trying to scare you off the case!"

Lockington said, "No, that was started by a disagreement over them blocking my car in the parking lot."

"Well, all right, but that guy in the black Stetson hat—he was following you, and he was a syndicate enforcer if I've ever seen one!"

"Not really. He caught up with me later in the day—he offered me a job."

"Cracking a blackmail case?"

"No, selling Kirby vacuum cleaners."

Barney's disappointment was obvious. "Well, dog*gone*, Mr. Lockington, there must be *some*thing going on!"

Lockington spread his hands the way you do when you're about to attempt to explain something you've never quite understood. "Look, Barney, the private detective racket is no different than the newspaper business, for instance—you have to be copy boy before you can become a reporter."

"You mean I got to serve an apprenticeship?"

"Yeah, something on that order."

"Okay, where do I start?"

"Right here at my desk, answering the telephone. I should be back by noon."

"All right, but how do I answer the phone—what do I say?"

"Just say, 'Confidential Investigations, Kozlowski speaking.' Try to sound gruff—you're giving the right impression when you sound gruff."

"The macho thing?"

"Right."

"Like this?" Barney lowered his voice, growling "Confidential Investigations, Kozlowski speaking." He sounded like an idling Diesel locomotive. "Like that?"

Lockington said, "That's *it*—right on the *money!*"

"Then I'll probably have to make a lot of notes."

"If they're still on the line, yes."

"But what if somebody comes in—*then* what?"

"Find out what he wants, get his telephone number, tell him that I'll get back to him shortly."

"And if it's a woman?"

"Same applies."

"Yes, of course, but what if she starts taking off her clothes?"

"Then you're on your own—why in God's name would she start taking off her clothes?"

"To *distract* me—that very thing happened to Joe Pilgrim in *Death Watch!*"

"By Ralph Collingsworth?"

"Yes, Collingsworth is one of my favorites—terse, hard-hitting."

Lockington left the desk, motioning Barney into the swivel chair. "Hold the fort, kid."

Barney seated himself, an aura of importance blossoming above his crew cut. He said, "Do you think we stand a chance of getting into a big international case one of these days?"

Lockington was putting on his hat. "International case—what *sort* of international case?"

"Well, you know—double agents, assassins, lots of intrigue—the kind that's got the CIA and the KGB all mixed up in it."

Lockington shrugged. "Extremely doubtful, but in this business you never can tell."

He went out, piling into the Mercedes to drive west to Meridian Road, then south toward Cornersburg and the Canterbury Arms retirement home, wondering if Barney Kozlowski represented an asset or a liability, deciding that he'd probably be both, but not a great deal of either. What the hell, he owed the boy something.

24 THELMA WAS AT THE DESK of the Canterbury
Arms retirement home, working on a drawer of
filing cards. Lockington said, "Working a
different shift?"

Thelma glanced up. She said, "No, just filling in for
Martha—she'll be in at noon. Her aunt died." She shoved the
filing card drawer into its cabinet. "Y'know, you remind me
of someone."

"Who might that be?"

"A fella who said he'd try to come back the other evening."

"And didn't."

"And didn't. Underline *didn't!*"

"Sorry, I got hung up."

"That's okay, I worked out a rain check for you—I'm off
on Sundays, and Saturday night's my night to howl."

"I'll let you know."

"*Do* that! I was just discussing you."

"With whom?"

"There was a policeman here—a man named Addison—
plainclothes detective—he left just a few minutes ago."

"How did I get into the conversation?"

"He asked if Abigail had been seeing men, so I told him
about you and Mr. Mawson—I *had* to—he was a *cop*."

"Mr. Mawson—when was Abigail with a Mr. Mawson?"

"Last night, I guess—at least, when she went out she told
me that he'd be waiting in the parking lot."

"You didn't get a look at him?"

"No, I didn't bother. Why *should* I?"

"Or his car?"

Thelma shook her head. "Our residents are in and out all
the time—relatives pick 'em up, take 'em home for dinner or
to a movie or something—they're free to go and come as they

100

please. Besides, it was after seven—it's beginning to get dark by that time."

"Would it be possible that someone else might have seen him—an employee, maybe?"

"Possible, I suppose, but darned unlikely—the parking lot's on the blind side of the building—no windows, just the entrance and the kitchen and linen storage—like that."

"All right, would you know if she received mail from Mr. Mawson?"

"Abby didn't get a lot of mail. She subscribed to Hustler Magazine, she belonged to Ecstasy Book Club and she received bulletins from there. She had a younger sister in Alaska—Anchorage, I think—once in a while she got a card from her—that was about it."

Lockington shrugged, lighting a cigarette. He said, "Well, it was worth a shot."

"Abby said that you're some kind of insurance investigator."

"Right—Mutual of Slippery Rock."

Thelma said, "She thought you were the cat's pajamas. Awful, the way she died, wasn't it?"

"Yeah, I heard about it on last night's late news. Who found her?"

"The desk clerk at the Belfry Motel, as I understand it—he's a live-in employee—works the desk twenty-four hours a day—sleeps in the office at night. Somebody told him that a door was open. He found her when he checked it out."

"Who told you this?"

"That detective who was here—but there are things he didn't know about Abby."

"What didn't he know about Abby?"

Thelma giggled. "Well, perhaps it isn't a proper subject for discussion in mixed company, but Abby liked to *tie* men on a bed, she told me—I mean, she'd spread-*eagle* 'em! She said she could drive a man crazy when he couldn't resist." Thelma gave the matter brief consideration, running her tongue across her bee-stung lower lip. "Of course, I suppose she meant crazy with *pleasure*—do you know what I'm saying?"

"Probably not," Lockington said. "Well, I'd better be moving along—things to do."

Thelma leaned across the counter top, lowering her voice to a purr. "Has a woman ever tied you to a bed and driven you crazy with pleasure?"

"Not if memory serves me correctly."

Thelma winked at him. "It might be fun, wouldn't you think?"

Lockington faked a yawn. "Well, yes, it might be, and then again, it might *not* be."

"Well, I suppose one never knows until one's tried it, don't you agree?"

Lockington didn't agree, nor did he disagree—not so Thelma could hear him, at any rate. Silence has its rewards, minuscule though they may be.

Thelma was saying, "That's where the clothes line came from—Abby's *handbag*! She told me that she carried it, just in case. Can you imagine a seventy-seven-year-old woman carrying on like *that*?"

"I guess it's horses for courses."

"I'm barely forty, you know."

Lockington said, "I had no idea."

He left the Canterbury Arms retirement home, mopping his brow. It was 9:45 in the morning, and already his ass was dragging.

25

THE OFFICE OF THE BELFRY MOTEL was approximately six feet by eight feet in size, Lockington figured. There was a counter, a stack of registration forms, a television set, a tattered beach chair, and a threadbare green rug in serious need of vacuuming. There was a fat guy sprawled in the beach chair with his nose jammed into a copy of The Sporting News. When the door slammed, he growled, "Wanna room?" He didn't bother looking up.

Lockington said, "Not just now, thanks."

"It says here that Carter has just about outlived his welcome with the Mets."

"Don't worry about Carter—he'll hook on somewhere."

The fat guy folded his Sporting News, dropping it into what remained of his lap. His eyes were bloodshot, he needed a shave, there was egg at a corner of his mouth, he was a mess. He spoke around a soggy cigar butt.

"You're a cop."

Lockington said, "You're sharp this morning."

"Don't have to be sharp—I can spot a cop from here to Washington, D.C."

"That'd be a good trick—there *ain't* no cops in Washington, D.C."

The fat guy said, "You're the second in the last hour—what's on your mind—the old Fleugelham broad who got scragged?"

"Yeah, I gotta go through the motions. What's your name?"

"'George,' if it makes any difference."

"It doesn't, but I gotta call you *something*."

"Okay, I'm George and you're from Scotland Yard—what can I do for you?"

"You can tell me who signed for the room the Fleugelham woman was murdered in."

"She signed for it."

"You must have seen who she was with."

"Was she with somebody?"

"Well, George, strangling yourself with forty feet of clothes line requires a bit of doing."

"Yeah, she probably had somebody with her but you sure couldn't prove it by *me*. She'd been here maybe six, eight times before and she always took care of the checking-in. Hell, I never pay no attention—you get all kinds in a roach ranch like this. If you ask me, that old chick was around the bend."

"Why?"

"Just the impression I got—she had a wild gleam in her eye."

"Her companion for the evening waited in his car?"

"Reckon so—they always have."

"Well, thanks, George—just running a routine check."

"No problem, I got nothing better to do. Y'know, I'll lay three to one that them ball players go on strike again."

Lockington said, "Yeah, well, you should try to see their side of it—what the hell, would *you* work seven months a year for a lousy two million?"

"Wouldn't *think* of it!"

Lockington drove away from the Belfry Motel, liking George. He was a bird of Lockington's feather.

26 LOCKINGTON DROVE EAST on Route 224 to Fritzi's, which was closed until 6:00 P.M., the sign said. It was nearly eleven o'clock when he doubled back, swinging north onto Meridian Road, heading for his office, knowing not a helluva lot more than he'd known when he'd left it. Unlike the story-book detectives, he'd never been able to get into a case from a distance. Sherlock Holmes had possessed that capability, so had Charlie Chan and Mr. Moto and Philo Vance, but Lockington worked better at close quarters, grinding it out inch by laborious inch, hitting dead-end streets, getting hung up in revolving doors, following wrong trails and cold tracks, arriving eventually but not always in time. If he was going to be late in locating Gen. Alexi Fedorovich, there'd probably be no point in getting to him at all.

Lacey Lockington wasn't a brilliant man, but he was smart enough to realize that he *wasn't* brilliant, and that knowledge had stood him in good stead over the years. He'd made a firm practice of intentionally overrating adversaries, known or unknown, real or suppositional, always giving them the benefit of every doubt—one of the reasons for Lockington being alive and in tolerable health at the ripe old age of forty-nine.

When you turn your back on a man you suspect, you probably deserve to get killed, but when you turn your back on the neighborhood Baptist minister you may get your fucking brains blown out whether you deserve it or not, because there's always an excellent chance that the innocent-appearing guy isn't as innocent as he appears. Lockington was from Chicago where there exists a constant awareness of that fact—it hovers in its polluted air—but in Youngstown, Ohio, the atmosphere is different, the pace is slower, the natives are friendlier, easier going, less wary. A hard-bitten ex-police

105

detective from Chicago might mellow in such surroundings, becoming a trusting and gullible soul.

Lockington wasn't ready for such transformation—not yet—which was why he was keeping a sharp eye on the fast-closing pink Cadillac convertible that'd just appeared in his rear-view mirror. Pink Cadillac convertibles are not the ideal vehicles for tailing purposes, but people from Chicago know that in Chicago you can get tailed by a guy in a Santa Claus suit, driving a hearse.

He turned east on Mahoning Avenue, watching the pink Caddy convert continue north on Meridian Road, noting that there was an elderly nun at its wheel. He pulled into the plaza lot, finding a parking space in front of his office—a possibly favorable omen for the rest of the day, he thought. Usually, he ended up parked twenty feet east of Grant's Tomb. The October noonday was warm, better than seventy degrees and getting warmer, but his office door was closed. Lockington kicked it open, starting in, then freezing on the threshold, holding the door ajar with his foot, staring. The straight-backed wooden chair had been moved from desk-side to the southwestern corner of the room, facing the wall, and a man sat in it, his hat smashed low over his eyes. In response to the sound of the opening door, the man had swung his head in Lockington's direction. He was unable to see through the band of his crushed hat, but he said, "*Help* me, for Christ's *sake!*" His voice gurgled like dishwater going down a half-plugged drain. From the swivel chair at the desk, Barney Kozlowski snapped, "Silence, creep!" He turned to Lockington. "No telephone calls, Mr. Lockington."

Lockington said, "*What* in the great eternal fuck is *happening* here?"

Barney jerked a thumb in the direction of the man in the straight-backed wooden chair. "Well, he came busting in here, looking suspicious, and right off the bat I spotted his piece!"

"The damned thing was hanging *out*—he's a *flasher?*"

The man in the wooden chair groaned.

Barney Kozlowski was saying, "His *heater*, Mr. Lockington—his cannon, his equalizer, his artillery." Barney popped open a desk drawer, producing a revolver, plunking it onto the desk top. "I relieved him of it."

Lockington said, "Oh, you're talking about a *gun*."

Barney smiled an efficient smile. "*Loaded*, too, by God! I figured that you'd want to run him through the grinder."

"'Run him through the *grinder*'?"

"I thought you'd probably want to *grill* him."

Lockington eased the office door shut, waving Barney to silence, walking to the man in the corner. He said, "Who are you, chief?"

The man struggled to remove his battered hat, accomplishing this by rotating it right to left three or four times. He was in Lockington's age group, probably fifty, he was baldheaded, there was consternation in his eyes and a rapidly swelling blue welt on the point of his chin. He croaked, "My name's Addison—Frank Addison. You're Lockington?"

"That's right—what can I do for you, Frank?"

"Well, for openers, you can prepare for a fucking seven hundred and fifty million dollar lawsuit!"

Lockington shrugged. "Would you settle out of court for lunch?"

Addison weighed the matter for a few moments. Then he nodded. "What the hell, it's the best offer I've had all day."

"You came here to see me—about what?"

"You were with a woman named Abigail Fleugelham the other evening?"

"For a few pops, yes."

"You're working that case?"

"Not really—it just might tie in with another matter."

"What would that be?"

"It'd be something I can't go into at the moment."

Frank Addison got to his feet. He was wobbly, clutching at Lockington for support. He shook his head, trying to clear the cobwebs. He said, "The girl at the Canterbury Arms gave me your name. I phoned downtown and they checked you out in the license file."

"All right, what about it? You got something on the Fleugelham business?"

"Not yet. That's why we should talk." Addison stuck out his hand. "I'm a sergeant of detectives—Youngstown Police Department."

27 FRANK ADDISON HAD A BLUE '86 Chrysler 4-door. "It belongs to the department," he said, but it has civilian plates—no point in advertising." He drove them to Tonto's Golden Sombrero, a run-down Mexican joint on the north end of Market Street.

Lockington said, "Thanks for the service—I'm from Chicago—not all that familiar with Youngstown yet."

"Youngstown's a nice city if you stay on the West Side."

"Chicago's okay if you keep off the North Side, the South Side, *and* the West Side."

"The East Side's good?"

"Just fine—the east side is Lake Michigan."

Addison was a chunky man, bushy-browed, with a pockmarked face and jutting jaw—twenty years on the Youngstown force, he told Lockington. He'd spent some time in Tonto's Golden Sombrero, obviously—a chunky waitress brought him a margarita before she said hello. Lockington asked for a double Martell's. Addison said, "I ain't supposed to drink on duty, but I've been through the mill this morning."

Lockington studied Addison's swollen jaw. "What kicked off the argument, anyway?"

"*Argument—what* argument? I didn't say a Goddamned *word*—I just walked in and I was taking out my wallet to identify myself. My jacket was unbuttoned and he must have seen my shoulder holster. Next thing I knew, the lights went out and when I woke up I was sitting in a chair with my hat smashed down to my nose! Who *is* this character?"

"Kid named Barney Kozlowski—he wants to break into the private investigation field."

"Yeah? Well, the next time he coldcocks *me*, he'll be wanting to break *out* of the fucking Mahoning County Jail!"

109

"He meant well," Lockington said.

"So did Don Quixote."

Lockington was silent, concentrating on lighting a cigarette.

Addison said, "So tell me about Abigail Fleugelham."

Lockington shrugged. "Seventy-seven-year-old sex fiend."

"Nothing more than that?"

"My God, isn't that *enough*?"

"She took you to bed?"

"No, but she tried."

Addison's smile was wry. "Love, your magic spell is everywhere."

"Nice number—sing a chorus."

"Can't—I'm under contract to Columbia Records—no gratis gigs."

Lockington said, "I suppose you've heard about a guy named Mawson."

"Yeah, according to the girl at the Canterbury, Abigail went out with him last night. You think she propositioned him?"

"Abigail Fleugelham would have propositioned a bull gorilla!"

"Mawson accepted?"

"Of *course*, he accepted!"

"All right, what do we have on Mawson?"

"A first degree murder rap."

"No doubt, but what do you know about him?"

"Nothing—nobody's laid eyes on him, so far as I can determine."

"At the Canterbury I was told that Abigail liked some gin mill on 224."

"Yeah, Fritzi's—I was there an hour ago. It was closed."

"You've hit the Belfry Motel?"

"Nothing there—the room jockey didn't see the guy she was with."

Addison ordered another margarita, Lockington another Martell's. Addison said, "You don't care to talk about your business with her?"

"I'm trying to locate a party that Abigail knew a long time ago. I thought that she might have information I could use. She had next to nothing—she amounted to a link that didn't pan out."

"That's all?"

"That ain't all, but it's all you're gonna get."

After a few minutes Addison had another margarita and a burrito. Lockington settled for one more double Martell's. During their drive back to the office Lockington said, "Abigail was a nice old lady—her pants were on fire, but she was a nice old lady."

"Mawson didn't think so. Okay, we have *your* connection with her—what was Mawson's?"

"Probably ditto to mine."

"You're looking for the same person?"

"Got to be."

"But you'd already questioned Abigail—if Mawson was trying to shut her up, why the hell would he hit her *after* she'd talked to you—why not *before*?"

"Because he didn't *get* to her before, and to make damned certain she didn't talk to anyone *else*." He lapsed into silence and they were turning into the plaza before he said, "I wonder what that sonofabitch *looks* like."

Addison pulled up close to the office door. He said, "He can't be pretty."

28 WHEN FRANK ADDISON PULLED AWAY, Lockington went into his office, finding Barney Kozlowski sitting on the window bench, staring disconsolately into the parking lot, looking very much like an abandoned basset hound. Lockington said, "Any calls?"

Barney shook his head. "Hey, look, Mr. Lockington, I'm really awful sorry about what happened to Mr. Addison."

"So is Mr. Addison, but he's going to let it ride." He clapped a hand on Barney's broad shoulder. "Y'know, kid, I can't think of a valid reason for you going around trying to impersonate the fucking Fifth Armored Division."

"Mr. Lockington, I regard a gun as a potential threat and I have a tendency to respond to threats—it's a reflex thing with me, I just can't help it—you know how it goes."

"Not at all—how does it go?"

"Well, I guess I'm sort of like Joe Pilgrim."

"Joe Pilgrim?"

"Joe Pilgrim—the P.I. in the Sin City Series."

"The Sin City series—that'd be by Ralph Collingsworth, of course."

"Yes—you see, Joe Pilgrim never takes chances with an armed man—Joe swings first and he asks questions later!" The subject of Joe Pilgrim had brightened Barney around the edges.

Lockington said, "How many police detectives has Joe Pilgrim slugged?"

The question dulled Barney's glow. "But I didn't have the slightest idea that Mr. Addison was a police detective!"

"Neither did Mr. Addison, for a while. Mr. Addison probably thought that he was on the ten ayem rocket to Venus." Lockington liked Barney Kozlowski, a sincere boy, playing a dream role to the hilt—he didn't want to bust the kid's bubble, but he felt that there should be some mention of the incident.

Barney was saying, "I didn't hit Mr. Addison all that hard."

Lockington said, "Well, that may be true, but there ain't no way you're gonna prove it by Mr. Addison."

"Would you believe that Mr. Addison has the same kind of revolver that Joe Pilgrim carries—a Smith & Wesson?" Barney had changed the subject, scrambling back to Joe Pilgrim like a rabbit to a briar patch, and Lockington didn't bother to get in his way—he could see no advantage in whipping a dead horse. Barney said, "Only time Joe Pilgrim didn't wrap things up with his Smith & Wesson was in the last couple chapters of *Death on Pocahontas Street*. That was the time he used his Martin's Ferry Elite."

Lockington frowned. "I've never heard of a Martin's Ferry Elite."

Barney was in his own ballpark now, discussing things that he knew how to discuss. "A Martin's Ferry Elite is a deadly accurate .303 rifle with an infrared scope. Joe Pilgrim was trying to stop a sniper who was picking off pedestrians from the roof of the Pickwick Hotel on Pocahontas Street in Sin City."

"I'll bet Joe nailed that sucker."

"Oh, sure, it was no contest! He took his Martin's Ferry Elite to the seventh floor of an office building across the street from the Pickwick Hotel, and he shot the sniper right through his medulla oblongata."

Lockington said, "Which probably didn't improve that sniper's sex life a great deal."

"Got him between the eyes!"

"Oh."

Barney snapped his fingers, making a gesture of finality. "When you get shot through your medulla oblongata with a Martin's Ferry Elite, you're *outta* here! By the way, the sniper turned out to be a bellhop at the Pickwick Hotel. He was pissed-off at the mayor of Sin City—the mayor was shacking up with the bellhop's grandmother at the Pickwick—Room 457."

"Yeah, those bellhops are a bad bunch—back in Chicago I knew one who booked *horses!*"

"Besides that, the mayor was a bum tipper."

Lockington said, "One question—why was this bellhop shooting pedestrians—why didn't he just blast the mayor and get it over with?"

Barney said, "Y'know, Joe Pilgrim was wondering about the very same thing."

Lockington nodded. "Good old Joe."

29 NATASHA WASN'T WAITING at the door when he came in. She was at their kitchen table, drawing eight-spoked wheels, filling the spoke gaps with letters, jotting numerals around the wheel rims. Lockington dropped a rose on the table and Natasha tossed her ballpoint pen to one side, glancing up at him. "*Thank* you, sir!"

"You're *welcome*, ma'am!"

She reached for his hand, pressing the back of it to her lips. She said, "*Hello*, Lacey!"

Lockington said, "Well, by God, the lady *remembers* me—that's a step in the right direction!"

Natasha picked up the rose, slipping it into her hairdo. "Lacey, I know that I've been preoccupied recently—try not to be angry with me."

"I hadn't noticed any difference." The hell he hadn't. He said, "What's with all the wheels?"

Natasha's shrug was discouraged. "I'm trying to be helpful."

"To whom?"

"To *you*, of course."

"In what way?"

"In finding General Fedorovich—I've been playing a longshot."

"Longshot players die broke." He studied the stack of paper on the table. "What do the wheels have to do with Fedorovich?"

Natasha was fixing vodka martinis. "You're home a couple of hours early."

"The Kozlowski kid's watching the office, I've given him a key—if anything pops he'll call me. What about the wheels?"

She picked up her papers, arranging them, pushing him into

the living room. "Get out of here—you're cluttering up my kitchen."

Lockington sat on the sofa, lighting a cigarette, wondering about everything in general and nothing in particular, watching Natasha bring the martinis. She sat across from him in the overstuffed chair. She crossed her legs. She was wearing a short navy blue skirt. Lockington enjoyed watching Natasha cross her legs in a short skirt whether it was navy blue or not, especially when she sat facing him. She raised her martini glass to him. "Did you see something that appeals to you?"

"It appeals to me if I see it or if I don't—that's *quality*. Tell me about the wheels, and the numbers and the letters. Are we into cryptography?"

She was lighting a cigarette, squinting against the smoke. She said, "It's probably a bad hunch, but when I was a girl in Odessa, my brother and I used to play a game. In Odessa there isn't much to do on winter evenings, so we'd amuse ourselves with it. It was my father's idea—he told us that it'd stimulate our thinking processes, but we suspected that it was to keep us quiet so he could read. My father read a great deal . . ." Her voice trailed off, a pensive smile of recollection twitching a corner of her mouth.

Lockington said, "This game—wheels were involved?"

"Yes, wheels and numerals and letters—it's best adapted to the English language, and my father said that English would eventually become the global tongue. He insisted that we use it as often as possible."

"How does the game apply here—how is it played?"

"It's relatively simple—I mean its *basis* is simple—it's finding the key that's difficult."

"The *key*?"

"The triggering device—with its discovery, a ten-year-old can handle the problem with ease."

"I'm not sure that I'm with you."

"It wasn't so much a game as it was a puzzle, but my brother and I played it competitively, and that made it a game. In the winter we played it almost every evening."

"And you won every time."

"Not *always*, but usually. We believed that my father had invented the pastime."

"But he hadn't?"

"I rather doubt it—it was probably a common enough time-killer—you know the Russian penchant for chess and games that require patience, but at that time we attributed its creation to him." She stared at the carpeting for a few moments. Then she said, "When we're young and impressionable we tend to embrace the improbable—then, when we grow up, we learn better."

Lockington scowled. "You're trying to tell me that there ain't no Santa Claus?"

Lockington loved her lopsided smile. She said, "In my case, there never *was*—Santa doesn't exist in the Soviet Union. Now, looking back, I feel cheated—but perhaps he'll get there someday."

"Back to this game, or puzzle, or whatever—you're into it up to your ears."

"Well, you see, I'd *forgotten* it—the wheels on the dust jacket of General Fedorovich's book returned it to mind. It comes under the heading of coincidence, it would appear."

"What did you think it would concern, if it concerned *anything*?"

"It occurred to me that it might have something to do with General Fedorovich—his location, possibly. That was a wild goose, I suppose."

"Much ado about nothing?"

"In all probability, yes." She got up to mix more martinis. When she came back she said, "Why don't we go out for dinner tonight?"

"To get away from the wheels?"

"Not necessarily—I'm in the mood for spaghetti. Could we do that?"

They drove south on Raccoon Road to a small Italian

restaurant Lockington had discovered during his earlier visit to Youngstown. They took a red-covered candlelighted table in a dim corner of the place. When Natasha was seated Lockington checked the jukebox, finding a few numbers, pumping coins into the slot. He returned to their table amid the strains of "Sunrise Serenade," winking at Natasha. "Remember *that* one?"

Natasha listened, her brow wrinkling. "*Should* I?"

"Why, certainly—it's 'Natasha's Eyes,' written by Leonid Gruschev, a noted Russian composer—appropriately named, I think—it's gently moody, but it has a certain sparkle."

Natasha was staring at him. "Lacey, are you trying to get me into bed?"

Lockington shrugged. "Well, quite frankly, that thought has crossed my mind."

Natasha placed her elbows on the red tablecloth, leaning in Lockington's direction. "You *chawrtuh*, that's 'Sunrise Serenade,' composed by an American pianist named Frankie Carle!" She accepted Lockington's proffered cigarette and a light. She leaned back, inhaling deeply, blowing smoke in Lockington's direction. "But I'll go to bed with you, anyway."

Lockington said, "The end justifies the means."

"Do you really believe that?"

"In this case, yes."

"In this case, so do I."

Their waitress came and they ordered a chilled bottle of Chianti wine. When they'd finished it they ordered another, and then one more, making occasional small talk, listening to the soft throb of the jukebox, "Moonlight Mood," and "Melancholy Baby," and "I Only Have Eyes for You." Lacey Lockington was so deeply in love that he didn't know whether he was on foot or on horseback.

30 A YELLOW DISHPAN-SIZE MOON rode high in a black velvet October sky. Lockington drove slowly north on Raccoon Road, singing "Cecilia." Lockington liked "Cecilia." He sang it again. Natasha interrupted the second chorus. "I wonder if there *was* a Cecilia—a Cecilia who inspired the song."

Lockington said, "I knew a Cecilia in Chicago—Cecilia Zoop—Sheridan Road hooker, fifty, maybe fifty-five, peroxide blonde, brown-eyed, heavy in the vest, ass like a forty dollar cow—thirty bucks, but she'd take five, your place or hers. She—"

"Lacey, will you shut up, for *God's* sake?"

"For *God's* sake? Communists don't believe in God."

"Some do, some don't," Natasha said. "By the way, the spaghetti was excellent."

Lockington said, "I guess it all depends on how you look at it."

Natasha said, "At what—spaghetti or Communists?"

"Damn right!"

"You're drunk."

"I know it. So are you."

"Just a little, maybe. Should we have a nightcap before we go to bed?"

Lockington said, "I knew a guy who drank nothing but nightcaps. What do they *put* in those things?"

Natasha said, "You'd better have one—you're going to need it."

"Was that a threat?"

"No, it was a promise."

They pulled into the drive of the little white house on North Dunlap Avenue, getting out of the Mercedes, pausing to study the heavens. There were a million stars up there and the moon was drifting behind a frothy screen of tattered white clouds. Natasha took his hand. She said, "Just think, that very same moon is shining on Odessa."

"No, it ain't—different time zones."

"Why split hairs?"

"*Hairs*? You're talking thousands of *miles*!"

Natasha said, "Well, excuse *me*!"

Lockington said, "Okay."

She slipped an arm around his waist, squeezing hard. She was very strong. She said, "Lacey, I love you."

Lockington tilted her chin, making wordless response by kissing her.

They went into the house and down the stairs to the little basement bar. Natasha perched on a stool, rapping briskly. She snapped, "Service, *please*!"

Lockington poured a short glass of vodka, then cognac. They toasted each other. Lockington turned on the eleven o'clock local news. The announcer was saying that a Youngstown fireman, Kevin O'Malley, had taken full responsibility for the rash of false fire alarms that had resulted in the systematic near-destruction of the Youngstown Board of Education building. Fireman Kevin O'Malley appeared on the screen accompanied by two large men in white coats. Kevin O'Malley's hair was in his eyes and he was waving his arms. He said that he'd taken great pleasure in getting into that bleeping Board of Education building and kicking the bleeping bleep out of the joint. He mentioned that Christ would return to earth, probably within a week, and he announced that the Philadelphia Phillies would win the 1989 National League pennant.

Natasha looked at Lockington. She said, "He's insane."

"*Obviously*! The Phils don't have a *prayer*!"

Natasha didn't say a word.

Lockington was sorry for Fireman Kevin O'Malley. He told Natasha about this.

Natasha said, "So am I." She let it go at that.

Lockington raised his cognac glass, holding it above his head. "I do now propose a toast to Fireman Kevin O'Malley."

O'Malley was still talking. He was saying that when the roll was called up yonder he'd be there. He added that stars would be falling on Alabama one of these nights.

They toasted Fireman Kevin O'Malley.

Lockington put his hand on Natasha's knee. He said, "You are a lady of good will and great compassion."

Natasha said, "I am aware of that. I am also a stem-winding, ring-tailed bitch-kitty in bed."

Fireman Kevin O'Malley had departed the television screen. The news announcer said that a prominent Youngstown psychiatrist, Dr. Luman J. Griswold had been consulted regarding his case. The scene shifted to Dr. Luman J. Griswold's office in downtown Youngstown where he was shown stroking his beard. Dr. Griswold didn't mince words. He said that Fireman Kevin O'Malley's time in Youngstown's public schools was undoubtedly responsible for his pitiful condition. He opined that O'Malley was harboring a grudge and a desire to avenge an injustice real or imagined, perhaps a detention period undeserved or an embarrassment at the hands of an insensitive faculty member. He said that this had probably brought about a deep-rooted resentment over which O'Malley had no control whatsoever, that he may have had no vivid recollection of the provoking incident, but that his anger had not yet subsided. Dr. Griswold noted that his knowledge of such cases stemmed from personal experience, that he'd had a fifth grade teacher named Miss LaVerne Pastor who'd made him stand in a corner until he'd urinated in his pants. Dr. Griswold's hands were twitching and his eyes had taken on a rather dangerous glint. He stated that the Atlanta Braves would win the 1989 National League pennant going away. He sang a chorus of "Down Among the Sheltering Palms."

Lockington turned to Natasha. "Do they get many false fire alarms at the Kremlin?"

"I can't say. I've never been to the Kremlin."

"Now *there's* a coincidence—neither have *I*!"

Natasha nodded acknowledgment of the fact that Lockington had never been to the Kremlin.

Lockington proposed a toast to Dr. Luman J. Griswold.

They drank.

The news announcer said that a fifty-year-old woman, a Candice Hoffman, had been found bludgeoned to death in her home at 24 North Brockway Avenue on Youngstown's West Side, and that the possibility of foul play was being given serious consideration.

Lockington lurched to his feet, suddenly stone-sober. He turned off the television set. He said, "Candice Hoffman knew where to find Olga Karelinko!"

Natasha was nibbling on her lower lip. She said, "Tell me about this business, tell me all about it—I mean *all*."

Lockington did that, starting with the moment Gordon Kilbuck had stepped into his office, bringing it up to the present, every move, every contact, every word, as he remembered them.

Natasha listened, nodding occasionally but asking no questions, making no comment, and when he was finished she said nothing. Nothing at all.

31 USUALLY, NATASHA ROLLED OUT of bed at 7:30 sharp, Lockington a few minutes later, but on that Friday morning he stirred shortly before 7:00, reaching for Natasha, and finding no Natasha. He slipped into his robe and went thumping barefoot through the hallway and into the living room. Natasha was at the kitchen table, frowning perplexedly. Gen. Alexi Fedorovich's book was in front of her and she was paging rapidly through it, jotting notes on a legal pad. She glanced up. "Coffee's ready."

Lockington poured a cup before seating himself across from her. "Back to the wheels? Why?"

"Why *not*? What do we stand to lose?"

"What do we stand to *gain*?"

"Probably nothing, but there's always a chance."

"You think Fedorovich's life's at stake?"

"I'm sure of it."

"You're worried about the KGB?"

"If you're Russian you worry about the KGB—even the KGB worries about the KGB, or about *Mawlniyuh*, which is a *branch* of the KGB."

Lockington said, "I don't speak Russian."

"*Mawlniyuh* translates to 'Lightning'—it's the equivalent of an American police department's internal affairs investigative unit."

"The KGB's KGB."

"Right."

"How does it function?"

"Quietly and efficiently. If you're KGB you don't know who's working for *Mawlniyuh* and who *isn't*."

Lockington nodded. "If *Mawlniyuh* comes across a bad apple in the barrel, he's reprimanded and kicked out of service."

123

Natasha said, "Well-l-l, yes, which is to say he's shot in the back of the head."

"Summarily?"

"Certainly. *Mawlniyuh* is a brass-tacks organization."

"It concentrates on corruption?"

"Earlier, that was its principal service, but recently it's become concerned with a KGB faction that's intent upon doing things its own way—the *old* way."

"Hard-line?"

"Yes, *very*. In his third chapter, General Fedorovich states his belief that Mikhail Gorbachev will be ousted from power within the next two or three years—probably by assassination, and if it's assassination, the general is of the firm opinion that it'll be implemented by *Krahsny Lentuh*."

"I still don't speak Russian."

"I'm talking about the KGB splinter group that the general regards as untrustworthy—*Krahsny Lentuh* means 'Red Ribbon'—it's a radical element, and it believes that the Soviet Union should regress to the repressive policies of the Stalin era."

"All right, why doesn't *Mawlniyuh* kick *Krahsny Lentuh*'s ass?"

"Because it can't put its finger on *Krahsny Lentuh*'s people— they're deeply imbedded in the fabric of the KGB."

"A big outfit?"

"Big enough. How many does it take to rock the boat?"

"This must work wonders for KGB trust and cooperation."

"There's no surface friction, no obvious suspicion—Kremlin orders are carried out to the letter in what appears to be a spirit of harmony. It's the *undercurrents* that disturb *Mawlniyuh*."

"A *Krahsny Lentuh* man could be moonlighting, following Kremlin instructions with one hand, violating them with the other—the mysterious Mr. Mawson, probably."

"Absolutely! Chapter three of *The Wheels of Treachery* gets into the subject of *Krahsny Lentuh*, revealing its aspirations and this has placed General Fedorovich in grave danger. He was born in Youngstown and he'll *die* here if Mawson finds him!"

Lockington shrugged. "Olga Karelinko appears to be the only loose thread."

"And the woman who told you about Olga is dead—so is the woman who picked up Olga's mail."

"Gordon Kilbuck knows about her, and he's still among the living."

"Yes, but for how *long*? Lacey, you're going to need *help*!"

"You're volunteering?"

Natasha said, "I'm not bad—I can offer excellent references."

"Yeah, and a guy named Lockington is one of them—you ran rings around him last spring!"

"Can you use me?"

"When I need help, I'll whistle."

"Lacey, you may not *have* to whistle." Her pale blue eyes were sparkling. She was taut, like a thoroughbred filly in the starting gate, much as she'd been when he'd met her, and Natasha Gorky had been nothing short of superb when he'd met her.

32 WHEN LOCKINGTON ARRIVED at his office, he found Barney Kozlowski leaning against the north end of the desk, peering into the parking lot. Barney's expression was grim. He said, "We may have trouble here!"

Lockington hung his hat on its favorite nail, yawning. "Is that right?"

"Yeah, there's a horse-faced guy in an '87 blue Caddy out there. He was there when I got here, and he keeps staring at the office. He's probably armed—guess I better go out and take him."

Lockington turned, following Barney's gaze, locating the blue Cadillac. He said, "Look, kid, you got real lucky with Frank Addison, but one of these days you're gonna swing at an armed man, and he's gonna pump a pound of lead into your navel!"

"But we just can't *sit* here!"

"*You* can—*I* can't."

"*You're* gonna take him?"

"I'm gonna *talk* to him—he's a client."

Lockington snatched his hat from the nail, jammed it onto the back of his head, and went out to Gordon Kilbuck's Cadillac, getting in. Kilbuck said, "Who's the guy at the desk?"

"A member of my staff—he's in charge of aerial reconnaissance."

Kilbuck didn't smile. "Got anything?"

"I had a couple of decent possibilities—lost both of 'em."

Kilbuck shook his head disapprovingly. "Well, dammit, Lockington, how did you manage to do *that*?"

"It was easy. They got killed."

Kilbuck blinked, his jaw sagging. "Oh, my *God—sorry*, Lockington!"

126

"So am I."

"They were *murdered*?"

"Rather thoroughly, I'd say."

"On account of this—this Fedorovich business?"

"Ten'll get you twenty."

"The KGB?"

"I've discounted the Mormon Tabernacle Choir."

Kilbuck whistled. "Jesus H. Christ—*now* what?"

Lockington said, "Well, as I figure it, you drive down to Polly's Place and play a few innings of grab-ass with Nanette, and I get back to looking for Alexi Fedorovich."

"There's still a chance?"

"There's always a chance, but some chances are better than others. So far, I've been stuck with the others."

"All right, whatever you say."

Lockington said, "Watch yourself, Kilbuck—there's a few heavies mixed up in this."

Kilbuck nodded, Lockington got out, and Kilbuck peeled rubber leaving the Mahoning Plaza parking lot. Barney was standing in the office doorway, thumbs hooked in his belt in the Hollywood-established fashion of Dodge City gunslingers.

Lockington gave him an okay sign, getting into the Mercedes to drive east on Mahoning Avenue. He turned left at the big red-brick church, pulling to a stop across the street from 24 North Brockway. The driveway of 25 North Brockway was a narrow uphill thing and he climbed it to go to the rear of a small gray dwelling, knocking lightly on the door.

A heavy-set elderly woman with horn-rimmed spectacles responded. She wore a pink bathrobe and fuzzy blue bedroom slippers and a wart on the end of her nose. She looked him over. "Cop?"

Lockington nodded. "May I come in for a few minutes, ma'am?"

She stepped clear of the doorway, allowing him to come in. "I heard there was cops all over the neighborhood last night, but I was playing bingo at St. Ann's—Friday night's my bingo night."

Lockington said, "It was Candice Hoffman's, too." He sat gingerly on a rickety chair at a wobbly table. There was a crossword puzzle book on the table and an ancient Sessions clock ticked loudly on a wall. The kitchen was neat. It smelled of nutmeg, Lockington thought—or maybe it was ginger. He didn't know one spice from another. He said, "Is it okay if I smoke a cigarette, ma'am?"

"It's okay if you got one for *me*—I'm fresh out." Lockington gave her a Camel, holding a match for them. He said, "Sorry, no filters."

She sucked on the cigarette, inhaling, permitting smoke to trickle from her nostrils. This one appreciated tobacco. She said, "Filters are for fairies. I ain't no fairy!"

"May I have your name, ma'am?"

"Mabel Johannsen, what's yours?"

"Poirot, ma'am."

Mabel Johannsen said, "I'm a widow, my kids are in California, I got no dogs, no cats, no job, no prospects." She considered her situation. She said, "Shit!" Then she said, "But I keep a clean house, which is more'n I can say for *some* people." She slipped a cheap glass ashtray onto the table at Lockington's elbow.

"Before this happened, have you noticed anything that appeared suspicious across the street?"

"Sure have—Mrs. Gossman's out of town—Kansas City, I think—and there's been a woman coming there in the afternoons and she stays two, three hours. If you ask me, old Vern Gossman's got another iron in the fire!"

"I meant at Candice Hoffman's house."

Mabel jerked a chair from under the kitchen table, seating herself with a resounding thump. "Like *what*?"

Lockington pushed the ashtray in Mabel's direction. "Oh, like maybe Candice is entertaining gentlemen callers."

"No, nothing like that, but what's suspicious about entertaining gentlemen callers? Hell, I entertain a couple every week, and, mister, when *I* entertain 'em, I guess they *stay* entertained! The bastards never come *back!*"

Lockington said, "Well, then, *any*thing that would seem to be slightly out of the ordinary?"

Mabel shook her head. "I hardly ever look over that way— I watch a whole bunch of TV, and I mind my own business, which is more'n I can say for *some* people."

"What can you tell me about Candice Hoffman—did you know her well?"

"Oh, not *real* well, but well as most, I'd say. Candice ain't been home much this summer—probably visiting her mother. Candice took care of her own, I gotta say *that* for her—can't say it for *some* people."

"She was married?"

"She *was*, yes, until her old man got drunk and ran his car into a bridge abuttment out in Columbiana County."

"Dead?"

"If he ain't, they buried somebody what looked exactly like him." Mabel chuckled. She'd liked that line.

"Where does Candice's mother live?"

"I don't know—never asked her, but it can't be too far from here—sometimes she ain't gone much over an hour. I suppose the old woman's sick."

"Her father—is he still living?"

"She's never mentioned him. I suppose he's gone. Her mother's got to be in her sixties, and men-folks usually go first—ever notice that?"

Lockington nodded. "What was Candice's maiden name, do you know?"

"No idea."

Lockington snuffed out his cigarette. "She had no friends— no visitors?"

"Just neighborhood people, far as I know—Candice was

well liked—I've been over there lotsa times for coffee. Candice made damn good coffee, which is more'n I can say for *some* people."

Lockington got to his feet. "Well, thanks, Mabel—sorry to have messed up your morning."

"No problem, officer. Candice's daughter used to come around once in a month of blue moons—maybe you could talk to *her*."

Lockington sat down. "She had a daughter?"

"Yeah, her only kid, I think—Brenda—real good looker. Brenda's in her late twenties, I'd say."

"Brenda—Brenda Hoffman?"

"Not now—Brenda's been married two, three times—can't hold onto a man. *I* had *my* husband for thirty-one years—all depends on how you treat 'em."

"What's Brenda's latest married name?"

"Damned if I know—it was Carpenter the first time, but that one went bust in hurry. Carpenter drank and chased floozies, Candice said, but then what man *don't*? You wanta keep your man, you gotta look the other way now and again."

"Brenda has kids?"

"Never heard of any—Candice would of mentioned 'em—Candice was crazy about kids. Anyway, Brenda's a nympho, and them nymphos got no time for kids—kids take 'em outta circulation."

"Who told you that Brenda's a nympho?"

"Candice did—only she didn't come right out with it—she just talked around it, but you couldn't miss what she was driving at."

"How long had Candice lived here on North Brockway?"

"Well, let's see—since '81 or thereabouts."

"Brenda was living with Candice then?"

"No, she got married early—probably right after she graduated from high school, if she even graduated—you know how today's kids are—can't wait to get married, can't wait to get divorced. I didn't get married till I was twenty-eight—

Jake was thirty-one—it pays to wait, I always say."

"Any information on Candice's wake?"

"Sure—Sabatini's over on South Avenue—tonight, six to ten."

"You're going?"

"Oh, *hell*, no—wakes depress me—*some* people *enjoy* 'em!"

Lockington nodded, getting up, thanking Mabel again, tipping his hat to her as he went out, remembering that he'd forgotten to take the damned thing off. There was a man leaning against the right front fender of the Mercedes. Lockington said, "Good morning, Frank."

"I recognized your car," Addison said.

"I got the only black '88 Mercedes in Mahoning County?"

"You got the only black '88 Mercedes with 987–KN plates."

"Where's *your* car?"

"Around the corner."

Lockington unlocked the Mercedes. "Get in."

"Don't mind if I do."

Lockington rolled down the windows. He said, "Frank, you got a cigarette? I left mine on Mabel Johannsen's kitchen table."

"Well, hell go back and *get* 'em!"

"Naw—Mabel was fresh out."

33 BORTS FIELD IS YOUNGSTOWN, Ohio's principal West Side recreational facility—baseball, football, swimming, tennis—bounded by Connecticut Avenue to the north, Oakwood to the south, Millet to the west, Belle Vista to the east. Frank Addison had suggested that they drive down there and Lockington had done so, parking on Millet Avenue. They sat in the third base line bleachers, soaking up the mid-October sunshine, sucking on cans of orange soda they'd bought from an Oriental lady in a little store on Oakwood Avenue. Addison was gazing over the deserted expanses of Borts Field, smiling. It was a nostalgic smile—Lockington knew a nostalgic smile when he saw one, he'd smiled a few of his own. Addison was saying, "I got some memories here—one time I hit a homer with two men on in the ninth and we won it 4–3. That baseball traveled three city blocks."

Lockington thought about it. "Some wallop—damn near half a mile."

Addison chuckled. "Back in those days, a lotta guys hit 'em that far." He pointed east toward Belle Vista Avenue. "Those chain-link fences weren't out there then, so if you busted a liner into right-center, sometimes it'd bounce through the hedges along the perimeter, and if it got through the hedges, it'd roll down the embankment to Belle Vista Avenue."

"That ain't no three city blocks."

"No, but Belle Vista runs downhill to the north, and that damn ball would roll across Connecticut Avenue and keep right on rolling."

Lockington said, "I see," knowing that when a guy Addison's age gets to talking about the sports heroics of his youth, it's hard to get him stopped.

Addison was rambling on. "I was hitting third in the lineup and do you know what that number-four hitter said when I crossed the plate?"

Lockington shook his head.

"He told me that if *I* hadn't done it, he *would* have!"

Lockington shrugged. "Well, he *could* have."

"Goddammit, Lockington, there was two *outs*—if I'd struck out, that sonofabitch wouldn't have got a *chance* to do it!"

Lockington nodded, letting the subject fade. The sun was hot and they took off their jackets, draping them over the splintered green benches of the bleachers. They watched a flock of pigeons wheel from the west to land on the infield. In a minute or so, Addison glanced at Lockington. "Do you like pigeons?"

Lockington said, "Sure—doesn't everybody? What's wrong with pigeons?"

"I didn't say there was anything wrong with 'em, I just asked if you liked the rotten little bastards."

Lockington yawned, "Okay, so I like pigeons."

A couple of teenage kids on bicycles came rolling down the hill from Oakwood Avenue, riding directly at the birds, frightening them to flight. Addison glanced at his watch. "Those kids oughta be in school."

Lockington said, "They oughta be in *jail*—they spooked the *pigeons!*"

Addison finished his can of soda. "You believe in God, don't you, Lockington?"

"Yeah—what's your point?"

"No point, but anybody who likes pigeons just gotta believe in God."

"And you're wondering why I'm looking into Candice Hoffman's murder."

"I ain't gonna ask—I'm gonna let you *tell* me."

Lockington's smile was dismal. "It's pretty much the same

story you heard at the Golden Sombrero—I'm looking for an individual that Abigail Fleugelham knew a long time ago. It's possible that Candice Hoffman was remotely connected with him."

"A long time ago?"

"No, recently."

"*How* recently?"

"About as recently as you can get."

"You're looking for a 'him'—you didn't tell me that earlier."

"Candice Hoffman was alive earlier."

Addison sat hunched forward on the bleachers bench, elbows on his knees, chin cupped in his hands. After a while he said, "So, what's it all about?"

Lockington said, "I can tell you this much—I think that there's a human trail leading to the guy I'm trying to find, and I think that somebody's on the trail with me."

"Who's in the lead?"

"He beat me to Candice Hoffman, didn't he?"

"Fleugelham, then Hoffman—apparently he's eradicating the trail. Why?"

"Possibly to slam the door on a *third* tracker."

"Who would the third guy be?"

"I don't know—I'm not concerned with a third man—it's the second sonofabitch that worries me. He's *close!*"

"If *he's* close, *you're* close!"

"Which is why he'll probably try to kill me." The pigeons were back. Lockington said, "I like that gray one with the white chest—the one on the pitcher's mound. Proud-looking cuss, ain't he?"

"Forget the pigeons. If this other man finds the guy you're trying to locate, will he kill him?"

"Certainly."

They got up, leaving the bleachers, walking a few yards to Oakwood Avenue, turning west toward Millet and the

Mercedes. Addison said, "Look, Lockington, if it's any of my business, why did you take this case?"

"Why did the chicken cross the road?"

"It wasn't a chicken, it was a pigeon."

Lockington said, "That's why I took the case."

34

CAYUSE BRESNAHAN WAS SEATED at the wheel of his brown Ford Escort just east of Lockington's Mahoning Plaza office. He beeped his horn when Lockington got out of the Mercedes. Lockington ambled over to the Escort. Bresnahan's black Stetson had been pushed to the back of his head at a rakish angle, his sunglasses resting high on his forehead—he looked weary, Lockington thought. Bresnahan frowned. He said, "That brontosaurus is sitting at your desk!"

Lockington said, "I know it."

"He *works* for you?"

"That's right."

"Then I think maybe we better talk out *here*!"

"Suits me, if we can find something to talk about."

"You've made no progress—none at *all*?"

Lockington rested his forearms on the roof of the Escort. "What'd you expect in forty-eight hours: bands? Wild horses? Naked women?"

"No, but I expected *some*thing!"

Lockington said, "You hired me—you can fire me."

"Aw, now don't go off half-cocked! When do you expect a break in this thing?"

"The very moment I can force one—possibly tonight, possibly not."

"What's happening tonight?"

"I'm going to a wake."

"No levity, please."

"No levity intended."

"A wake—there's a connection?"

"I believe there is."

"Lockington, I'm under big pressure."

"Check with me tomorrow morning."

"What *time* tomorrow morning?"

"Look, Bresnahan, I stopped punching clocks before I left Chicago. Keep trying until you get me."

"Okay, *okay*, no offense, but you know how it goes—I get paid for results and if I don't produce 'em, somebody else *will!*"

"And I do the best I can with the cards I get. That wasn't a straight flush you dealt me."

"What's with this wake?"

"I'll know when I get there."

"Well, play it cool—we don't want publicity—we want Alexi Fedorovich."

Lockington stepped away from the Escort and Bresnahan backed from his parking place.

Barney Kozlowski was peeking around a corner of the office doorway. He said, "You didn't have a thing to worry about—I had my eye on him all the way!"

Lockington said, "Anybody call?"

"Yeah, the painter. He said that he'll be here around the middle of November."

"What for?"

"To paint your office—he said that your office gets painted once a year—it's in your lease. You get your choice of sixteen shades of eggshell white, he said."

"*White?* White ain't a color—white is the *absence* of color."

"All I know is what he told me. Say, Mr. Lockington, isn't there something I could be helping you with? I ain't cut out for a desk job—I want to be out where it's *happening!*"

"Where it's happening—where *what's* happening?"

"Don't kid me, Mr. Lockington—I know you're working on a major case!"

"I *am?*"

"Damn right—I can *feel* it!"

"Uh-huh. How does it feel?"

"Well, I'm sort of jingly in my stomach. You've never felt jingly in your stomach?"

"Kid, I haven't felt jingly in my stomach since July of '83."

"In July of '83 you probably got into a big shootout with a bunch of Mafia guys."

"No, I got into a big dose of ptomaine at Mamma Mia's Pizzeria."

He'd lied, of course. He'd never gone through the doors of Mamma Mia's Pizzeria, and he'd been feeling jingly in his stomach since he'd first laid eyes on Natasha Gorky. But Lockington wouldn't have described that sensation as "jingly." He'd have likened it to King Kong teeing-off on a church belfry with a telephone pole.

35

IT WAS 5:00. Barney Kozlowski would be closing the office, Lockington was at the kitchen table with Natasha, and Natasha was eyeing the stack of yellow legal paper in front of her, shaking her head ruefully. She was saying, "I'm not sure that there's anything here—if there *is*, I can't find the key."

Lockington said, "The book's dust jacket hooked you."

Natasha nodded. "It may have been nothing more than happenstance and wishful thinking—those wheels intrigued me."

"The puzzle, or game—just how was it set up when you learned it?"

Natasha sketched three eight-spoked wheels on her legal pad, circling them with numbers, filling the spoke gaps with letters. She said, "This way," pushing the pad to Lockington. He studied the arrangement:

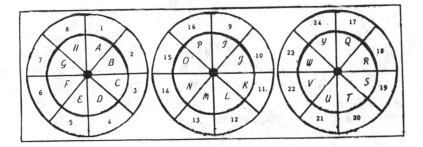

After a while he said, "You matched the numbers to the letters in the gaps?"

"Yes, three wheels, twenty-four spokes, twenty-four letters

between the spokes—*X* and *Z* were omitted, *Q* indicated a space, or the end of the message."

"The letters run clockwise in proper order—was that standard procedure?"

"That's how it was introduced to my brother and me. That's the easy way, of course—the letters could have been entered in random fashion, but in that case the number of combinations would be *staggering!*"

Lockington slid the legal pad back to Natasha. "Yeah, twenty-four multipled by twenty-three, that total multiplied by twenty-two, and *that* total multiplied by—Jesus Christ, you'd need a *computer!*"

"At home we kept it simple—it was just as you've seen it. The *trick* was to find the *key*."

"How did you go about finding it?"

"My father would place tiny dots under a book's page numbers, or under its index numbers—he made it difficult, but not *too* difficult—after all, he was dealing with children. Under the numerical and alphabetical arrangement you've just looked at, 8-5-12-16 would translate to *HELP*, but there'd be longer messages, like *DON'T FORGET TO FEED THE CAT*. It was a time-consuming exercise, that's all."

"There's nothing that resembles a key in Fedorovich's book?"

"Well, yes, there's a special list of footnote numbers in the introduction, divorced from the main body of footnote references—there are seventeen of these, and they're jumbled, all out of order. There are *five* repetitions, and numbers repeated usually represent vowels, *A, E, I, O,* or *U,* but not so in this instance. Applying that string of numbers to this lettering system results in mumbo jumbo."

"What about the footnotes on the special list—what do they make reference to?"

Natasha turned her attention to an isolated sheet of paper, rattling off the numbers in rapid-fire fashion, "20-24-9-20-2-14-20-4-17-1-3-6-15-22-24-3-17. All correspond to the

General's estimates of Warsaw Pact and NATO combat losses at various points of certain encounters, in the Fulda Gap and at the Danube, for example—planes, tanks, artillery pieces, communications gear—and troops, of course—General Fedorovich predicts astronomical loss of life."

"During the third world war."

"Or what will most certainly *provoke* it!" Natasha's voice was small.

Lockington said, "Does he pick a winner?"

"No, he picks a dozen losers, including the Soviet Union."

"Well, if there *is* a message, and if there *is* a key, who the hell would General Fedorovich be trying to reach—and *why?*"

"At this juncture, these are two more unknowns."

Lockington shrugged, lighting a cigarette. "Okay, so to hell with it—I have time for a fast sandwich, then I gotta cut out for Candice Hoffman's wake."

Natasha got up, busying herself with the construction of a sandwich. "Where will the wake be held?"

"A joint on the South Side—Sabatini's on South Avenue."

"What's the point—why bother going?"

"I just might run into Candice Hoffman's daughter."

"Would that be good or bad?"

"Good, hopefully—Candice picked up Olga Karelinko's mail—Olga Karelinko has been Fedorovich's postal contact—Candice's daughter may know something of Olga, Olga certainly knows something of Fedorovich. That's why it might be good."

"What's Candice's daughter's name?"

"Her first name's Brenda—I don't know her last name."

"It isn't Hoffman?"

"No, she's been married a few times, I've heard."

"She's young, obviously."

"Approaching thirty."

"Pretty?"

"So they say."

"Still married?"

"Not as I understand it."

Natasha spun away from the sinkboard to slam Lockington's sandwich plate onto the table. She pointed an authoritative finger at him, her eyes snapping pale blue sparks. She hissed, "Lacey Lockington, you be home not one damned moment later than eleven o'clock, do you *hear* me?"

Lockington grinned. "*Da.*"

Natasha said, "Never trust an American who speaks Russian!"

Lockington bit into his cheddar cheese sandwich. A man up to his ears in love rarely knows if he's eating cheddar cheese or moose dung. Nor does he care.

36

THE NIGHT STREETS of Youngstown's South Side are for the weak of mind, the strong of heart, or the fleet of foot. Being none of the three, Lacey Lockington checked his .38 before taking Route 680 to the South Avenue exit.

Sabatini's Funeral Home was a three-story gray frame building in an excellent state of repair. Its front lawn was neatly manicured, its windows were bordered by stained-glass panels, its front porch was the length of a bowling alley. Back in the twenties or thirties it'd been a mansion, Lockington figured, but since the war the neighborhood had gone downhill on roller skates and its occupants had packed up to light out for the tall timber. As a residence it was outdated, as a funeral home it was okay, as funeral homes go, which wasn't a great distance in Lockington's book.

He swung the Mercedes into the wide blacktopped drive that looped the big gray house, backing into a parking place in the north corner of the parking lot, noting that his was the only automobile in sight save for a brace of black Cadillac sedans nosed against the red-on-white EMPLOYEES ONLY sign tacked to the rear of the building. He glanced at his watch—5:50. He lit a cigarette, settling back on Mercedes leather to watch late afternoon begin its long blue slide into twilight. They'd be rolling back the clocks in a couple of weeks and that wouldn't serve to accomplish a great deal other than to disturb the nation's sexual and drinking rhythms. Lockington had never been able to see the advantages of clock jockeying, putting the practice down as just one more change for the sake of change. He turned on the radio, tuning to 1390 on the AM dial, listening to Nat Cole sing "A Blossom Fell," the likes of which hadn't been composed in more than thirty years.

At 5:58 an '87 gray Buick Skyhawk slipped into the Sabatini

parking lot. Its driver, a woman, wheeled the car southward to the opposite side of the expanse, where she left it to cross the blacktop and enter the funeral home through an entrance at a rear corner of the building. She had a nice gait, Lockington thought—free-striding. He was unable to get a head-on look at her, but her profile was promising. Her hair was chestnut, wavy, cascading to her shoulders. She wore a form-fitting, black satin, short-skirted dress and three-inch-heeled black sling pumps. Her legs were excellent, in Lockington's opinion. She had a gray sweater slung over her left forearm and she carried a small black patent leather clutch-purse. She was slim, trim, closing in on thirty, but certainly not that far along yet. Lockington was confident that he'd just witnessed the arrival of Candice Hoffman's daughter, Brenda Who-the-hell-ever.

He waited in the Mercedes, smoking, listening to WHOT. At 6:30 there were no other cars in the Sabatini parking lot, nor were there any at 7:00. By 7:30 mid-October darkness was blanketing the city, and the parking lot lights had clicked on—blindingly bright, *too* bright, Lockington thought, but then considering the neighborhood, perhaps not. Candice Hoffman wasn't attracting a standing room only turnout. Two men in dark suits left the building to drive away in the black Cadillacs—Sabatini and son, probably. At 7:45 the Mercedes and the Skyhawk were still the lot's only occupants, and when Brenda hadn't emerged by eight o'clock, Lockington went in.

Sabatini's Funeral Home possessed the facilities for two wakes. On Lockington's right the first suite of rooms was deserted. Farther down the hushed hallway he forged into Candice Hoffman territory—to his left a small room lined with uncomfortable-looking wooden chairs and pedestal ashtrays, to his right an amber casket resting on a black velvet-draped stand. The casket was closed. They can't do much for a woman who's been bludgeoned to death. There was a single modest flower arrangement in a white wicker basket. Somewhere in the dim recesses of Sabatini's Funeral Home a pipe organ recording was playing "Jesus Savior, Pilot Me." Good taste, Lockington thought—beat hell out of "Darktown Strutters' Ball," not that Candice Hoffman gave a damn one way or the other. Funeral homes depressed Lockington, not so much because another soul had departed this world for the next as for the fact that the undertaking industry was a ravenous beast growing fat on heartbreak. Lockington rated undertakers on a level with lawyers and used car dealers—there wasn't a drop of genuine mercy in the lot. Over the years, he'd had occasion to shoot a few people, but he hadn't shot a lawyer or a used car dealer or an undertaker. He regretted that. He was seating himself in the smokers' alcove when he heard a female voice. "You knew her?"

Before he turned, Lockington said, "Not long."

The woman's eyes were large, dark brown, with flickers of gold in their depths. Her nose was short and upturned, her mouth full-lipped. She was smiling. It was a smile to be remembered. She said, "You were her lover?"

Lockington shook his head. "Did she have a lover?"

"Well, my God, I *hope* so." Lockington didn't say anything.

She sat beside him, crossing her legs, her short black skirt hitching to within six inches of where the panther pissed in the pea patch. "I'm her daughter, Brenda Willoughby."

The pipe organ recording had drifted into "Just As I Am." Brenda had put out her hand. Lockington had taken it. He said, "I'm Lacey Lockington—how are you?"—the question having nothing to do with the title of the pipe organ selection. Brenda was looking him full in the eyes. She said, "That's right—you wouldn't know."

Lockington grabbed the brass ring. "If I knew, I wouldn't ask."

"I'm very good—*exceptional*, really."

"From here, I believe that."

Under the circumstances, the conversation had taken an unusual turn, Lockington thought, but grief sometimes turns glows into bonfires. Whatever the reasons prompting her approach, Brenda hadn't minced words, she'd laid it right on the line.

She said, "You can't tell a book by its cover."

"No, but you can come close."

"'Close' counts only in horseshoes."

"It's a long time between ringers."

"Not if you practice."

"'Practice makes perfect'?"

"Well, not *perfect*, perhaps, but I'll bet you won't know the difference."

Mabel Johannsen had said that Brenda was a nymphomaniac. Mabel might have been guilty of understatement—it appeared that he was on the shortest road to Rome.

"I'd like to talk to you, Ms. Willoughby" he said. "In private."

She popped to her feet. "He who hesitates is lost, wouldn't you say?"

"I might, if somebody else hadn't said it first."

Brenda Willoughby put her hand on his shoulder. "I'll be right back."

She left the room, returning within moments, carrying her gray sweater and her clutch-purse. She stood in front of Lockington, pigeon-toed in her black pumps.

Lockington said, "Ready?"

"You'll find out."

Lockington didn't doubt her, not even a little bit. "You aren't going to ask why I came?"

She reached for his hand, pulling him to his feet. "Later. First things first."

37 THEY WERE WALKING down the long corridor in the direction of the rear exit, Brenda at Lockington's side grasping his arm. It was the grasp of complete possession, however temporary. She was saying, "Nobody came—nobody but me. And you."

Lockington said, "Who *didn't* come?"

"Damned near everybody—they stayed away by the dozens!"

"I mean, did you expect relatives that didn't show?"

She was silent for a few steps. "No, I guess not."

Lockington said, "We should stop for a drink."

"*Why*? I have a bottle in the trunk."

"You're driving?"

She squeezed his arm. "Not far, just a mile or so south on Market Street—cozy little motel."

"Maybe I should follow in my car—this might be time consuming."

She nodded. "Never in haste—*never*!"

It would be a tough one to wiggle out of, and he couldn't squirm until he'd gotten around to the subject of Olga Karelinko. Brenda said, "You're a policeman, of course."

Lockington didn't say yes, he didn't say no. He busied himself with opening the door for her. They stepped into the parking lot. A breeze was sweeping from the west and leaves were pinwheeling across the broad span of blacktop, making tiny little scratching sounds in their hurry. Brenda was saying, "The police have been around, I've been told, but you're the first I've seen."

Lockington said, "No questions from *any*one?"

"I had a telephone call from a detective at the funeral home the moment I arrived."

"What was his name?"

"Mawson, I think he said—Lieutenant Mawson—he—"
There was a dull plopping sound from the south, like someone
had dropped an empty shoe box. Brenda was spinning,
staggering. Lockington grabbed for her, missing. She went
down, flat on her back, one hand to her face. On the side
street to the south there was the roar of an engine and the
scream of spinning rubber. Lockington knelt beside Brenda
Willoughby. Her right eye was missing. She'd been dead
before she hit the blacktop.

38 NATASHA WAS SEATED at their basement bar, chin in her palms, a yellow legal pad between her elbows. Lockington said, "Could a man get a cognac in this establishment?"

She got up, pouring a double for him. "Lacey, I'm seeing wheels in my *sleep!*"

"Progress?"

"Not a blessed inch." She perched on the stool behind the bar, watching him down the cognac, refilling his glass. She said, "There was trouble tonight." It was a statement, not a question. She knew him well.

"I saw a woman killed."

"Brenda?"

Lockington nodded.

Natasha's facial expression didn't change. "How?"

"Shot—she was two feet from me."

"There's nothing that'll connect you to this, is there?"

"Not that I know of—I was out of there in nothing flat."

"*Krahsny Lentuh!*"

"Look, why don't you just say *KGB?*"

"Because it *isn't* the KGB, damn it—not the KGB *I* worked for—*Krahsny Lentuh*'s out of *bounds!*"

"Okay, so *Krahsny Lentuh*'s a berserk splinter group—Brenda's still dead."

Natasha pulled the legal pad to her, drawing wheels in sets of three, adding numbers. Without looking up, she said, "Death gets under your skin, doesn't it, Lacey?"

"*Unsolicited* death, yes."

"But you've killed."

"I've killed people who were asking for it—that didn't faze me. And you? You've never told me."

"Three, all in Europe."

"And one in the United States—Devereaux."

"Indirectly." She poured vodka into a short glass, sipping at it. "Brenda was your last link to Olga Karelinko?"

"She introduced herself as Brenda Willoughby—if I can locate her husband, there's a chance. I'll tackle that in the morning."

"She was shot in the funeral home parking lot, I assume."

"Yeah—we'd just stepped outside."

"At that point you'd learned nothing?"

"Just that her name was Willoughby—I was going to follow her to a tavern for a drink or two—I wanted to inquire about Olga Karelinko. So did somebody else."

"Who?"

"She told me that she'd had a call at the funeral home before I came in—a police detective named Mawson. This guy Mawson really gets around!"

"What did she tell him, did she say?"

"She didn't get the chance."

"Our Mr. Mawson is a *Krasny Lentuh* operative, *depend* on it! He was ascertaining that she was *at* the funeral home."

"He's a killer—he'll be the man who brained Candice Hoffman."

"Likely, but Mawson may not have wanted Brenda Willoughby—he may have missed his target."

"He meant to get *me*?"

"It's worthy of consideration, isn't it?"

"I doubt it."

"Quite frankly, so do I—it was just a thought."

Lockington said, "If *Krasny Lentuh* doesn't know Fedorovich's location—"

"Which it *doesn't*—he'd be *dead*, if it knew."

"And if it knows that I'm looking for Fedorovich—"

"Which it *does, believe* me!"

"All right, then—why kill *me*? Why not use me, watch me, let me lead the way to him?"

"That's the strategy—then kill *both* of you. No tracks."

Lockington shrugged. "We'll cross that bridge if we ever get to it."

Their glasses were empty and Natasha was filling them. "I'd say that Mawson believed that you'd already gotten the important information, thereby reducing Brenda to the status of complicating factor, more liability than asset."

Lockington frowned. She was a furlong in front of him.

The tautness had left her lips, her lopsided smile had returned. She raised her glass and Lockington raised his. She said, "To Mr. Mawson—until *Mawlniyuh* catches up with him."

"Which may be three years after the cow jumps over the moon."

"No, Lacey, he's on his last legs—he'll be dead within a week. Mawson's good, but *Mawlniyuh*'s better--*much* better!"

They drank, and there was silence. Natasha turned off the bar lights. She reached across the bar to take his hand. "Mr. Lockington, you're an excellent detective. How are you in bed?"

"With limited capabilities, I do the best I can."

Natasha was on her feet. "Last one stripped is a sissy!"

Lockington finished second, and there was nothing new about that. He'd been finishing second since he could remember, and he'd been willing to settle for it—second isn't all that bad. He rolled into bed and into Natasha's waiting arms. She stroked the side of his face. She whispered, "There's a first time for everything, isn't there?"

"I suppose so." He kissed the end of her nose, wondering what she was leading up to, but not for long.

She said, "That point having been agreed upon, Lacey, here you *go!*" She had him by the ears, tugging his head gently downward to the swell of her breasts and southward. His lips brushed her navel and in a moment he was there. She held onto his ears, cocking a leg, lifting her buttocks, pulling his face into the hot V of her, holding him in place. "Welcome to perestroika."

Lockington said, "Perestroika has hair?"

"Perestroika is a word indicating the beginning of a new era. *This* is the beginning of a new era!"

"Well, whaddaya *know!*"

Natasha murmured, "More than four months, and you've never been there."

"I didn't know that you *wanted* me here."

"Enough conversation! Are you going to do it or aren't you?"

"I'm going to do it."

Natasha's voice was hoarse. "Then do it, for God's sake, *do* it, I—I—yes—yes—yes-s-s—that's right, *that's* right—that's *right*—wonderful—*wonderful*—WONDERFUL-L-L-L!" A prolonged shudder was racking Natasha Gorky's tawny naked body, she jack-knifed in Lockington's direction, grabbing him by the hair of his head, gasping, "Oh, but that was quick—*so* quick—too damned quick!" She released her hold on him, falling back to her pillow, the tension gone out of her. She said, "Don't you think?"

"Don't I think what—that it was too damned quick?"

"Yes—too damned quick."

Lockington shrugged as best he could in that position. He said, "I don't know—it's a moot point, probably."

"Do you have objections?"

"None that come readily to mind."

"Might I ask you a question?"

"You might—in fact, you probably will."

"Would you do it again?"

"When?"

"There's no time like the present." She reached for Lockington's ears. "Mary Manley said that."

"She did?"

Natasha said, "Yes, possibly at a moment like this, wouldn't you say?"

"I wouldn't say—I'm not an expert on the subject."

Natasha had grasped his ears. She said, "Well, you certainly could have fooled *me!*"

Lockington's response was strangely muffled.

39 NATASHA HAD SLEPT soundly through Lockington's Saturday morning alarm. Considering the previous evening's hectic bedroom activities and Natasha's demands for encores, that was understandable, as was the crick in Lockington's neck. At eight-thirty he'd left the house quietly, driving to a small coffee and doughnut shop in Austintown, west of Meridian Road. That was where Frank Addison caught up with him. Addison said, "Well, doggone, Lockington, fancy meeting *you* here!"

Lockington crunched down on a chocolate doughnut. "Knock it off, Addison, you were parked on Burbank Avenue, watching for me."

Addison's smile was sheepish. "Yeah, well, I didn't want to wait at your office—I haven't established a great deal of rapport with your hired man." He slumped onto a chair, ordering a jelly doughnut and a cup of black coffee.

Lockington gave him a quick once-over. "You look like there was a hole in your parachute."

Addison shook his head wearily. "I was up half the night—homicide on the South Side."

"From what I know of the South Side, that ain't grounds for a congressional investigation."

"Woman killed in the parking area behind Sabatini's Funeral Home on South Avenue. We found a thirty caliber rifle casing on the street north of there—she was probably shot from a parked car."

"Local woman?"

"Yeah, a Brenda Willoughby—man, she must of been some kind of cat! There was a dozen condoms in her clutch-purse!"

"Well, one never knows when opportunity will strike."

"She lived in an apartment on Wick Avenue—we checked

153

with neighbors—she was a divorcée. She threw her old man out last spring. He rolls an eighteen-wheeler for Moffitt Red Ball Express east of Canfield—he's out of town—left on a run to Chicago night before last."

Lockington drained his coffee cup, studying Frank Addison over its tilted rim. He said, "This is none of my affair, is it?"

Around a bulging mouthful of jelly doughnut, Addison said, "Maybe yes, maybe no. Probably yes."

"Why yes?"

"We went through the identification stuff in her purse—driver's license, social security card, that sort of thing, and the person to be notified in case of emergency was Brenda's mother, a Candice Hoffman of 24 North Brockway Avenue."

Lockington yawned. "Then she was at her mother's wake."

Addison said, "Point of interest—how would you know where Candice Hoffman's wake was to be held?"

"The old gal across the street from the Hoffman house told me yesterday morning."

"And you forgot to mention it to me."

"Slipped my mind."

"I'd think that you should have been at Sabatini's, just to see who came around."

"I was considering stopping there tonight—most wakes are two-night affairs. Things are usually more settled on the second night."

Addison grabbed a napkin from a chromed holder on the table, wiping a smear of jelly from a corner of his mouth. "Well, actually, the reason I'm here is because you're looking for Mr. X, and you seem to think there was a connection between him and Candice Hoffman, and Brenda Willoughby was Candice's daughter, so I thought you might want to talk to Cy Willoughby."

"I might, yes."

"Well, he's due in at the Moffitt terminal this morning—

hour, hour and a half, give or take. Wanta ride along?"

"Why not?" Lockington grabbed Addison's check.

"Much obliged."

"My pleasure."

It was raining when they left the doughnut shop.

40 FRANK ADDISON TOOLED the blue Chrysler west through the rain, turning north on Route 11. He said, "Y'know, Lockington, I been thinking about what you told me at Borts Field yesterday morning."

"That I like pigeons?"

"No, that there's a human trail leading to the guy you're trying to find, and that somebody is erasing it."

Lockington said, "Well, if it ain't that way, I've just run into the Goddamndest set of concidences I've ever run into."

"Okay, but he's erasing it *behind* you, never *before* you get there, always *after*!"

"How about the Willoughby woman, wasn't he ahead of me?"

"My ouija board tells me *wasn't*."

"Then you better get a new ouija board."

"Well, anyway, you got the right idea. You said that old Abigail Fleugelham knew your man, and Abigail gets throttled with a plastic clothes line. Candice Hoffman was mixed up in this thing somehow, and Candice gets her brains knocked out. Brenda Willoughby was Candice's daughter, she had to know something of Candice's affairs, and Brenda takes a thirty through the eye. Care to take it from there, Lockington?"

"If I could take it from there, I wouldn't be *here*."

"Who are you working for?"

"No dice, Addison."

"You don't have to give me a name."

"I don't have to give you *any*thing."

"I could run you in, you know that."

"On what charge?"

"I could come up with one—material witness—obstruction of justice—*some* damned thing."

156

"Run me in and you're gonna have an office full of pissed-off feds."

Addison grinned. "Well, that helps just a bit—you're *government!*"

"No, but I know people who *are.*"

"And you're working for them."

"I didn't say that."

"This guy you want, he's a fugitive?"

"Not exactly."

Addison lit a cigarette, rolling down his window, pitching the match into the rain. He was silent for half a mile. Then he said, "Jesus Christ, Lockington, don't tell me that this is an *international* thing!"

"Okay, I won't tell you that this is an international thing."

They turned west on Route 224, passing a string of fast-food joints and restaurants. Lockington couldn't equate fast-food joints with restaurants—you can't get a vodka martini in a fast-food joint. Addison was saying, "I'll tell you what—you could be getting into a matter involving the KGB, couldn't you?"

"I could also be getting into a matter involving the Salvation Army, couldn't I?"

Addison was slowing the Chrysler, spinning south between eight-foot barbed wire-topped gates and onto a blacktopped acreage fanning in front of a corrugated metal garage more than a hundred feet in length. The building had four overhead doors, one of them open. To their left, twenty or more trailers were parked in orderly fashion along the perimeter of the blacktopped area. Fifty feet off to their right, a small white-frame enclosure occupied a corner of the apron—Moffitt Red Ball's dispatching office, apparently.

Lockington checked his watch. "We're early."

Addison said, "So, we'll wait—I'm not scheduled to address the Senate until this afternoon."

"Put in a few words for me."

"I'll do that—I'll mention that you're a hard-headed

sonofabitch." Addison pulled onto the graveled shoulder, stopping, killing the engine. He said, "You'd better start looking over your shoulder. A green T-bird followed us all the way from the doughnut shop."

Lockington said, "If he's watching you, he's probably a hit man—if he's watching me, he's a bill collector."

"It wasn't a 'he.'"

"Okay, so there are female bill collectors."

"She continued west into Canfield."

Lockington didn't reply, and they sat in the Chrysler, listening to the rattle of rain on the roof. Lockington whistled absent-mindedly. After a while, Addison said, "Ain't it the truth?"

Lockington stopped whistling. "I don't follow you."

"You were whistling 'I Get the Blues When it Rains'."

"I guess that's a habit."

"A Freudian thing, maybe."

"No, it was written by Klauber and Stoddard—we used to sing it at Mike's Tavern."

Addison said, "I was referring to spontaneous psycho-physical responses."

"Sounds like classical stuff—we never got into classical."

"Fuck you, Lockington."

They watched a big man in a gray jacket come out of the office carrying a small overnight bag. He entered the garage through its open door and a few moments later a blue Peterbilt tractor snorted onto the macadam, swung left, stopped, backed toward the row of trailers to the east and coupled with one. Addison said, "Where do you suppose he's headed?"

Lockington shrugged. "Christ knows, but there'll be a chickie waiting when he gets there."

"Yeah, these over-the-road guys all got chickies at the other end of the line—*any* old line." He thought about it. "How's about you, Lockington—you got a chickie?"

"Yeah, I got a chickie."

"Permanent?"

"Hope so."

Addison said, "Hell, *nothing's* permanent. I got a little barmaid at Dinty's Wharf on Hubbard Road, but that's a temporary thing—she's got a female-dominant complex. You know about female-dominant complexes?"

Lockington shook his head. "Look, why don't we hit the office? Willoughby might have busted down in Indiana."

Addison started the Chrysler, pulling up to the office door. They got out, Addison leading the way, climbing the steps in the rain. They went in. A portly baldheaded man in a peppermint-striped shirt sat at a paper-cluttered desk, munching on the stump of a cigar, talking on the telephone. He glanced up, placing a forefinger across his lips for silence. He was saying, "Yeah—yeah—okay—okay, I'll jump right on it and I'll call you back." He banged the telephone into its cradle. "Gents, I'm Nate Slifka—what can I do for you?"

"Youngstown police—Frank Addison—I spoke with you earlier this morning."

"Uh-huh. About Cy Willoughby, wasn't it?"

"That's right—he should be in shortly, shouldn't he?"

Nate Slifka said, "Yeah, he *should* be, but he ain't *gonna* be— Cy Willoughby's dead."

Lockington checked his surprise meter. It hadn't so much as quivered.

Frank Addison was saying, "I'm a sonofabitch—*where*?"

"Chicago—that was the Chicago cops on the line."

Addison said, "Wreck?"

"Naw, they found him in the pissery of some gin mill near the Mohawk West terminal—he'd been knifed." Slifka shook his head. "Jesus, what a way to go—knifed in a tavern shithouse!"

Addison said, "When did this happen?"

"Late last night—he was scheduled to be on the road one o'clock this morning."

"They get the guy who knifed him?"

"If they did, they didn't say so."

"Who do you notify?"

"All I got is his ex-wife—they busted up sometime last spring, as I recall. Cy was outta West Virginia—he got no immediate family in these parts, far as I know. Was he in some kind of trouble?"

"No, we wanted to talk to him about his ex-wife—she was killed last night."

"Holy Christ—it never rains but what it pours! I've met her—cute cookie—Brenda, I think. Well, maybe I can get hold of his mother-in-law."

Addison said, "She's dead, recently."

Slifka said, "Well, what the fuck do I do *now*?"

Lockington said, "There aren't too many trucking terminals in Chicago proper—most of 'em are in the suburbs. What's Mohawk West's address?"

Slifka said, "It's someplace on Grand Avenue—I got it here—we make six runs a week to Mohawk—Mohawk takes it through to Denver." He was riffling through a stack of invoices. "I'll find it—hang on a minute."

Lockington said, "There ain't no Mohawk West terminal on Grand Avenue—you're thinking of Great Lakes Central."

"Great Lakes Central sold to Mohawk West in August."

"Then Willoughby probably got knifed in the Roundhouse Café."

"Yeah, by God, that was it—Roundhouse Café! You must be familiar with Chicago!"

"I've been there."

"You know this Roundhouse Café?"

"It's half a block from the truck terminal, across the street from the Amtrak coach yard."

"You've been *in* it?"

"A few times—it's a railroader-truck driver hangout—rough joint."

"Good spot to pick up bimbos?"

"Not bad."

"Figures—Cy Willoughby was cunt-struck."

Addison said, "Well, we gotta roll—lots of luck, Nate."

Nate said, "Thanks for nothing."

They went out. The rain was coming down in gray sheets. There's nothing more depressing than an October rain, Lockington thought, unless it's a November rain.

41 ON ROUTE 11, returning to Youngstown, Addison braked the Chrysler to a near halt, swerving sharply to the side of the road to let a black Ford pickup truck whiz by. Lockington said, "What was *that* all about?"

Addison was back in his lane, rolling north. He said, "The sonofabitch got on my ass the minute we left the Red Ball terminal, and it *stayed* there!"

"I didn't notice. Man or woman?"

"Man, this time—guy wearing sunglasses. How about that—sunglasses in all this *rain!*"

They left Route 11, turning east toward the Youngstown line. Addison was squinting into his rear-view mirror, grinning. "He's back there, three cars deep—determined bastard, ain't he?"

"What plates is he carrying?"

"Pennsylvania, but I can't make 'em out—they're splotched with mud, just like the T-bird's. Odd coincidence."

At the Austintown doughnut shop Lockington climbed into the Mercedes, heading for the office, dreading the telephone call he'd have to make.

"NOTHING MUCH HAPPENING," Barney reported. "A guy called—didn't give his name—I told him that you'd be in shortly."

Lockington nodded. Probably Cayuse Bresnahan, frothing at the mouth. "Barney, why don't you go out and grab a bite of lunch?"

"Because it ain't even ten-thirty yet."

"All right, make it breakfast."

162

"I already *had* breakfast—orange juice, oatmeal, ham, pancakes, apple pie, and two glasses of milk."

"Then go out for coffee."

"I don't like coffee. If I liked coffee, I'd have had coffee for breakfast."

"Maybe a bromo?"

"I don't need a bromo."

"Then just go *out*, will you?"

"What for?"

"About half an hour."

Barney said, "You know what I think?"

"You think that I want you to get the hell outta here."

"Sure, because something's gonna happen that you don't want me to know about!"

Lockington said, "Son, you're showing genuine promise. One of these days you're going to be a top-notch private investigator."

Barney went out, head down, obviously miffed. Lockington slipped into the swivel chair, grabbing the telephone. Here went nothing. He dialed. The phone in Chicago rang twice before a raspy voice said, "Classic Investigations."

"Hello, Moose."

Moose Katzenbach said, "Who's—*Lacey*, is that *you*?"

"Yeah, Moose, it's me."

"Well, what the hell's going *on*—how come you never got back from Ohio?"

"I came back for a day, but it's better in Ohio, Moose, cleaner, quieter—there are *trees* here."

"You ain't coming back to Chicago, even for a *visit*?"

"Maybe for a visit one of these days. Look, Moose, you still get into the Roundhouse Café occasionally?"

"Once in a while, sure—not as often as I used to, but now and then."

"I'm looking into something that happened there last night."

"Yeah, Buck Payson was telling me about it this morning—

some truck driver got knifed—Buck was there when they found him. Real professional job, Buck said. How did you find out about it in Ohio?"

"The truck driver was *from* here."

"I'll be damned—small world, ain't it? I *knew* the guy—just well enough to speak to, but I knew him—Cy Willoughby, right?"

"What did you know about him?"

"Well, not much—Chicago was his regular run from Ohio, two, maybe three times a week. He'd hit the Roundhouse looking for stray quiff—he managed to score, usually—hell, if you can't score at the Roundhouse, you're all washed up."

"You hear anything on who might have done him in?"

"Naw, but I ain't been all that interested. You want me to dig into it?"

"If you wouldn't mind, yes."

"Sure thing! I still got connections on the force—I think maybe Kalmer and Krakow worked that one."

"The K-Boys—they're a good team."

"Okay, Lacey, tell you what—I'll call Jack Kalmer, then I'll take a run up to the Roundhouse. You got a number where I can reach you?"

Lockington gave him the Confidential Investigations telephone number.

Moose said, "How long you gonna be there?"

"Till five."

"Shouldn't take that long."

"Thanks, Moose. How's the agency going?"

"Surviving. I get a couple divorce cases a month—the wolf's out there but he ain't at the door yet. I'll call you, Lacey, one way or the other." Moose hung up.

Lockington leaned back, relieved. Edna Garson hadn't been mentioned, which was just as well. Edna Garson had been a long time ago.

42 CAYUSE BRESNAHAN CAME IN as Lockington was hanging up the telephone. He wasn't foaming at the mouth but Lockington thought he could detect wisps of steam oozing from beneath his black Stetson. Bresnahan sat on the bench near the window. His eyes were gray slate.

"All right, Lockington, I want a peg that I can hang my hat on! Tell me *any*thing—tell me that Fedorovich was kidnapped by Martians, tell me that he went to take a crap and the hogs ate him, tell me that the sonofabitch is playing oboe with the fucking Minneapolis Symphony, but for Christ's sake, tell me *some*thing!" He was haggard and he needed a shave.

Lockington yawned. "Okay, how's about four people getting murdered since I hired out to find Alexi Fedorovich—that good enough?"

Bresnahan snapped, "I like the one about the Martians—more credibility."

Lockington said, "Maybe so, but the statement stands."

"Cut the comedy—I'm *serious*!"

"You wanta *count* 'em?"

"Yeah, I wanta count 'em—I got a call to make this afternoon, and I better say something besides 'Hi, there'."

"All right, get out your abacus—there was a retired schoolteacher named Abigail Fleugelham and a woman named Candice Hoffman and a hot-crotched divorcée named Brenda Willoughby, and Brenda's ex-husband, a pussy-chasing truck driver named Cy Willoughby. That's four, ain't it?"

Bresnahan leaned back on the bench, grinning, slapping his knee. "Well, God *damn*, Lockington, that's great, just *great*!"

Lockington said, "You'd have been a real riot during the Spanish Inquisition."

"No, you misunderstand me—what I mean is, you must be

165

rattling a few cages. These were people you've talked to?"

"I've talked to two of 'em."

"Then you're getting *close!*"

"I'm not one step closer than when I *started.*"

"The hell you aren't—you just don't *know* it! You can back this story up?"

"Ask Frank Addison."

"Who's Frank Addison?"

"A Youngstown police detective—I left him less than an hour ago."

"How did Addison get into this thing?"

"He's investigating three of the murders."

"Why not all four?"

"Cy Willoughby was the fourth—he was killed in Chicago."

"When?"

"Last night."

"He was one of the two you didn't talk to?"

"Yes—Candice Hoffman was the other."

"You're thinking KGB all the way, aren't you?"

"Aren't *you?*"

"Yeah—they gotta want Fedorovich so bad they can *taste* him." The telephone rang. Lockington stared at it, but he didn't reach for it. Bresnahan said, "Private business?"

"Maybe."

"All right, I'm down the road! See you shortly!" He went out, his black Stetson tilted to the side of his head, his step jaunty. Lockington watched him go. There's nothing like a few cold-blooded murders to brighten a rainy day.

43 Moose Katzenbach was on the line.

"I caught Jack Kalmer at home and he gave me all he had so I didn't bother going up to the Roundhouse."

"How did it play?"

"Well, Jack said they questioned everybody who was sober enough to be questioned."

"At the Roundhouse, that probably required all of thirty seconds."

"Yeah, it was Friday night and most of 'em was looped, but there was a Mohawk West driver who just got in from Denver and he was making sense—turns out he'd been sitting next to Willoughby at the bar and Willoughby was trying to con some hefty redhead into making the run to Ohio with him, said he'd have her back in Chicago in a couple days. He was giving her the usual jaw-job and he'd just about sold the package before he got up to hit the washroom. The Mohawk West driver said that he noticed a guy leave the bar to follow Willoughby into the can, and he said that they were in there quite a while, but he didn't think much of it, even when the guy came out and Willoughby didn't. Then this redhead asked the Mohawk West driver to check on Willoughby because he'd been gone such a long time, and he went into the john along with Buck Payson. Willoughby was flat on his face and they figured he'd passed out till they rolled him over."

Lockington said, "Could the Mohawk West man describe the guy who followed Willoughby into the washroom?"

"Not real good—skinny guy, he said—you know that route, Lacey—you ask five people, you get five different descriptions."

"Anything on a vehicle?"

"Yeah, and that's where it looks promising—the Mohawk

167

driver had been sitting near the window and he said that when the guy came out of the men's room he went straight through the door and drove off in an '87 baby blue Audi sedan."

"It was an Audi, he was certain of that?"

"*Positive*—he said he noticed the car when he came in because he got one just like it, only his is black."

"They have an APB out on the car?"

"Sure—they got no plate numbers, but how many baby blue Audis can there *be*?"

"Okay, Moose—if you get more on this, let me know, will you?"

"Sure will—look, Lacey, one of these days, you and me gotta sit down and have us a long heart-to-heart."

"What about, Moose?" Lockington knew what about.

Moose hesitated. Then he said, "Well, about this agency for one thing. You just hauled off and vanished, and I took it over, and I'm making a living, so I *owe* you for it."

"Not a dime! I got it for nothing—be my guest."

"I *knew* that's what you'd say! How're *you* doing, Lacey—you own this Confidential Investigations?"

"Yeah, more or less—it's a partnership, sort of. I'm getting by."

"Good! There was one other thing, Lacey, but we'll talk about it later."

Lockington said, "Moose, all the 'one other things' would fill the Grand Canyon. Don't worry about it."

"Okay, Lacey—we're probably on the same railroad."

"Probably. I'll be listening, Moose." Lockington hung up. The one other thing would be Edna Garson, of course. Lockington didn't want to talk about Edna Garson, that was one thing he'd just as soon not look back on.

44

THE PHONE WAS RINGING again—Kilbuck, or Addison, or Bresnahan, or maybe Moose Katzenbach. Lockington jerked the jangling instrument from its cradle. He snapped, "Okay, whaddaya have?"

Natasha Gorky's voice drifted dreamily over the wire. "Lacey, if you don't know what I have by *now*, I've wasted time and energy—especially energy."

"Sorry—I thought it might be someone else. What's up?"

"I have an absolutely *wonderful* idea!"

"You had an absolutely wonderful idea last night—you had about *twenty* absolutely wonderful ideas last night."

Natasha's laugh was silvery. "Would you believe that I slept until nearly nine-thirty?"

"And would *you* believe that my neck is out of joint?"

"Poor baby—and you did so very well—you were *sensational*!"

"That's what they intended to tell the guy who went over Niagara Falls on a bicycle."

"About my absolutely wonderful idea—the rain's due to clear this evening, and tomorrow's supposed to be *scrumptious*—sunny and in the high seventies!"

"Thanks for the weather report."

"Well, can you think of one earthly reason why we shouldn't go on a picnic tomorrow?"

Lockington was unable to think of one earthly reason why they shouldn't go on a picnic tomorrow.

Natasha said, "We could go to that park southeast of here—Mill Creek Park, is it?"

"That's right, Mill Creek Park—beautiful place."

"You see, after all, it's the middle of October and tomorrow could be the last nice Sunday of the year."

"All right, should I pick up some picnic stuff on the way home?"

"No, I've already done that—I just got back. I bought ham and cheese and buns and mustard and lettuce and pickles and olives and I'm going to bake a dozen cupcakes. Did I forget anything?"

"What kind of cupcakes?"

"What kind do you want?"

"Lemon."

Natasha made a little kissing sound and hung up. Lockington replaced the telephone, a warm feeling sweeping over him, not a strange sensation—he'd been experiencing it since late May.

MOOSE KATZENBACH called back. "Got the wrap-up for you, Lacey. Jack Kalmer just phoned me—they found the cat who killed Willoughby."

"Did he resist arrest?"

"Not enough to notice—he was dead."

"Where was he?"

"The Audi was parked behind an abandoned railroad shanty in the old Galewood freight yard west of Central Avenue—he was under the Central Avenue Bridge, shot through the back of the head. He had to be marched there at gunpoint—execution-style thing. The coroner's office says he got it late last night."

"Who was he?"

"Guy named Ivan Leonid—worked for the Chicago Polish Consulate. He'd rented the Audi under the name of 'Dayton.' He had a six-inch switchblade in his pocket—there were traces of blood on the blade and the lab matched 'em up with Willoughby's."

"It wasn't a robbery?"

"Not a chance—he had over two hundred in his wallet. He's your boy."

"That does it, Moose—thanks a million."

"Glad to be of help. You got a minute?"

"Sure, Moose." There'd be no evading it—Moose had to get it off his chest.

"Lacey, look, about me and Edna—I'd lost Helen and I was lonely—you were out of town and Edna was hurting—it was just one of those things, Lacey—I don't know how the hell it happened, but it did."

"No problem, Moose—all's well that ends well."

"It didn't end so well, Lacey—Edna dumped me in August. They hired a new barkeep at the Shamrock and he's got her now. Serves me right, huh?"

"No—you deserved better than that." Lockington meant it.

"Thanks, Lacey." The line went dead.

Lockington hung up, dragging his mind to more verdant pastures—Natasha's Sunday picnic. He hadn't been on a picnic since shortly after the big war. It'd been in the summer of '46, he'd been seven years old, there'd been ham and cheese sandwiches and olives and pickles and lemon cupcakes—a family Sunday afternoon affair at Humboldt Park in Chicago. Most of Lockington's memories were in Chicago—Chicago and Vietnam. Vietnam had been the safer of the two but there'd been more cognac in Chicago, and a man can't have everything.

Barney Kozlowski opened the office door, sticking his head in. "Coast clear?"

Lockington said, "Sure, kid—my apologies, but I was dealing with a serious matter."

Barney stalked to the desk, his eyes narrowing "What was it? Extortion? Counterfeiting?"

"No, I've been invited to a picnic."

45

THAT EVENING during their vodka martini session, Lockington gave Natasha the story of his rainy day—the round trip to Moffitt Red Ball's Canfield terminal, Frank Addison's suspicions that he'd been followed both ways, Cayuse Bresnahan's visit to the office, and Moose Katzenbach's reports on Cy Willoughby and Ivan Leonid.

Natasha said, "Are you in the market for an opinion?"

"I already *got* an opinion—I got an opinion you and I better move to San Juan Capistrano!"

Natasha ignored the remark. "In the first place, *Addison* wasn't followed, *you* were followed. You're the bellwether."

"*Krahsny Lentuh*, needless to say."

"Directly or indirectly, yes—*Krahsny Lentuh*'s laying back."

"*Krahsny Lentuh*'s laying *back*? Jesus Christ, Natasha, it's murdered four people in five days! What happens when it really gets down to business? Where's this *Mawlniyuh* outfit you've been talking about—they're supposed to be the *good* guys, ain't they?"

"*Mawlniyuh* is *functioning*! Ivan Leonid was a *Krahsny Lentuh* man, obviously. *Mawlniyuh* executed him—a bullet in the back of the head is *Mawlniyuh*'s trademark, and you'll be in no danger until you've found General Fedorovich."

"Uh-huh—that's providing that *Krahsny Lentuh* doesn't find him *first*!"

"*Krahsny Lentuh* isn't *looking* for him—it's letting *you* do the looking!"

"Fedorovich is with Olga Karelinko—*I* know that, *you* know that, *Krahsny Lentuh* knows that, the fucking Duke of Buckingham knows that, the—"

Natasha cut him off. "And so does *Mawlniyuh*, believe me."

Lockington tilted his martini glass, draining it, "What a mucking fess."

"Lacey, this is coming into focus now—something *has* to break, and it'll be *soon!*"

Lockington said, "Christ will return to earth 'soon'."

"You'll find General Fedorovich before Christ returns to earth."

Lockington glared at his empty martini glass. He said, "Your confidence is genuinely appreciated."

Natasha got up, taking his glass. She said, "Another vodka martini?"

"Usually, you don't have to ask."

"Usually, four is your limit. This'll make six."

"Usually, I don't have a bum neck."

Natasha leaned down to kiss his forehead. "I hope I don't live long enough to become *usual*."

Lockington said, "If you do, have a happy five hundredth birthday."

46 THEY'D LEFT THE HOUSE at noon sharp on Sunday, driving south on Belle Vista Avenue, turning east slightly beyond Calvary Cemetery, beginning the long descent to Lake Glacier on a winding leaf-strewn road. They were walled in by trees— maple, pin oak, birch, pine, buckeye—towering on either side. There was a perceptible change in temperature, so dense was the shade. At the bottom of the hill they emerged from the multihued tunnel, Lake Glacier sparkling blue ahead of them, diamond-bright in October sunlight.

Lockington turned south along the rim of the lake. To their right was more forest than Lockington had seen in his Chicago lifetime, a rolling mass of autumn colors, red, maroon, orange, flaming against a backdrop of fleecy white clouds. Natasha pointed excitedly toward the lake shore. "*There*, Lacey—there's a nice spot, under that big tree!"

He spun the Mercedes across the road and into a U-shaped parking area. They got out, Lockington carrying Natasha's big wicker picnic basket, Natasha following, toting the gallon thermos jug she'd filled with lemonade and "just a touch" of vodka. Knowing Natasha, Lockington figured that would translate to something in excess of a quart. They trudged across a broad grassy expanse, pulling up at a rough-hewn table at the foot of a giant sugar maple near the lake. They sat on splintered benches across from each other, and Natasha looked around, her pale blue eyes wide with wonder. She said, "Oh, but it's *lovely* here—it reminds me of *Odessa*!"

Lockington said, "You're in Youngstown, Ohio's claim to fame—this is the biggest city-limits park in the United States."

"Really, *is* it? Who told you that?"

"I forget." He hadn't forgotten, it'd been Pecos Peggy Smith on a night in late spring, but Lockington considered it a subject best avoided.

A gaggle of Canadian geese stalked sedately along the water's edge fifty or so yards to the south. Two white-haired black men were fishing from a small rowboat a few yards clear of the shoreline, chatting, laughing, catching nothing, having a wonderful time doing it. The surface of Lake Glacier was dotted with ducks, probably more than a hundred, floating, drowsing, minding their own damned business. Lockington liked ducks—like pigeons, they were too intent on their own affairs to meddle with those of others.

Natasha poured plastic cups of her lemonade-vodka mixture, bumping her cup against Lockington's. She said, "To *us*, Lacey."

Lockington winked at her and they drank. It was excellent stuff, Lockington thought. They sat in Mill Creek Park's profound silence, Natasha watching clouds, Lockington watching Natasha. She gestured urgently over his shoulder, to the north. "There's a cloud that looks almost exactly like a *dragon*!"

Lockington turned to peer at Natasha's cloud. "Having never seen a dragon, I'm in no position to make comment."

"Well, dragons look like *that*, only their tails are longer."

"How *much* longer?"

"That would depend on whether you're talking about a big dragon or a smaller dragon."

"I was under the impression that all dragons are big."

"Yes, of course, but big dragons have to be smaller dragons before they can become big dragons."

Lockington leaned across the table to kiss her—he just couldn't help it.

Natasha said, "Thank you very much!"

"You're welcome very much."

A silent half-hour went by. There were occasional comments—these subdued out of respect for their surroundings—and Natasha smiled at him half a dozen times, Lockington noting that her fourth smile had been the best of the bunch, barely edging out her sixth. People in love notice things like that, he thought. Fifteen feet above their heads a chunk of bark was ripped from the sugar maple and a split-second later from high to the west there came a sound like the breaking of a distant balloon. Lockington's reaction was spontaneous, almost devoid of thought. He was on his feet, vaulting the table, grabbing Natasha's left arm, jerking her from the bench, dropping her on the lake side of the maple, pinning her to the ground, her head close to the tree trunk, throwing himself on top of her. She lifted her head to stare at him. There was a grass smudge on her cheek. She said, "Well, I'm flattered, I must say, but I don't like this location! Can't you wait until we get home?"

Lockington snapped, "Stay *down—sniper*!"

Natasha's gallon thermos jug disintegrated on the table, the lemonade-vodka mix streaming between the weathered planks. Natasha said, "Yes, now that you've mentioned it, I see what you mean."

"That's two, and that'll be all—thank the Good Lord for sugar maples!"

The black fisherman were staring at them. Lockington waved and they waved back, grinning. Lockington hoped that they weren't thinking what he knew damned well they were thinking. Natasha was saying, "This doesn't *fit*—did he want *you* or *me*?"

Lockington said, "Me, if he wanted *any*body, which I doubt."

"Why *you*? You're the trailblazer! *I'm* the one who walked out on the KGB—*Krahsny Lentuh* would see me as a traitor!"

Lockington got to his feet, extending a hand to assist Natasha. "He'll be long gone—only suicide-mission snipers hang around."

Natasha was dusting the seat of her slacks. "Who says that he isn't a suicide-mission sniper?"

Lockington shook his head. "He's a lousy shot, or he's an excellent shot *pretending* to be a lousy shot, and I'll take the latter."

"*Why?*"

"Because that's Mr. Mawson up in the woods. Mawson put a slug through Brenda Willoughby's *eye*, and he missed *us* by five *yards*, *that's* why!"

"His *second* shot didn't miss by five yards!"

"His second shot came after he'd given us time to get behind the tree." He walked to the table, grabbing the picnic basket, opening it. "Ham or cheese?"

47

THE HOLIDAY HAD GONE flatter than a politician's promise. Natasha had been strangely subdued throughout the remainder of their Sunday afternoon in Mill Creek Park. She'd sat looking across Lake Glacier, nibbling detachedly on a sandwich, then a cupcake, saying little. The biggest part of their picnic lunch had been contributed to the Canadian geese.

They'd driven directly back to Dunlap Avenue where Natasha had gone to the kitchen table to sit poring over eight-spoked wheels until Lockington had given up and hit the hay. In the small hours of the morning he'd felt her slip in beside him, snuggling close, caressing his chest, but he hadn't stirred—the crick in his neck had been letting up and he'd seen no future in aggravating it.

Shortly after dawn he left her sleeping, moving quietly so as not to disturb her, showering, shaving, dressing to go into the kitchen and start a pot of coffee. He was leaning against the kitchen door, staring morosely into the misty woods behind the house, sipping a cup of black coffee when Natasha came into the kitchen barefoot in her robe, blinking, shaking her head. She murmured, "Sorry, Lacey—I didn't get to bed until after three-thirty." She seated herself at the table, lighting a cigarette, yawning.

Lockington sat beside her, putting his hand on her shoulder. "Don't worry about it—one of these evenings we'll work on those wheels together—we'll figure it out."

"No—we can't have many evenings left, and I don't believe that we can do it."

"The hell we can't—it's just a matter of covering all the possibilities!"

She grimaced. "We'd be lucky to *live* that long—not if you mean that we should try every letter in every spoke-opening."

178

"Well, sure—that's the only way it can be done, isn't it—trial and error?"

"Probably, and if that's the only way it can be done, we're up against a *googol*, possibly a googol*plex*!"

Lockington squinted at her. "If we're gonna discuss this, let's discuss it in *English*."

"A googol contains one hundred and one digits—look it up."

"Uh-huh, and if that's a googol, what's a googolplex?"

Natasha clamped her hands against her temples. "Lacey, I can't comprehend a *googol*! For*get* googolplexes!"

"Well, who knows? We might get lucky."

Her laugh was brittle. "I've been trying to get lucky for nearly a *week!*"

"Those jumbled footnote reference numbers—they don't help?"

Natasha shrugged. "They're probably the text of what General Fedorovich has to say, *if* he has *any*thing to say, but we won't know until we find the key, if there *is* a key!"

"Which there probably isn't, so don't knock yourself out. How about a slice of toast?"

She made toast and they ate in an atmosphere of gloom before Lockington got up to put on his jacket and hat. Natasha kissed him. "Try to bear with me, Lacey—I'll put this thing behind me, *honest*, I will!"

Lockington said, "Why don't you let me have a copy of those footnote numbers? If I run into some spare time I could give it a shot."

Natasha nodded, returning to the kitchen, scribbling rapidly on a legal pad, ripping the sheet free, folding it, stuffing it into his shirt pocket. She said, "You know the basic version—first wheel, *A* through *H*—second wheel, *I* through *P*—third, *Q* through *Y*—*X* and *Z* are eliminated—*Q*'s a space. Okay?"

"Got it."

She put her arm around him, accompanying him to the door. He drove to the Mahoning Plaza without the slightest intention of bothering with the wheels. He'd made the offer to boost Natasha's sagging morale, and he'd been thinking of Barney Kozlowski—the puzzle would give the kid something to occupy his mind. Lockington felt a trifle guilty. But just a trifle.

48 WHEN LOCKINGTON ENTERED the office, Barney was leaning against the desk, frowning, yawning, hands clasped in front of him, rotating his thumbs. Lockington got the drift—the boy was bored stiff and the pained expression on his face indicated that he was on the verge of saying so. Lockington beat him to the punch.

"Kid, I have an important assignment for you."

"I've already swept the floor, Mr. Lockington."

"I'm *serious,* son."

Barney was lighting up like a Budweiser sign. "We'll be going out on something of *consequence?*"

"Well-l-l, *we* won't be going out, but there's a matter of importance that I'd like you to tackle."

"A matter of importance—how important is it?"

"A man's life may depend on it—that would make it important, wouldn't it?"

Barney was standing erect now, the slouch gone from him. "*Whose* life?"

"A Russian defector's—a bigshot Soviet general who took it on the duffy out of East Berlin."

Barney slammed his hands together, creating a sound similar to a clap of thunder. "And the KGB's after him!"

"Right!"

"And he's in the Youngstown area!"

"Right!"

"*Damn,* then you *are* into a blockbuster! I had a *hunch* on that!"

Lockington motioned to the bench near the window and they sat there, Barney studying the wheels Lockington sketched in his pocket notebook, leaning forward, watching intently as Lockington jotted letters into the spoke-gaps,

181

numerals around the rims. Barney said, "It's a secret *code!*"

Lockington said, "It's *secret*, all right."

"But are you sure that the letters are supposed to come in the right order like that? If it's a crypto thing, I'd think that they should be all mixed up."

"Maybe they *should*, but we have to start *some*where, don't we?"

Barney was shaking his head. "We'll need more than *this*—there has to be a *key!*" Suddenly, there was an authoritative air about the youngster.

Lockington produced the sheet of legal paper bearing the scrambled footnote numbers, explaining that X and Z were to be eliminated, that Q would probably indicate a space, going on to describe the mechanics of the problem as Natasha had detailed them. He said, "It's just possible that these numbers constitute a message." He handed the sheet of legal paper to Barney. "Want to take a whack at it?"

Barney said, "Why, *sure!* I've done a lot of reading on espionage, and I ran into a cipher system like this in Ralph Collingsworth's *Here's to the Next Man Who Dies.*"

Lockington said, "I haven't read it."

"Want me to tell you about it?"

"I doubt that we'll have time for that, Barney—this is a pressing matter."

"Well, anyway, it was one helluva story—World War I background—France, 1917—Spads, Bristols, Fokkers, German spies all *over* the place—"

Lockington broke in on him. "Yes, I'm sure it was all very exciting."

"Yeah, but what I'm driving at is that this sort of coding was common during the First World War—you see, *googols* are probably involved! You know about googols, Mr. Lockington?"

Lockington stifled a false yawn with the back of his hand. "Googols? Yeah, I was *raised* on 'em." Then he said, "There's scratch pads in the bottom desk drawer."

49

HE LEFT THE OFFICE, his smile sly. Barney Kozlowski would be busy for a while—*quite* a while. He drove into Mill Creek Park, checking his rear-view mirror occasionally. Nothing there. There'd been cars behind him yesterday, several, but on a sunny October Sunday, they'd been expected—*Krahsny Lentuh* didn't own every automobile in Youngstown. He parked where he'd parked on Sunday afternoon, walking to the table they'd occupied, studying the trunk of the sugar maple. The bullet had grooved the tree west to east at a slightly downward angle, the deepest portion of the gash being its western tip, indicating that the shot hadn't been fired from dead west, but probably from just a shade to the north.

He walked directly west, crossing the road, beginning the climb up the hill, forging into the trees. The forest was silent, dense, damp, cool, and he reached the crest of the hill, puffing just a bit, his shoes wet with dew. He looked down in the direction of Lake Glacier, seeing nothing but trees. He found a stump and sat on it, lighting a cigarette, considering yesterday's situation. Sunday traffic along the western side of Lake Glacier would have been reasonably busy—a man with a rifle would have stood a good chance of arousing curiosity, but a man carrying an oblong case might have gone unnoticed—he could have passed for a tree surgeon or possibly a trombone player out to commune with nature. No matter how Mawson had worked it, he'd been in the forest on the hill, the sonofabitch.

Lockington departed the stump, heading north, crunching through an ankle-deep carpet of leaves, pausing frequently to look to the east, his view always obstructed by trees. He walked approximately fifty yards before descending the slope of the hill a few feet and doubling back to the south. The process

183

went on. He crisscrossed the steep slant several times, dropping down toward the road on every lap, tripping over fallen branches, slipping, sliding, sweating, cussing, but finding what he'd been looking for—a small barren spot more than halfway down the hill. Kneeling there, Lockington could see the Sunday table perhaps one hundred and twenty yards distant. The gap was narrow but adequate for rifle fire.

He pawed through the leaves until he struck brass, a thirty caliber casing, and in the damp soil he found the tripod's indentations. He studied the cartridge. There was no identifying print around the firing cap. He combed the area thoroughly in search of its mate, finding nothing but twigs, toadstools, and a few rain-discolored Marlboro cigarette butts, a couple of which were lipstick-smeared. The secluded spot would have provided a fine setting for love in the afternoon— or in the morning, or when-the-hell-ever—the cover was excellent, the leaves soft.

Once upon a spring afternoon he'd found a small forest clearing with Natasha, and they hadn't left it until dusk. And early on the following morning, a man with a rifle had been killed in the clearing. By other men with rifles.

50

DRIVING NORTH on Belle Vista toward Mahoning Avenue, he wondered why he'd bothered returning to Mill Creek Park. Surely he hadn't expected to find Mawson's address carved into the trunk of a buckeye tree. As it'd turned out, he'd come across more than he'd hoped for—a spent thirty caliber rifle casing, make and vintage unknown, which established nothing and led nowhere.

Barney looked up from a desk cluttered with sheets of scratch-pad paper, all bearing sets of eight-spoked wheels.

"You had one call." He glanced at a notation on a wheels sheet. "Kilbuck—he left a number."

Lockington said, "Okay, take a half-hour break, and I'll catch up on a couple of matters."

Barney left the desk, sauntering wordlessly through the office door, not looking back, reminding Lockington of a whipped puppy. Lockington shook his head. The kid wanted to move in on the ground floor and there just wasn't room for him, not at *this* stage of the ball game.

He dialed the number Barney had given him. Nanette answered the phone. Lockington said, "Nanette, let me speak to Gordon Kilbuck, will you?"

Nanette said, "Howja know it's *me*?"

"Your voice—you have such a sweet voice."

Nanette giggled. Lockington winced. He'd heard sweeter voices in the lion house at Chicago's Lincoln Park Zoo.

Gordon Kilbuck got on the line. "Lockington?"

"Yeah, what's happening?"

"Funny thing—I wanted to ask you the same question."

"Well, for starters, somebody took a shot at me yesterday afternoon."

"Oh-oh!"

"That's what *I* said."

"Where?"

"Down in Mill Creek Park."

"You're bugging people! Any idea who?"

"Not yet, but buckle up—this teapot is gonna blow shortly!"

"*How* shortly? You're about due for another payment."

"Maybe before then."

"That'll be *great*!"

"Maybe it will and maybe it won't." Lockington hung up, leaning back in his swivel chair, lighting a cigarette, blowing smoke at the ceiling. He was marking time, Mawson was just a whisker off the pace, and the telephone was ringing. Cayuse Bresnahan's voice was terse. "Lockington, I think I'm onto something!"

"Concerning?"

"Concerning what happened yesterday afternoon."

"What happened yesterday afternoon?"

"I'm talking about target-practice—know what I mean?"

"Uh-huh—so let's hear it."

"Not on the phone. Can you be at the Valencia Café in an hour?"

"I can be there in five minutes."

"I can't."

"Where are you?"

"We'll talk when I see you."

"Okay, then—Valencia in an hour."

"Good boy! We just caught a break!"

"That's what Neville Chamberlain said when he got back from Munich."

Bresnahan chuckled and Lockington heard the phone clatter onto the hook.

Fifteen minutes later, Barney came in. He said, "I've been out in my car, doing some figuring. Do you know how many permutations could be in this wheels thing?"

Lockington said, "Break it to me gently—I'm operating on one slice of toast."

Barney said, "Upwards of a septillion, as I see it."

"Is that a googol?"

"If it ain't, it'll do till one comes along."

"I'll take your word for it."

"I may have to take the sonofabitch *home* with me!"

51

HE PARKED THE MERCEDES in the bumpy lot behind the Valencia Café, going in several minutes ahead of schedule for two reasons, the first being that Cayuse Bresnahan might get there early, the second being that Lockington was thirsty. Bresnahan had implied that he had knowledge of Sunday's events. How he'd learned of them puzzled Lockington, but *how* he'd learned wouldn't be as interesting as *what* he'd learned.

The Valencia Café was running slow. There was an old man at a table, nursing a glass of wine, and another in a booth, sleeping. The elderly lady behind the bar gave Lockington a smile. Obviously she was in a better mood this time around. "Weren't you in here the other day with a guy whose shirt was half-missing?"

Lockington said, "Yeah, that was Bresnahan—his twenty-foot crocodile attacked him."

"I wouldn't have a crocodile in the house!"

"Neither would Bresnahan—he keeps his in the garage."

The elderly lady said, "I'm Clara—who're you?"

"The biggest liar in Mahoning County."

"You ordered Martell's cognac and we were out."

"And you're *still* out."

"That's right—brandy okay?"

Lockington nodded and Clara poured brandy before going to the other end of the bar where a television set was belching a soap opera. On the screen a half-naked blonde woman was in bed with a half-naked dark-haired man. The blonde woman was saying, "Holy Toledo, what if Mary finds out about us?"

The dark-haired man said, "We won't worry about Mary, will we?"

"Maybe *you* won't, but *I* will! Holy Toledo, Mary has a *gun*!"

188

"Mary has a gun, but she doesn't know how to use the damned thing."

The blonde woman said, "Holy Toledo, are you *sure!*"

The dark-haired man said, "Sure, I'm sure.

The bedroom door was swinging silently open. A slender redheaded woman stepped into view. She was carrying a revolver. She said, "*Bastards!*"

The dark-haired man sat up in bed. He said, "*Mary!*"

The blonde woman sat up in bed. She said, "*Holy Toledo!*"

The slender redheaded woman walked to the foot of the bed. She raised her revolver. She shot the blonde woman seven times. Then she shot the dark-haired man thirteen times. The scene faded and a commercial for Debutante Sanitary Napkins flashed on. Clara was back, refilling Lockington's glass. She said, "Mary's been onto 'em for over a month."

"Mary was the dark-haired guy's wife?"

"No, Mary was his mistress. The blonde woman was his wife."

Lockington said, "Uh-huh."

Clara said, "This one's over, but 'Despair and Desire' is on next. 'Despair and Desire' got a whole bunch of sex in it."

"To hell with it."

Clara arched her eyebrows. "Sex?"

Lockington said, "Not now—too early in the day."

Clara retreated to the other end of the bar. "Despair and Desire" was coming on.

Lockington waited, nipping at his brandy, glancing at his watch. Bresnahan was late.

52 Two BRANDIES and fifteen minutes beyond the appointed meeting time, Lockington dropped a five dollar bill on the bar, waved to Clara, and left the Valencia Café through its front door, walking around the building to its rear, stopping short there. Cayuse Bresnahan's brown Ford Escort was in the parking lot, squeezed close to Lockington's Mercedes. Bresnahan was seated in the Ford, his black Stetson tilted over his eyes. Lockington strode rapidly toward the little brown car, waving. Bresnahan didn't move. Dead people hardly ever do. There was a small bluish black bullet hole in his left temple. A fluid scarlet ribbon had trickled down the side of his face, twining into his collar. Bresnahan's eyes were open, glazed, staring into eternity or whatever may be out there.

Lockington looked around the Valencia Café's parking lot. A couple of automobiles, but no movement of any sort. He got into the Mercedes, driving slowly and carefully back to the Mahoning Avenue Shopping Plaza. Barney Kozlowski sat hunched at the desk, scowling, feverishly drawing eight-spoked wheels. He said, "Golly, Mr. Lockington, this is certainly *interesting!*"

Lockington said, "See any cracks?"

Barney grinned. "Not yet, but I don't quit easy!"

"Look, kid, this thing could take a while. Work on it at home where you can be comfortable. I'll finish out the afternoon."

Barney scrambled to his feet, gathering his papers, rolling them, shoving them under a brawny arm. "See you in the morning, Mr. Lockington!" He went out, his outlook definitely improved.

Lockington sighed, sinking into the swivel chair, firing up a cigarette, turning on WHOT and the music of a generation that'd fought two wars, both of which Lockington had missed. But he hadn't missed Vietnam and, somehow, he wished that he had. How can you brag about serving in your country's only losing action? But the men who'd fought it hadn't surrendered, it'd been America's turncoat politicians—hawks on Friday, doves on Monday, assholes seven days a week. Lockington shook his head. The bewildered mind is the Devil's playground.

The door opened and Barney was back. He said, "I was crossing Schenley Avenue when I saw a couple police cars and a paramedics' van in the Valencia Café's parking lot."

Lockington shrugged. "Probably a tavern brawl. You came back to tell me *that?*"

"No, the reason I came back was to ask you if it's possible that these wheels *turn.*"

Lockington frowned. He said, "Hell, I don't *know,*" amazed that the thought had never crossed his mind, remembering Gen. Alexi Fedorovich's lines at the beginning of his book— "The wheels of treachery turn slowly, one click at a time—" "Click?" Was it possible that Fedorovich had meant "notch," declining to use the word because it would have been too obvious? And if *stationary* wheels could produce a googol of possibilities, what astronomical total would result if they *turned,* altering all values with every shift in position? Lockington's mind reeled he'd just brushed shoulders with infinity.

Barney was saying, "The wheels—where did they *come* from—a picture, maybe?"

Lockington said, "Right—a picture of some people pushing a six-wheeled cart."

Barney's eyes were slits. "Were they pushing the cart from right to left or from left to right? Try to remember, Mr. Lockington—it could be real *important!*"

"Left to right, I guess—yeah, left to right."

"Thanks, Mr. Lockington—thanks a *lot!*" Barney Kozlowski was going through the door like he was busting into an enemy high school's backfield. Lockington heard an engine roar. He watched Barney's Mustang turn east on Mahoning Avenue, defying the laws of centrifugal force.

Then, having witnessed Barney's departure, he turned his attention to Frank Addison's arrival.

53

ADDISON SAT on the window bench facing Lockington, lighting a cigarette.

Lockington said, "So what's new?"

"Interesting happening down the street—guy found dead in his car, shot through his left temple."

"When was this?"

"Less than an hour ago."

"Suicide?"

"Not unless he shot himself in the head and disposed of the weapon."

"That'd be a nifty trick."

"Sure would."

"I've heard nothing of it."

"You *won't*. It's been squelched."

"Who squelched it?"

"The same people who squelched the shooting at Sabatini's Funeral Home."

"That right?"

"Yep—Uncle Sam's boys— heavy government pressure— you know anything about government pressure, Lockington?"

"Damn right! Couple years ago I owed the IRS sixty-two dollars. The bastards were gonna impound my car, only it wasn't worth sixty-two dollars."

"You aren't talking about that black Mercedes, obviously."

"No, at that time I had an old Pontiac."

"How did you come by your Mercedes?"

"Won it in a raffle."

Addison's smile was one-half smirk. He said, "You have anything on this shooting?"

"Should I?"

"Shouldn't you?"

Lockington shrugged. "None of my damned business."

"You're probably working with the feds and this guy carried a National Security Agency card—Robert Bresnahan. You acquainted with anybody named Bresnahan?"

"No, and I've never heard of the National Security Agency."

"It deals primarily in the field of cryptography—busting Eastern Bloc ciphers, protecting our own—you know the route."

"Uh-uh—explain the route, if you will."

Addison shook his head. "It's a circuitous sonofabitch and it runs through Chicago. Hear anything on Cy Willoughby's murder?"

"Yeah, Willoughby was killed by a guy named Ivan Leonid, a Chicago Polish Consulate hand."

Addison said, "Well, that gives this thing a nice international flavor, doesn't it? The Chicago cops nailed Leonid?"

"No, they ran second. He was dead when they found him."

"Uh-huh, and this Chicago business is connected to the guy you're trying to find?"

"I'd say so."

"Who's your boy, Lockington?"

Lockington shook his head. "Not yet."

Addison's slow smile was the smile of a weasel in a chicken coop. He said, "All right, let's ditch the peekaboo routine and play 'Let's pretend.' Let's pretend that you're looking for a Soviet general who went over the hill—a guy named Alexi Fedorovich."

"I'd rather play 'Pin-the-tail-on-the-donkey'."

Addison chuckled. "You're a good one, Lockington—a real *good* one!"

Lockington said, "If I'm so good, why ain't I rich?"

Addison got to his feet, "Okay, have it your way, but if you need help—"

Lockington said, "If I need help, I'll let you know."

Halfway to the door Addison turned. "I saw your minotaur pull out of here—I think he was prepping for the Daytona 500."

"No, he was going out to beat up on a few cops. He stays in shape that way."

Addison eased the door shut behind him. WHOT was playing "*La Cumparsa*." Lockington didn't recognize the band, but it was a great number and it took him back to the senior prom at Kelvyn Park High School in Chicago and to Minnie Larsen. Minnie had been the daughter of Nels Larsen, a Scandinavian bricklayer. She'd been tall, blonde, good-looking, and she'd had a snapper, the real thing, or that'd been the opinion of the majority of guys in Kelvyn Park High's senior class. Lockington had never managed to verify the story, but he'd come close. It'd been a hot June night, the gymnasium windows had been open, the band had been playing "*La Cumparsa*" when Minnie had taken Lockington's hand to guide him across Kilbourne Avenue and into the park. The band had been playing "*La Cumparsa*" when Minnie Larsen had dragged Lockington into the bushes. It'd still been playing "*La Cumparsa*" when Nels Larsen had dragged Lockington out of the bushes and kicked Lockington's ass up around his ears. Almost every song is accompanied by a memory. Some memories are better than others.

Lockington switched off the radio and picked up the telephone. He dialed Chicago.

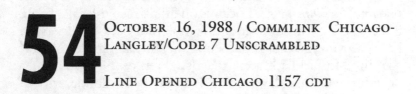

54

October 16, 1988 / Commlink Chicago-Langley/Code 7 Unscrambled

Line Opened Chicago 1157 cdt

Chicago-Langley / Attn Massey / 1158 cdt
Begin Text: Contact From Lockington 1149 cdt This Date / End Text / Carruthers

Langley-Chicago / Attn Carruthers / 1259 edt
Begin Text: Contact Through Whom? /End Text/ Massey

Chicago-Langley / Attn Massey / 1159 cdt
Begin Text: Direct / End Text / Carruthers

Langley-Chicago / Attn Carruthers / 1300 edt
Begin Text: Be Advised Lockington Coded Birddog / See May Memo / Future References Must Comply / End Text / Massey

Chicago-Langley / Attn Massey / 1201 cdt
Begin Text: We Have That Here / Sorry / End Text / Carruthers

Langley-Chicago / Attn Carruthers / 1301 edt
Begin Text: Contact Regarding What? / End Text / Massey

Chicago-Langley / Attn Massey / 1202 cdt
Begin Text: Birddog Reports Govt. Man Murdered

196

YOUNGSTOWN APPROX 1200 HRS EDT THIS DATE / END TEXT
/ CARRUTHERS

LANGLEY-CHICAGO / ATTN CARRUTHERS / 1303 EDT
BEGIN TEXT: FOXFIRE & CHECKMATE ONLY TWO AGENCY
PEOPLE IN YOUNGSTOWN THIS TIME / IDENTIFY VICTIM
/ END TEXT / MASSEY

CHICAGO-LANGLEY / ATTN MASSEY / 1204 CDT
BEGIN TEXT: ROBERT BRESNAHAN / SUPPOSEDLY
EMPLOYED NSA / END TEXT / CARRUTHERS

LANGLEY-CHICAGO / ATTN CARRUTHERS / 1307 EDT
BEGIN TEXT: CROSSFILES SHOW NO ROBERT BRESNAHAN
WITH NSA / WHERE DOES BRESNAHAN FIT IN? / END TEXT
/ MASSEY

CHICAGO-LANGLEY / ATTN MASSEY / 1208 CDT
BEGIN TEXT: HIRED BIRDDOG TO LOCATE ALEXI
FEDOROVICH / END TEXT / CARRUTHERS

LANGLEY-CHICAGO / ATTN CARRUTHERS / 1309 EDT
BEGIN TEXT: BE ADVISED ALEXI FEDOROVICH CODED
WIZARD / SEE JUNE MEMO / END TEXT / MASSEY

CHICAGO-LANGLEY / ATTN MASSEY / 1209 CDT
BEGIN TEXT: WE HAVE THAT HERE / SORRY / END TEXT
/ CARRUTHERS

LANGLEY-CHICAGO / ATTN CARRUTHERS / 1310 EDT
BEGIN TEXT: BRESNAHAN LIKELY KGB / END TEXT / MASSEY

CHICAGO-LANGLEY / ATTN MASSEY / 1211 CDT
BEGIN TEXT: AGREED / BIRDDOG REQUESTS TWO
OPERATIVE YOUNGSTOWN IMMEDIATELY / END TEXT /
CARRUTHERS

LANGLEY-CHICAGO / ATTN CARRUTHERS / 1312 EDT
BEGIN TEXT: **WHAT PURPOSE?** / END TEXT / MASSEY

CHICAGO-LANGLEY / ATTN MASSEY / 1213 CDT
BEGIN TEXT: **WASN'T EXPLICIT / WOULD SAY BIRDDOG
EXPECTS EARLY BREAK WIZARD MATTER** / END TEXT /
CARRUTHERS

LANGLEY-CHICAGO / ATTN CARRUTHERS / 1314 EDT
BEGIN TEXT: **THIS OFFICE HAS NOT AUTHORIZED HIRING
OF BIRDDOG** / END TEXT / MASSEY

CHICAGO-LANGLEY / ATTN MASSEY / 1214 CDT
BEGIN TEXT: **DITTO** / END TEXT / CARRUTHERS

LANGLEY-CHICAGO / ATTN CARRUTHERS / 1315 EDT
BEGIN TEXT: **IF CLIENT DEAD WHY BIRDDOG STILL
INVOLVED?** / END TEXT / MASSEY

CHICAGO-LANGLEY / ATTN MASSEY / 1215 CDT
BEGIN TEXT: **PRESUMABLY BROUGHT IN BY FOXFIRE** / END
TEXT / CARRUTHERS

LANGLEY-CHICAGO / ATTN CARRUTHERS / 1316 EDT
BEGIN TEXT: **PRIOR TO BRESNAHAN?** / END TEXT / MASSEY

CHICAGO-LANGLEY / ATTN MASSEY / 1217 CDT
BEGIN TEXT: **PROBABLY / BIRDDOG GAVE NO INDICATION
FOXFIRE CONNECTION / CONTACT WITH FOXFIRE
TENUOUS / CHECKMATE PHONED YESTERDAY / SAYS
BIRDDOG CLOSING FAST / SITUATION DELICATE** / END
TEXT / CARRUTHERS

LANGLEY-CHICAGO / ATTN CARRUTHERS / 1320 EDT
BEGIN TEXT: **DISPATCH OPERATIVE YOUNGSTOWN**

PRONTO / SHOULD HOOK UP WITH CHECKMATE /
BIRDDOG GAVE RENDEZVOUS PARTICULARS? / END TEXT
/ MASSEY

CHICAGO-LANGLEY / ATTN MASSEY / 1221 CDT
BEGIN TEXT: AFFIRMATIVE / FLAMINGO LOUNGE
MAHONING AVENUE YOUNGSTOWN 1000 EDT 10/17/88 /
WILL SEND DELLICK WITHIN HOUR / ASSUME FOXFIRE
WILL LAY BACK UNTIL SHOWDOWN / END TEXT /
CARRUTHERS

LANGLEY-CHICAGO / ATTN CARRUTHERS / 1322 EDT
BEGIN TEXT: SHOULD COME SHORTLY / WHEN BIRDDOG
REQUESTED ASSISTANCE IN JUNE MATTER RESOLVED
WITHIN HOURS / END TEXT / MASSEY

CHICAGO-LANGLEY / ATTN MASSEY / 1222 CDT
BEGIN TEXT: WILCO INSTRUCTIONS / WILL KEEP YOU
POSTED / END TEXT / CARRUTHERS

LINE CLEARED LANGLEY 1323 EDT 10/16/88

55 HIS RADIO WAS ON again but Glenn Miller's arrangement of "Along the Santa Fe Trail" seemed a thousand light years away. He lit a cigarette, not wanting the damned thing but lighting it anyway. It was something to do.

He'd never been superior at anything—marbles, mumblypeg or Ping-Pong—adequate, usually, but never a standout. He'd had decent speed but he'd been the *third* fastest kid on the block. He'd played American Legion baseball and he'd never hit better than .250. As a sandlot halfback his longest gain from scrimmage had been for fewer than twenty yards and he'd been hit from behind and fumbled. In straight pool he'd had a run of thirty-eight balls but that'd been a once in a lifetime thing. As a bowler he'd rolled a 660 series, but his season average had been the same, year after year—165. He'd played some chess during his service years and once he'd beaten a guy who'd claimed to be the Florida state champion. He'd taken considerable pride in that accomplishment until he'd realized that you can become the Florida state champion by beating one Seminole and two alligators.

He'd been outsmarted in his time, but never twice by the same party. In the spring he'd taken a thorough mental shellacking from a woman he'd loved like he'd never thought he could love a woman—the same woman he *still* loved like he'd never thought he could love a woman—but he had his share of pride, and he didn't want that to happen again, if he loved her or if he didn't.

He locked the office, picking up Natasha's rose before driving home, checking his rear-view mirror every half-block. Natasha was in the front yard, cultivating around an azalea bush, if it *was* an azalea bush—Lockington's chances of being enshrined in the Horticultural Hall of Fame stood at something south of zero. Natasha came to the car, accepted her rose, frowning, searching his face. She said, "It's heating up, isn't it?"

Lockington nodded. He said, "Sister, could you spare a martini?"

She left her trowel on the top rail of the white trellis fence, leading the way into the house. When she'd made martinis they sat in the living room facing each other and Natasha didn't cross her legs.

"Lacey, I've told you that I'll try to help. The offer stands."

Lockington got a cigarette going before he said, "Tell me something, will you?"

"Certainly—if I can."

"Are you happy—in this house—in Youngstown, Ohio—with me?"

Natasha's gaze was level. "Happier than I've ever been—happier than I have a right to be. Lacey, you should be able to *sense* that!"

"Then let's not rock our boat—I don't want to see you dragged into this affair."

She shook her head. "Understand me, *please*—I don't intend to leap astride a white charger and go galloping wildly in all directions, but I *do* have experience in this sort of thing—you know that, of course."

"Yes, I know that very well." And he did. *Very* well.

"People have been killed, we've been shot at, the General Fedorovich business is coming down to its crucial stages, and you haven't asked for help, not *once!*"

"I've asked for your opinions, haven't I?"

"I don't know that you've *asked* for them, but I've given them."

Lockington clinked his martini glass onto the coffee table. He said, "All right, give me one more." He told her about the death of Cayuse Bresnahan.

Natasha reached for his cigarette, lighting hers from it, returning it. She said, "This is opinion and opinion *only*, but

I doubt that Bresnahan was a National Security Agency man."

"Why doubt that? He knew my life *story!*"

"Your life story isn't difficult to come by—neither is that of the neighborhood barber—they call for thorough research, that's all. I believe that Bresnahan was a KGB operative, a member of *Mawlniyuh* who was watching you or having you watched because he knew that *Krahsny Lentuh* was trailing you. I believe that he learned the true identity of our Mr. Mawson, and that Mawson murdered him for his trouble."

Lockingon was nodding. "Plausible." Then he asked the question that he didn't want to ask. "Natasha, are you out of the KGB—really *out?*"

He'd expected an explosion, or tears, or sullen anger. He got none of the three, just a pale blue-eyed stare.

"I suppose you had to ask that. All factors taken into account, it's a fair question. Lacey, I struck a deal with the KGB in June—I'm sure you remember."

"Yes, I remember—you were a KGB agent, working out of Chicago's Polish Consulate, and so was the guy who knifed Cy Willoughby—Ivan Leonid. Did you know Leonid?"

"Not by that name—people came and went through the Polish Consulate, there were countless aliases—I've had a few myself."

"Okay, when you left the consulate, had there been mention of the Fedorovich defection?"

"I wasn't privy to such matters—I was a hired hand, I was given assignments, the Devereaux case for one—I had little knowledge of events that influenced KGB policy."

"Well, look—according to Gordon Kilbuck, Fedorovich defected in the spring of this year. According to Bresnahan, Fedorovich spent three months under CIA questioning before he was placed in a home just outside of Rochester. Now, Kilbuck has no firm dates and Bresnahan may have been lying through his teeth, but it would appear possible that Fedorovich hit Youngstown at approximately the same time we got here. Don't you see that as being just a trifle on the odd side?"

Natasha came out of her overstuffed chair like a tawny javelin. She took his head in her hands, tilting it, peering down into his eyes. "Lacey, do you believe that I'm working *against* you?"

"You were working against me last spring."

"I was *not* working *against* you—our goals were identical."

"At the outset, perhaps, yes—certainly not at the end."

Natasha released his head, stepping back, pointing a finger at him. "I'm in *love* with you! Devereaux intended to *kill* you! *Any*body who wants to kill *you* is fair game in my book, and *that* includes Mr. *Mawson!*"

Lockington didn't say anything, knowing that he'd just seen a tigress on the verge of snapping her leash.

Natasha said, "Another martini?"

Lockington said, "Damn right."

56 HE'D SPENT EIGHT HOURS in bed, but he'd netted less than six hours of sleep. He'd comforted himself with the thought that he wasn't alone in his situation. Surely there were other forty-nine-year-old men doing their damndest to keep sexual pace with thirty-one-year-old redheads from the Ukraine—*millions* of them in all probability. He'd blundered into the kitchen at eight o'clock, finding Natasha at the table, up to her elbows in eight-spoked wheels. She'd said, "Sit down before you *fall* down!"

Lockington had said, "Coffee, ere I perish!"

She'd poured him a cup of black coffee. She'd lit a cigarette, inserting it between his lips. She'd stroked his cheek. She'd said, "*Behdny bahtuh!*"

Not having the slightest idea what *behdny bahtuh* meant, and not being of a mind to take any damned fool chances, Lockington had smiled silent response, concentrating on his coffee, and Natasha had returned to her wheels, working silently.

Later, during his second cup, he said, "Do you still see possibilities?"

"*Only* possibilities—a few days ago I believed I could see *probabilities.*"

"Well, look, Barney came up with an interesting question yesterday—he wanted to know if the wheels rotate. *Do* they?"

Natasha dropped her ballpoint pen, pushing her papers away from her. She licked her lips contemplatively. "They were stationary when I was a child—but then, when I was a child, I *thought* as a child..." Her voice faded into the morning silence of the kitchen.

Lockington said, "If they turned, would that increase the number of combinations?"

Natasha's brow was furrowed. "If *everything* turned, *nothing* would change—if the *numbers* stood still and the *letters* rotated—no, I don't believe it'd be more difficult than it already is. How *could* it—we're into *googols*, aren't we?"

"Fedorovich spoke good English, they say."

"*Excellent*—or so I've heard—he was American-born, and I'd think that he'd have retained that ability."

"Do you remember his words at the beginning of his book?"

"'The wheels of treachery turn slowly, one click at a time'? That *could* have been more aptly put, I thought."

"Maybe not—'one revolution at a time' wouldn't have conveyed the proper meaning—'one click' *says* it, *if* we're on the right track."

Natasha said, "Let me think about it." She got up to walk with him into the living room. He put on his jacket, then his hat, wincing slightly. She was watching him. "Your neck again?"

"*Still.*"

"I'm *so* sorry!"

Lockington said, "Sympathy won't help—*pray* for me!"

"*Khawdish!*" She opened the door, pushing him out of the house. He climbed into the Mercedes, hurting just a bit, but deeply in love. If you're deeply enough in love, a pain in the neck doesn't matter, and Lockington was in deeply enough.

57 A CHILL DRIZZLE was riding a light gray wind out of the west and Lockington thought of Helen Hunt Jackson's lines about October's bright blue weather. They'd been true enough if Helen had been speaking of *early* October because early October is a virgin lass. On the other hand, *late* October is a full-fledged woman, gaudy but aging, given to bitchy spells, and she was in vile spirits on the morning of Tuesday the 17th.

Barney Kozlowski was nowhere to be seen, the office was locked, and Lockington let himself in. The place was uncomfortably cool and damp, so he didn't take off his jacket. Or his hat. He sat in the swivel chair, wondering about Barney. The kid had been annoying at times, at others a genuine nuisance, but Lockington missed him. The rain was pelting the windows now, a nasty downpour. He turned on the radio, stacking his fists on the desk top, leaning to rest his chin on them, lapsing into thought.

Apparently the hour of the grande finale was at hand and he was beginning to feel like the last replacement to reach the Alamo. He counted his allies—Natasha, of course, first and always, Barney Kozlowski, and probably Frank Addison. Natasha would be at home, drawing wheels, and then she'd go shopping because it was Tuesday—not because the cupboard was bare, or because there were any stupendous bargains to be had, simply because it was *Tuesday*. Barney would be somewhere on the planet, Lockington assumed, but *where* on the planet was a mystery at the moment. He might have joined the Junior Secret Service Cadets—you could do that by mailing in the top from a box of Toasted Wheat Zingers, and you got a badge and a ring with a built-in whistle. Frank Addison was an intelligent, sincere, hard-working

Youngstown flatfoot, efficient enough at the local law enforcement level, but hardly qualified to go up against the likes of *Krahsny Lentuh*. And the leader of this disjointed safari, the great white hunter, was none other than the fabled Lacey Lockington who was sitting on his dead ass in a store-front office in Youngstown, Ohio, where rain was falling like a cow pissing on a flat rock, listening to Stone Age music, and trying to figure out which fucking end was up.

WHOT's melodies came and went, Mahoning Avenue's traffic roared and faded, the rain continued, Lockington's mind swarmed with questions, and there wasn't an answer in sight. Something had tripped the last of the floodgates, a word, a mistake, an event. Cy Willoughby's murder in Chicago—had *that* been it? Lockington clawed into a jacket pocket in search of a fresh pack of cigarettes, considering that possibility. Cy Willoughby had been small potatoes—or *had* he? This Leonid fellow from Chicago's Polish Consulate—had he learned something from Willoughby, something of importance? If so, *what*? And if he'd gained information of consequence, *why* had Leonid killed the poor bastard after he'd gotten it? Lockington scowled into the smoke of his new cigarette. To hell with the *what*—get the cart out in front of the horse—concentrate on the *why*. Sometimes it works a little better that way.

There'd be more than one possible *why*—two came instantly to mind—Leonid hadn't wanted another party to become cognizant of the knowledge he'd received from Willoughby *or* he hadn't wanted Willoughby to reveal that he'd divulged it in the first place. Lockington wasn't sure that he was pleased with those choices. They weren't all that compelling.

All right then, it was probably a matter of guesstimating Willoughby from the ground up—who *was* he, anyway? He was a pussy-pursuing over-the-road truck driver, and that failed to qualify him for the *Guinness Book of World Records*. Okay, who *else* was he, or what else had he *been* before he'd stopped a switchblade in the men's room of a fourth-rate

Chicago boozery? Well, first and foremost, he'd been Brenda Willoughby's ex-husband, and *that* was undoubtedly the motivating factor, directly or indirectly. Slowly now, one step at a time—Brenda Willoughby had been Candice Hoffman's daughter and Cy Willoughby had been Brenda's husband and this had made him Candice's son-in-law for however brief a span. Lockington's eyes narrowed a trifle. According to old Mabel Johannsen who lived across the street from the Candice Hoffman residence, Candice's mother had been ill, and Candice had visited the old lady frequently—not a long trip, Mabel had told him—Candice had rarely been gone for more than an hour. So what can a doting daughter do for an ailing mother? She can drop in every couple of days, she can bring candy and flowers, she can help tidy up the house, she can do some shopping, she can be cheerful, tell funny stories, play the banjo if she knows how, and—and—the flat of Lockington's hand came down on the desk top with a spanging sound—and *she can pick up the mail at the post office!* Candice Hoffman was the daughter of Olga Karelinko just as sure as God made Eve's little green apple. Why in the *hell* hadn't he seen that *earlier?* Not that it would have altered the equation to any great degree because he still didn't know Olga's location, but she wasn't *ill*, she was lying *low!* That was how it went now and then—you look for the *why* and you trip over the *what*.

Brenda Willoughby's ex-husband had known *exactly* where Grandma Olga lived. It was a lead-pipe cinch that Gen. Alexi Fedorovich was *with* Olga, and if Ivan Leonid had acquired Olga's address, Fedorovich's life wasn't worth a busted bucket of borscht! The information would have been telephoned from Chicago to Youngstown within minutes of Cy Willoughby's demise *if* Ivan Leonid had managed to get to a phone before he'd been killed, and maybe he hadn't made it. He might have piled into the blue Audi to discover that he had an unexpected passenger. Ivan, please be so kind as to drive us to Central

Avenue—I'd like you to see the old Galewood freight yard.

The minutes had jelled into nearly an hour—it was pushing ten o'clock. Lockington turned off the radio in the middle of Frank Sinatra's "Roses of Picardy." He hated to do that. "Roses of Picardy" had been Sinatra's very best number.

58 THE SKY WAS DARKENING in the west, the wind
gaining in strength. John Sebulsky's white Olds
Cutlass was parked behind the Flamingo
Lounge, tight against the building. A beige '88
Toyota Camry stood in a corner of the lot. It carried Illinois
plates. Lockington parked next to the Camry, entering the
Flamingo at ten o'clock sharp. The tavern was virtually silent.
Two well-dressed young men sat in a booth, playing chess
on a pocket-size board that had holes to secure the bases of
the tiny red and white pieces. White was in trouble.
Lockington brushed by the booth, walking directly to the
bar, and John Sebulsky lowered his Racing Form to belt
level. He poured a double hooker of Martell's cognac. Out
of a corner of his mouth he mumbled, "Watch yourself,
Lacey—the guys in the booth were talking, and I heard your
name mentioned."

Lockington nodded, picking up his glass of cognac and
headed for the booth. He slid in on the side of the man playing
red. "Good morning, gentlemen."

Steve Dellick smiled. He said, "Lockington, how are
you?"

Lockington said, "I don't know, and nobody better tell
me."

Dellick said, "You've met this fellow."

"I know him as Frank Addison."

They shook hands all around. Dellick said, "He's a
Youngstown boy, stationed in Seattle—they brought him
home for this business."

Frank Addison said, "I haven't seen you in damned near
twenty-four hours."

Lockington said, "Absence makes the heart grow fonder."

Dellick said, "Carruthers hustled me down from Chicago

210

yesterday afternoon. Got in around eleven last night."

"Good trip?"

"Not bad. Last time I saw you was up the road a piece at the New Delhi Motel—the Devereaux debacle—front end of June." Lockington didn't say anything. "That was one very hairy morning," Dellick added. Lockington still didn't say anything. "You're in Youngstown because of Fedorovich?"

Lockington shook his head. "I live here now."

Dellick winked. "*Sure*, you do." Frank Addison was yawning. "Carruthers said that you have Fedorovich in the sack."

"Carruthers speaks with forked tongue."

"Don't we all?" Addison put in.

Lockington said, "Man is born in sin."

Dellick said, "You got something to run on?"

"Not immediately."

Dellick said, "We're here to take orders. You're in charge."

"Who says so?"

"Carruthers. Carruthers got it from Massey at Langley."

"Who's Massey?"

Addison said, "I've never seen the sonofabitch."

Dellick said, "Neither have I, but nobody argues with him."

Lockington said, "All right, boys, you're on twenty-four hour alert."

Addison said, "I was *born* on twenty-four hour alert."

Dellick took out a pad, scribbling on a sheet, tearing it free, handing it to Lockington. "I'm at the Day's End on Belmont Avenue—Mr. Felix Martindale—I sell cook books—Room 108."

Addison said, "Call Mr. Felix Martindale—Felix can get hold of me."

Lockington eyed Addison. "Damned good thing I didn't call the Youngstown Police Department."

"Yeah, they already got *one* Frank Addison."

"What's he doing?"

"Ninety days—pimping for his grandmother."

Dellick said, "Helluva good way to starve to death."

Addison said, "Hey, you oughta see his grandmother!"

Lockington downed his double cognac. "Fellas, it's been a genuine delight." He went out, waving to John Sebulsky.

Sebulsky waved back, looking slightly puzzled.

59 AUTUMN WAS THE SADDEST of seasons and it wept inconsolably on that morning. Lockington stood at his office window, one foot up on the seat of the wooden bench, looking over the rain-drenched plaza parking lot into the sodden forests west of Meridian Road. It would be an excellent day for something, he supposed, but he couldn't imagine what that would be— a drawing-and-quartering, perhaps. He was powerless—he knew what to do and he knew how to do it, but he didn't know *where* to do it.

It was likely that Olga Karelinko lived within ten minutes' drive of his office, but from his office he could be in another *county* in less time than that. They were somewhere in the vicinity, perhaps two or three miles distant, old General Fedorovich and his woman, peeking through windows, watching every passerby, every automobile, reading sudden death into every midnight sound, waiting for the axe to come down, while the appointed savior of the situation stood motionless, staring out of windows while the whole damned dance hall came down around his ears. Barney Kozlowski's friendly swat on the shoulder spun Lockington, seating him roughly on the bench. Barney boomed, "Hi, Mr. Lockington—sorry I'm late!" If it wasn't the most unapologetic apology in history, it certainly ranked in the top ten.

Lockington lurched to his feet. "And that's why you just disconnected my gizzard from my appendix?"

Barney had turned away, oblivious to the question. The kid's morale had improved, obviously—he'd never been flippant with the boss. He'd crossed the room, taking a slim packet of white filing cards from a shirt pocket, placing it on the desk.

He glanced over his shoulder, grinning like an undertaker at the scene of an airliner crash.

"Mr. Lockington, would you step over here, please?"

Lockington approached warily, the way you approach a drunken grizzly bear. "Kid, this better be *good!*"

"You be the judge." Barney turned the top card, placing it face-up on the desk. "Tell me, is that the series of mixed-up footnote numbers you gave me yesterday morning?"

There was a string of numbers on the card—20-24-9-20-2-14-20-4-17-1-3-6-15-22-24-3-17. Lockington took one look and shrugged. He said, "I've been blessed with a lot of things, but a photographic memory ain't one of 'em. *You* tell *me—is* it?"

"It *is*—it's *identical!*"

"All right, if it's identical, it's identical."

Barney turned the next card on the stack, pointing to it, looking very much like Caesar at the Rubicon, Lockington thought, although he really didn't know how Caesar had looked—at the Rubicon, or anywhere else for that matter.

Barney said, "And is this the problem as it was presented to me—three eight-spoked wheels—first wheel, 1 through 8, *A* through *H*—second wheel, 9 through 16, *I* through *P*—third wheel, 17 through 24, *Q* through *Y*, *X* and *Z* eliminated, *Q* to indicate a space?"

Lockington bent to peer at the card, studying it briefly.

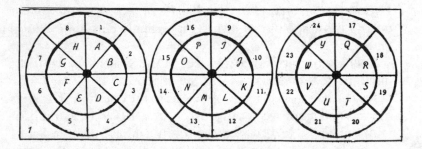

He said, "That's how it looked to *me*."

Barney said, "All right, 20 is the first in the series of footnote numbers, and what letter does it correspond to?"

"The letter in the 20 slot is *T*, and you're going to run into a whole bunch of gibberish—it just won't work that way."

"Only if we don't move the wheels." He flipped another card. "Now we've turned the wheels one notch from left to right, left to right being the direction in which you told me the cart was being pushed. The *numbers* haven't turned, just the *letters*—*A* has advanced from the 1 position to the 2 position, *I* from 9 to 10, *Q* from 17 to 18—see for yourself, Mr. Lockington."

Mr. Lockington saw for himself.

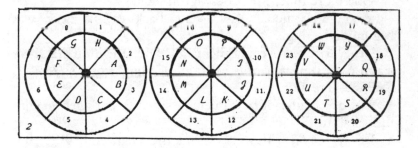

He said, "You're right."

Barney said, "The second footnote number is 24—what's the letter?"

"The number 24 letter is *W*."

"See how easy it is?"

"See how *easy* it is? So far, we got 'TW'—how many words start with 'TW'?"

"Quite a few." He was turning another card. He said, "Check me on this—*A* has moved to 3, *I* to 11, *Q* to 19—is that correct?"

Lockington looked.

He said, "You got it."

"And the third number is 9—give me the letter."

"That'll be *O*."

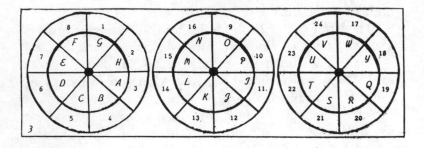

"Now we have '*TWO*,' don't we?"

"We do."

"One more time, Mr. Lockington—okay?"

Lockington said, "Okay." The back of his neck was beginning to tingle.

Barney snapped over another card. "Did I mention that there was a code similar to this in Ralph Collingsworth's *Here's to the Next Man Who Dies*?"

"Yes, as a matter of fact, I believe you did. Let's get on with this, shall we?"

Barney got on with it. "Give me the locations of *A*, *I*, and *Q*, if you will, Mr. Lockington."

Lockington checked the new card.

"*A*'s at 4, *I*'s at 12, *Q*'s at 20—they've moved up another

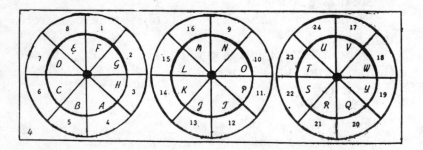

click. What happens when they've gone completely around?"

"They keep going around and around until you run out of key numbers. In *Here's to the Next Man Who Dies* the Allies encoded an entire chapter from the Bible—it was a code *within* a code, you see—it had to do with a hush-hush aerial operation which—"

"Later on that, kid—what's the next number?"

"The next number is 20, 20 corresponds to *Q*, and *Q* is a space, so our first word is '*TWO*'." Barney turned a card. He was having the time of his life, Lockington could tell. Barney was saying, "Our next number is 2."

Lockington said, "Looky, kid, I don't believe that we'll have time to go through the whole thing at this pace—how does it come out—what's the message?"

"I don't quite understand it, but it's an address, Mr. Lockington."

"Let's *have* it!"

"*TWO FIVE HACK ROAD—ROAD*'s abbreviated to *RD*."

"Hack Road—where the hell is Hack Road?"

"It runs off of Kirk Road—I got a friend who lives out that way."

"Kirk Road's south of here, isn't it?"

"Yeah, maybe a mile—you take Meridian Road to Kirk, turn west on Kirk until you hit Route 46—Hack Road pops up something like three-quarters of a mile after you cross 46."

"You know that area well?"

"I just came from there."

"You just *came* from there?"

"I was *reconnoitering*, Mr. Lockington."

Lockington said, "Good God, kid, I hope you didn't go out there wearing a cape and a deerstalker hat—I mean, you could attract *attention* that way! Were you *followed*?"

"No *way*—not at seventy-five miles an hour on Kirk Road, *both* ways!"

"Did you turn into Hack Road?"

"Naw, that would have been too obvious—I drove past it and turned around, but I took a good look going, and another one coming back!"

"How's the neighborhood?"

"On Hack Road? There *ain't* no neighborhood—that's *Gongaland*! Somebody must of been going to build a subdivision but I guess they ran outta money! Hack Road's half a block long and there's just one house on it—that's *gotta* be number 25!"

"What kind of house?"

"Little white bungalow, stuck back in the trees."

"Trees?"

"It's a *jungle* out there—trees to the north of the house, trees to the south, trees behind it, trees across the street! Hell, except for a couple foundations nobody ever finished, it's *all* trees!"

"Signs of life at 25?"

"Nothing the first time—second time I saw some old woman on the front porch, picking up a newspaper. Who *is* she?"

"Probably the luckiest woman in Ohio—so far."

"So *far*?"

"We're in the eighth inning—we gotta play nine." Lockington took a scratch-pad from a desk drawer, tore off a sheet and wrote rapidly on it. He handed it to Barney. "Call this guy—tell him to meet me here at 1:30 *sharp*—no earlier, no later. Got that?"

"You're *leaving*?"

"I should be back in twenty minutes."

"And then the shit hits the fan?"

"I think so."

Barney grabbed Lockington's arm. "Can I come along on it, Mr. Lockington?" The boy's eyes were beseeching, the eyes of a hungry hound.

Lockington said, "Kid, I wouldn't have it any other way." He meant it.

60 HE'D DRIVEN TO THE HOUSE at the north end of Dunlap Avenue. Natasha's car wasn't in the garage, and he'd anticipated that—the rain hadn't stopped her. Tuesday was Natasha's shopping day, that was etched in granite—to delay it by so much as an hour would have been difficult, to change it impossible, and on Tuesday, October 18, this had been a convenience because Lockington had wanted a handful of spare .38 cartridges and he hadn't wished to alarm her—lately she'd been wound tighter than a mandolin string.

He'd gone into the bedroom, digging into his dresser drawer to half-empty the little cardboard box of .38's into his jacket pocket. Then he'd looked for his Chicago police handcuffs. If General Fedorovich proved uncooperative, Lockington figured on handcuffing the old bastard to a water pipe until he could call in the reserves. No handcuffs. He'd shrugged— well, that was where he'd *thought* he'd last seen them. He'd gone into the kitchen to grab the phone and dial the Day's End number that Steve Dellick had given him. He'd asked for Room 108, and Dellick had answered on the first ring. Lockington had said, "Got him—I think."

Dellick had said, "Got him, you *think*?"

"We've got *some*thing, and it's probably Fedorovich."

"Damn! *That* didn't take long!"

"It took a week, that's long enough."

"Meet at your office?"

"Pronto."

"Flak jackets?"

"I'd think so. Did you bring slickers?"

"Yeah—we'll be there in fifteen minutes."

Lockington had hung up, pausing to peer at Natasha's pile of yellow legal paper on the kitchen table. There'd been

219

activity. Apparently she'd spent part of her morning on the wheels project, but he'd looked at the work sheet that was clear of the stack and the letters hadn't been shifted—*A* had been at 1, *I* at 9, *Q* at 17—no progress. Good. He'd been determined to keep Natasha out of it.

He'd climbed into the Mercedes, heading south. His plan came in three stages, and if it worked smoothly, Gordon Kilbuck would get his interview, Dellick and Addison would get Fedorovich, and Lockington would get drunk in a tavern he hadn't been in before. Lockington frowned. That might be the toughest part of it—finding a tavern he hadn't been in before.

He stopped at the bank.

61 STEVE DELLICK AND FRANK ADDISON came into the plaza parking lot on screeching rubber less than ten minutes after Lockington had returned to his office. He waved them in. He said, "This isn't going to take long." It didn't. Five minutes later, he watched them pull away in Addison's blue Chrysler, Addison at the wheel, Barney the guide in the front seat with Addison, smiling broadly, flashing Lockington an okay sign, Dellick hunched on the rear seat, glowering out at the rain.

Lockington slammed the office door, tilting back in his swivel chair, lighting a cigarette, waiting, watching for Gordon Kilbuck's dark blue Cadillac. It came at exactly 1:30. Lockington watched Kilbuck clamber out of the car, hobbling toward the office through the downpour, his limp more pronounced, his cane bumping on the blacktop. Wet weather's rough on bum hips. Kilbuck came in, shaking rain from his hat, his smile anxious, his muddy eyes feverish with anticipation. He sat on the bench near the window, facing Lockington's desk. There was a slight tremor in the hand holding the cane. He said, "You have something?"

Lockington nodded.

"You've found Fedorovich?"

"We know his probable location."

"'*We*,' did you say?"

"You and I—it's likely that he's living with Olga Karelinko in a lightly populated area west of here."

"Olga Karelinko—that'll be the woman with the post office box, the one I told you about."

"Right—Olga was Fedorovich's junior high school girl friend."

Kilbuck grinned from ear to ear. "Oh, *God*, isn't that *romantic*? What a note to finish my book on—the aging

221

Russian general and the sweetheart of his teens, together again—so many years, so many tears, so many miles—home is the sailor, home from the sea, and the hunter home from—"

Lockington said, "Don't get carried away, Kilbuck—we aren't sure that Fedorovich will even open the fucking *door*!"

"But, he *has* to—after all our effort, he simply *has* to!"

"Don't bet the barn on it."

"If I can just *talk* to him for a minute—I can be *very* persuasive! Good Lord, Lockington, Alexi Fedorovich is a living *legend*—why, they say that he killed at *least fifty* German soldiers, more than *half* of them in hand-to-hand combat—cold *steel*! They say that he was known as 'The Lion of Stalingrad'!"

"*Who* says that?"

Kilbuck's smile was a lame thing. "Stuff I've read on him from time to time—old Russian periodicals, articles from *Pravda*—things like that."

"Written before he hit the bricks, of course—by now he'll be the biggest coward in Soviet history. You read Russian?"

"No, this was translated copy—New York City's main library has *acres* of it on microfilm—it dates back beyond 1940. Believe me, I've made a thorough study of Fedorovich, and I can't *believe* that I'm about to *meet* the man! Fedorovich would have had a monument built in his *honor*!"

Lockington left the desk. "Let's roll—you're driving."

Kilbuck got to his feet. "Good—then I won't have to transfer my things."

"*What* things?"

"My attaché case and my tape recorder—you can't conduct an interview without a tape recorder. Do you know precisely where we're going?"

"If I did, *I'd* drive." They went out, getting into the Cadillac. The rain was letting up, there were jagged streaks of copper on the western skyline. Lockington motioned for a left turn on Meridian Road. Kilbuck was cramped forward over the wheel, looking for all the world like a praying mantis with a bellyache, Lockington thought. They swung west on Kirk Road. Kilbuck said, "How far?"

"I don't know exactly—when we get there, we'll stop."

At the Raccoon Road traffic signal Kilbuck said, "Are you armed?"

Lockington said, "Yeah—why?"

"Well, isn't it possible that the KGB will make an appearance?"

"It's possible that the KGB has *already* made an appearance." He checked his watch. They'd be deployed now—Steve Dellick in the trees behind the house, Frank Addison in the trees across the street, having reached their positions from east and west, undetected, he hoped. Barney would be waiting in Addison's Chrysler, watching for the arrival of Kilbuck's Cadillac, ready to seal off Hack Road.

They crossed Route 46 and Lockington said, "We're close now—slow down."

The Hack Road sign was readable from a half-block away, jutting from the weeds at a forty-five degree angle, badly in need of paint. Lockington signaled for Kilbuck to turn south on Hack and Kilbuck rolled the Cadillac into the narrow, rutted, dead-end street. Lockington spotted Addison's blue Chrysler at the side of the road, a block to the west, beginning to move east. Kilbuck pulled to a halt in front of the only house in sight. He turned to Lockington. "Apparently, this is it."

Lockington nodded, studying the tiny white bungalow surrounded by trees. "Helluva change for Fedorovich, wouldn't you think? No bands, no uniforms, no May Day parades, no hoopla, no prestige."

Kilbuck made a wry face. "Well, I'm not sure that those things would be important to him now. There's a verse of an old poem that says it so well. Care to hear it?"

Lockington said, "I doubt it."

Kilbuck gave it to him anyway:

"When all the world is old, lad,
And all the trees are brown;
And all the sport is stale, lad,
And all the wheels run down;
Creep home and take your place there,
The spent and maimed among:
God grant you find one face there
You loved when all was young!"

Lockington squinted across the spacious front seat of the Cadillac. "Did *you* write that?"

Kilbuck shook his head. "No, but I wish I had. Touching, isn't it?"

"Yes—where did you get it?"

"It's from something by Charles Kingsley, an English clergyman—a Socialist, by the way."

Lockington said, "Okay," willing to let the matter rest. He'd never heard of Charles Kingsley. The rain had stopped, its darkness traveling east.

Gordon Kilbuck was saying, "And isn't that how it's gone for Alexi Fedorovich? He's an old man now, it's all behind him, his heroics, his strategies—what's left but to come home?"

"Kilbuck, you're a rank sentimentalist."

Kilbuck had taken out a handkerchief, wiping his eyes, blowing his nose. He said, "I know it. So are you, but you *don't* know it." Lockington said nothing. "That verse would make one helluva windup for my book, don't you agree?"

Lockington said, "I can't say—I haven't read your book."

62 THEY LEFT KILBUCK'S CADDY, walking toward the house. There was no walkway, just quack grass. Lockington said, "Better let me take the point."

"It's all yours. Lockington, would you carry my attaché case, please? It's confoundedly heavy—notebooks, a ream of blank paper." Lockington accepted the case, walking ahead, Kilbuck bringing up the rear, lugging the big tape recorder, the tip of his cane making little sucking sounds when it was tugged from the wet ground. Lockington mounted the sagging front steps to the weatherbeaten front porch, turning to lend Kilbuck a hand. Kilbuck muttered, "Thanks."

Lockington saw no doorbell button, and he knocked lightly on the glass of the battered aluminum storm door. There was no response. They waited, exchanging glances. Lockington knocked again, louder this time. The inner door swung open just a crack. A woman's voice said, "Yes, what is it?"

Lockington said, "I beg your pardon, ma'am, but are you Olga Karelinko?"

"Yes, what do you want?"

"Miss Karelinko, my name is Lacey Lockington, and I have with me a nationally-known writer of biographies who is doing a book on General Alexi Fedorovich. He's been a long-time admirer of the general, and he'd be grateful if he could be granted a short interview."

There was a lengthy silence. Then from a distance a male voice called, "It'll be all right, Olga—permit them to come in."

The door opened slowly. He swung the storm door toward him, stepping into the living room of the little house, Gordon Kilbuck on his heels, breathing heavily.

The room was tidy, stuffy, dim. It was furnished in old,

comfortable pieces—a huge blue velvet-covered sofa resting on highly varnished mahogany lion's paws, an overstuffed chair with a rumpled flowered throw, a worn but solid-looking platform-rocker, a small wooden table on which rested a blue-shaded lamp and a black telephone, the dial type. Lockington saw no television set, just a Zenith cabinet model radio, circa 1940. There were a few pictures on the walls, one of a wolf sitting on a hilltop overlooking a village, another of a bony, aging Indian astride a spavined pony. Lockington recognized the picture of the Indian—*The End of the Trail*. Appropriate, he thought.

The door had closed behind them and an elderly buxom woman in a floor-length brown chenille robe said, "General Fedorovich is in his study." Her eyes were red and swollen—she'd been drunk or she'd been crying, or both. She was gesturing toward an open doorway to their left. Lockington said, "Thank you, ma'am," crossing the blue carpeted living room to enter the study. Kilbuck following closely.

There was a desk cluttered with papers, maps, and books, a padded swivel chair in better condition than Lockington's, a two-seat leather sofa, a floor lamp, and a large rocking chair in which sat an angular, rawboned, craggy-faced, silver-haired man, a gray afghan over his lap and legs—the great one at last, hero and prey. Lockington stared at him speechlessly. The man's thin-lipped smile curled over even tobacco-stained teeth. He extended his hand.

"Mr. Lockington, I know of you—I've heard nothing but good about you."

Lockington shook the hand. "General, I wasn't aware that you'd heard *any*thing about me."

Kilbuck had nodded to General Fedorovich, propping his cane against the desk, seating himself on the leather couch. He placed his tape recorder on the floor to his right, his attaché case between his feet. His hands were at the snaps of the attaché case when he turned to face the doorway, freezing in that position, his muddy eyes wide. A woman stood just inside the study. She wore a gray water-repellent jacket, gray slacks, and blue jogging shoes. She held a Mikoyan snub-nosed .32 pistol in her hand, its hammer cocked, its barrel directed unwaveringly at Gordon Kilbuck's chest. Her eyes were pale blue ice, her voice was splintered flint. She said, "When you open your attaché case, do it *slowly*, please."

63

GORDON KILBUCK'S FACE HAD BLANCHED to the color of wood ashes. "But there's nothing *in* it—just notebooks and spare paper—I can show you."

Natasha said, "Do that, please—open it and turn it over."

Kilbuck complied, spilling notebooks and paper onto the floor.

Lockington said, "Natasha—"

She waved him to silence, motioning to Kilbuck with her left hand. "On your feet—we're going for a walk." Kilbuck got up from the couch, groping for his cane. Natasha said, "Leave it, you won't be needing it." She pointed to the door, circling behind Kilbuck to pick up his tape recorder, following him toward the living room. Kilbuck gasped, "No, Natasha, *pukzhahlstuh!*"

She shook her head. "Turn, and I will shoot you between the eyes—run, and I will shoot you in the back of the head."

Lockington started after them. General Fedorovich held up a detaining hand. He said, "No, Mr. Lockington, this is a Russian matter—let Russians settle it." His afghan was on the floor next to his chair. There was a revolver in his lap. The old man had been ready. He still was.

The front door was creaking open, the storm door banging shut. Olga Karelinko tottered to the couch, seating herself there, shaking uncontrollably. General Fedorovich looked at Lockington. "As you say here in America, 'You win a few, you lose a few'."

Lockington managed a tight smile. "I thought that might be a Russian saying."

"In Russia, it differs somewhat—in Russia you win a few and you lose but *once*."

The front door slammed and Natasha came into the study.

She closed the door behind her, leaning against it. She said, "Now we'll learn if it was or if it wasn't."

There was quiet in the room, thick, nearly tangible. Then, from the road came high-pitched hoarse-voiced shouts— "*Puhmuhghat mnawyoo! Puhmuhghat mnawyoo!*" Olga Karelinko buried her face in her hands, sobbing audibly. Fedorovich plucked absent-mindedly at a bit of lint on his trousers leg. Lockington started to speak, then thought better of it. Natasha Gorky's shoulders were against the closed study door. She stared at the ceiling, her face expressionless.

The blast blew Natasha away from the door, halfway across the room where Lockington caught her. She looked up at him, smiling, her pale blue eyes bright. She said, "It *was!*"

General Fedorovich placed his revolver on a table to his left. He said, "All right, Mr. Lockington, you may go out now if you wish."

64 LOCKINGTON LEFT THE STUDY. The living room window had been shattered and the floor was a sparkling sea of broken glass. The pictures were off the walls, the telephone stand lamp was on the sofa, the overstuffed chair had been upended. Lockington waded through the wreckage, stepping on the front door which had departed its hinges. He stumbled onto the porch, skidding to a stop there. Gordon Kilbuck's blue Cadillac was a searing pond of orange flame, its roof half-gone, its windshield and trunk lid missing. Its doors had sailed twenty-five feet from the car in either direction. Barney Kozlowski was standing on the west side of Hack Road, motioning urgently to Lockington. Lockington waved back, leaping from the porch, shielding his face against the intense heat, skirting the blazing vehicle. Barney's face was pale, his eyes were unbelieving saucers. "My God, Mr. Lockington, I *saw* it—I saw *all* of it!"

"Take it easy, kid—*all* of it—all of *what*?"

Barney was struggling to collect himself. He said, "She brought him out of the house at gunpoint and she made him get into the car! She handcuffed him to the steering wheel. Then she picked up a big tape recorder and shoved it into the back seat and slammed the door, and when she went back into the house she didn't bother looking back! He was trying to break loose and then he started screaming—Holy Christ, they must of heard him in *Cleveland*! By that time I was running down here, but the Goddamned car blew up—the explosion knocked me flat on my ass! He's *in* there, what's left of him— if there's *anything*! What *caused* it?"

Lockington was tight-lipped. "Offhand, I'd say about five pounds of Czech plastic explosive in the tape recorder, probably on a sixty second timer wired to the play-record

230

switch. Try to put it out of your mind, kid." He grabbed
Barney by the arm, turning him toward Kirk Road, pushing
him in that direction.

Barney said, "Who *was* she?"

"I wasn't acquainted with *this* one—let's get back to
Youngstown."

"*How?* That ain't my car!"

Lockington said, "No problem—we'll just borrow it."

"But how are *they* gonna get back?"

They were getting into Frank Addison's blue Chrysler.
Lockington said, "Well, son, that's *their* problem, ain't it?"

Dellick and Addison had come pounding out of the trees.
Addison was waving his arms and hollering. As he drove east,
Lockington shoved his left hand out of the window, holding
it above the Chrysler's roof, clenching his fist, extending his
middle finger upward, wiggling it.

65 IN THE PARKING LOT of the Mahoning Avenue
Shopping Plaza Lockington turned to Barney
who was swallowing hard. "You gonna get sick,
kid?"

"No, but I came mighty close!"

Lockington said, "Look, they all don't turn out this way."

"What percentage, would you say?"

"Maybe less than fifty."

"How *much* less than fifty?"

"Not a helluva lot."

Barney said, "Jesus *Christ!*"

Lockington said, "You still wanta be a P.I.?"

"You think the CIA might be better?"

"Boy, *anything* would be better."

"How about the FBI?"

"There ain't that much difference. You got a college degree?"

"No."

"Then come down to earth and *get* one—criminal justice,
political science, crap like that."

"If I get a degree would I be accepted?"

Lockington said, "You get your degree and apply, and I'll
call in a few markers. If that don't work, I'll *blackmail* some
sonofabitch. *You'll be accepted!*"

"It costs something like ten grand to come out of
Youngstown State with a degree! Where am I gonna get ten
grand?"

Lockington reached for Barney's hamlike right hand,
turning it palm upward. He slammed a sheaf of bills into it.
"There's a good piece of it—I'm splitting my fee with you—
you busted the case."

Barney stared down at the money, blinking. He mumbled,
"Can I do something else for you, Mr. Lockington?"

Lockington said, "One thing."

"*Name* it!"

"It's pushing dinner time. Take your old man out for a steak." He started the engine. Barney got out, closing the door. Lockington drove to a plaza exit. Before he turned east on Mahoning Avenue he checked his rear-view mirror. Barney Kozlowski was standing in the parking lot, wiping his eyes with one hand, waving so long with the other.

Lockington tooted the horn.

66 HE HADN'T TAKEN THE TROUBLE to drive into the Flamingo Lounge parking lot. He'd left Frank Addison's blue Chrysler on Mahoning in front of the Flamingo and a no-parking sign. He was sitting at the bar talking baseball with John Sebulsky when Addison and Dellick came in. Lockington didn't turn, he watched their approach in the backbar mirror. Addison slapped a hand on Lockington's shoulder, spinning him around. He said, "How would you like to go to jail for automobile theft?"

Lockington said, "How would you like to wear your teeth for a necklace?"

"Taking off with my car was absolutely un*called* for!"

"I've had a bad day, Addison—don't fuck with me."

John Sebulsky was staring at Steve Dellick. He said, "By the way, if this comes to fisticuffs, *your* ass belongs to *me*."

Dellick glanced at Addison. Out of a corner of his mouth he said, "Better cool it, Frank."

Addison shrugged. "Yeah, what the hell." He pitched a twenty dollar bill onto the bar, motioning to John Sebulsky. "Can we get a pair of Buds and a double Martell's in a booth?"

Sebulsky nodded and they retired to a booth. Sebulsky brought the drinks and Addison's change. Addison said, "What the hell made you run off like that?"

"Habit of mine—I always leave when the show's over."

Dellick said, "Helluva show."

Lockington shrugged. "I liked *Lawrence of Arabia* better—not as much noise but the cast had class."

Addison said, "Lockington, you're pissed about something."

"Aw, I wouldn't say that—why should I be pissed? After all, everybody's played it straight with me, haven't they?"

Dellick said, "It was all in the game—there were a few things you couldn't be told—you'd have lost your effectiveness."

Addison said, "She drove us here—her car was on the next block east."

Dellick said, "Hell, Lockington, she was just doing her job."

"Well, she sure got it done—damned miracle she didn't blow the roof off the fucking Mahoning County Courthouse!"

Dellick said, "No matter—she *nailed* that sonofabitch! Hey, this Foxfire, she's a *world*beater!"

"'Foxfire'—you call her 'Foxfire'?"

Addison said, "That's right—in the spring she was coded 'Pigeon', now she's 'Foxfire.' What do you call her at home?"

"Too early to say—I ain't home yet."

Dellick said, "We invited her in for a drink but she said she had to go shopping."

Lockington said, "Yeah, *Tuesday*, y'know."

Addison said, "Massey told Carruthers to coax her out of retirement. She told Carruthers that she'd help on just this one case."

"Why just this one case—why didn't she agree to overthrow Castro and bomb the fucking South Pole?"

Dellick said, "Why the South Pole—what's at the South Pole?"

Lockington said, "I'll let you know—I'll be there by midnight."

Dellick waved for a round and Sebulsky delivered it. Addison said, "Well, anyway, Lockington, you did real good!"

Dellick said, "Yeah, I got a hunch you knew how it was going to play all along."

"Sure, I just strung it out to make it interesting."

Addison said, "There's a parking ticket on my windshield. Who's gonna pay it?"

Lockington said, "Get it fixed—you're a Youngstown cop, you told me."

67

SHE WAS WAITING FOR HIM at the living room door. She said, "My God, are you ever *drunk!*"

"I found a tavern I haven't been in before."

She tried to kiss him but he grabbed her, holding her away from him. "Madame Foxfire, is it?"

Natasha stared at him, snapping, "Don't manhandle me, Lacey!"

Lockington snarled, "Don't *manhandle* you? That was the most ruthless, coldblooded, merciless fucking execution I've *ever* run into—and with *my* handcuffs yet!" He released her, permitting her to lean against the living room closet door.

"If Gordon Kilbuck's tape recorder hadn't been loaded, there'd have *been* no ruthless, coldblooded, merciless fucking execution, with *your* handcuffs yet!"

"The man deserved a fair trial!"

"A trial for Gordon *Kilbuck*—on what *grounds*—what would the *charges* have been—what could have been *established*—where was the hard *evidence*? Lacey, you were a Chicago police detective—you know the courts! Tell me, would he have been *convicted*?"

Lockington shook his head slowly, simmering down. He said, "Never."

She pressed her advantage. "Kilbuck murdered Abigail Fleugelham, he murdered Candice Hoffman, he murdered Brenda Willoughby, he murdered Cayuse Bresnahan, he was highly instrumental in the murder of *Cy* Willoughby! He was about to finish the job—he'd have begun to interview General Fedorovich, he'd have activated his tape recorder, he'd have remembered something he'd left in his car, he'd have gone out to get it, and he'd have been on Kirk Road when the house was reduced to *toothpicks!* Olga Karelinko would be dead, so would General Fedorovich, so would Lacey Lockington! The

236

explosion would have been attributed to a gas leak in the basement, and you're talking about a fair trial for *Gordon Kilbuck*? Not to *me*, you aren't!" She flew at Lockington like a jungle cat, throwing her arms around his neck, kissing him until their teeth clicked together. Then she stepped back. She said, "What about Natasha Gorky—does *she* get a hearing?"

Lockington shrugged. "Why the hell not?"

She took his hand. "Let's go down to the courtroom."

68

THEY WERE SEATED at the basement bar, vodka in front of Natasha, cognac in front of Lockington. He said, "When did you get out to Hack Road?"

"Shortly after ten this morning, about twenty minutes after I'd experimented with Barney Kozlowski's idea. The wheels *turned*—that simplified things."

"I came home after you'd left. I looked at your wheels and everything was at the first position—I saw no signs that you'd accomplished anything."

"That's because there were seventeen footnote numbers requiring sixteen clicks of the wheels. Sixteen clicks rotated the wheels *twice*, returning them to their points of origin. I must do something for Barney Kozlowski!"

"I've already done something for him—I've given him half my fee. You were waiting on Hack Road, knowing that we'd come?"

"No, my primary purpose was to alert the general and attempt to persuade him to return to CIA protection, but I'd sketched a plan, just in case. Then you arrived, and I waited in the kitchen."

Lockington said, "The general was solid, Olga Karelinko flew to pieces like a seven dollar watch."

"Her daughter had been murdered—Olga wasn't tempered at Stalingrad. I request permission to address the court."

Lockington growled, "Granted."

She smiled her bewitching lopsided smile, winking at him. She had him now and she knew it. So did Lockington. She said, "Lacey, *Krahsny Lentuh* sentenced General Fedorovich to death, *not* because of his book—there was nothing of great import in it, it amounted to maybes, and *what ifs*—he was condemned simply because he'd *defected*."

238

"*You* defected, didn't you?"

"Yes, and so have countless others, but we're small fry—Gen. Alexi Fedorovich was *prominent*, he was a *name!*"

"And *Krahsny Lentuh* turned the execution over to Gordon Kilbuck, or whatever his name was."

"Totski—Georgi Totski. I knew him in Dzerzhinsky Square at the KGB Academy. If you'd mentioned that Gordon Kilbuck smoked a pipe and carried a cane, he'd have been dead a week ago. Totski was excellent at chess, probably the academy's best. He played a waiting game, looking for a mistake, as he did with you."

"And I made a dozen."

"No, you overlooked a few points, but you made only one mistake—that was when you took him to General Fedorovich. Fortunately, that was—well, *rectified*, shall we say?"

"With a bang."

"I'd think that Totski followed you to Princeton Junior High School, going in a few seconds after you came out, asking the same questions you'd asked, getting the same answers. He called Abilgail Fleugelham before you got to her, the next night he took her out for a few drinks, receiving her usual proposition. He accepted and strangled her, thereby shutting off that spigot of information before it leaked again. He'd learned that the Karelinko family had moved out of the Princeton district, and after chatting with Abigail, he suspected the reason for the move."

"All right, what was the reason?"

"Olga Karelinko was pregnant by Alexi Fedorovich!"

Lockington thought about it, nodding. "Yeah, back in those days, abortions weren't a dime a dozen."

Natasha said, "True, and an unmarried pregnant daughter was a catastrophic family disgrace. The Karelinkos moved to the North Side of Youngstown, representing Olga as a child bride whose husband had fallen down an elevator shaft. In such cases, any old story will do—nobody believes it, but it's better than no story at all."

"If Totski guessed that she was pregnant, then he knew that the child would have been born in late '38 or early '39."

"Yes. He probably hit the Mahoning County microfilm banks, learning that a Candice Karelinko had been born in January of '39, mother: Olga Karelinko, widow."

"It was getting easier."

"Certainly, just add another dash of arithmetic—Candice would have been eighteen years old in 1957. Totski made a tour of Youngstown's high schools, probably by telephone, learning that a Candice Karelinko had graduated from Rayen High School on Youngstown's North Side—June, '57."

Lockington said, "I'm looking more stupid by the minute."

Natasha shook her head. "Not at *all*—you'd already *found* Candice—you knew *where* she was, but not *who* she was, Totski knew *who* she was, but not *where* she was."

"He found her."

"Yes, he worked rapidly and hard, and locating Candice was a relatively simple matter. There'd be dozens of fiftyish Youngstown North Siders who'd remember Candice Karelinko, that she married a boy named Richard Hoffman in 1958, that she gave birth to a daughter, Brenda, in 1959. The Youngstown telephone directory shows a Richard Hoffman at 24 North Brockway Avenue—Richard is dead, but Candice never got around to changing the listing."

"And Totski closed in on her."

"There's no telling what ruse he used to get into the house—an inheritance settlement, perhaps; that usually opens a door in a hurry. At any rate, there he was, alone with Olga Karelinko's *daughter*, a woman who knew Olga's whereabouts—he was one short step away from Gen. Alexi Fedorovich!"

"And Candice clammed up."

"Undoubtedly. Candice knew her mother's situation, she'd been aiding in keeping the general and Olga undercover. Lacey, have you noticed that the most *patient* people have *violent* tempers? They don't surface quickly, but when they do—"

Lockington said, "It's 'Good morning, John, I brought your saddle home'."

"Exactly! Georgi Totski was a patient men, he *had* to be, but when he was thwarted mere inches short of General Fedorovich, it was more than he could handle. Something snapped, and he beat Candice Hoffman to death with his cane."

Lockington was refilling their glasses. "Totski recognized you—he called you by name. You were classmates at the KGB Academy?"

"Not classmates—I was a cadet, Georgi Totski was an instructor."

Lockington threw up his hands. "Wait a minute—don't tell me, let me guess! He was one of your sex course teachers!"

Natasha smiled, not her Sunday smile, just a run-of-the-mill smile—it wasn't even lopsided.

"No, Georgi was an expert on subversive activities—his specialty was packing tape recorders with Czech plastic explosive."

69 LOCKINGTON SAID, "How did you manage to put all of this together?"

"I didn't *have* to put it together—I had a long talk with Olga Karelinko this morning. What she couldn't tell me was easily filled in."

"What about Brenda Willoughby—how did Totski track her? There was brief mention of Candice Hoffman's death, but beyond that, the media had nothing to say."

"Totski didn't *track* her, he did what *you* did—he *waited* for her at Sabatini's Funeral Home. You knew where the wake was to be held, Totski *didn't*, so he called a few undertakers, ascertaining that it'd be at Sabatini's. He knew that there'd been a daughter, Brenda, and discreet inquiry from an 'uncle' or a 'nephew' revealed that she'd be in attendance, also that Candice's ex-son-in-law was out of town on a trucking run, that he was unaware of the tragedy, but that he'd be notified at the Mohawk West trucking terminal in Chicago, and that it was hoped that he'd be on hand for the second night of the wake. This last bit of intelligence spelled the end of Cy Willoughby—Totski relayed it to Ivan Leonid in Chicago."

"All of that information from a hired hand at a funeral home?"

"Oh, yes, that and more, and *not* from a hired hand. It came from Mario Sabatini himself. Mario is the most obligingly garrulous man I've ever talked to."

"You called him?"

"Immediately after you left for Candice Hoffman's wake. I was a 'cousin' from Cleveland—'Celeste Goldensnatch'."

"'*Copper*snatch' would have been closer to the truth."

"That's nobody's business but *yours*. There'd been calls from other relatives, he told me—Totski and Cayuse Bresnahan, of course. Totski drove to Sabatini's but he couldn't afford to be seen—you were there ahead of him. He was locking all doors behind him—he figured that you'd already acquired the pertinent information, so he killed her, assuming that all he'd have to do would be keep an eye on *you*, which he was doing, I assure you! I'll venture to say that at least half a dozen private investigations agencies had operatives following you!"

"One of 'em in a black pickup truck with Pennsylvania plates."

"Why not? We're just sixty miles from Pittsburgh. Your every move was known to Totski."

"Well, why all the convoluted bullshit? Why didn't he just hire those agencies to find Olga, and leave me alone?"

"He was confident that you'd get to her in due time. There were numerous links between Totski and *you*, but only one between Totski and *Olga*—it's easier to kill one man than to wipe out the personnel of several private investigations concerns. Totski didn't intend to leave a discernible trail—that's in keeping with KGB policy."

"It was Totski who shot at us in Mill Creek Park—that goes without saying."

"Of course—you had that one right, 'an excellent shot pretending to be a lousy shot'—a ploy to divert suspicion from himself. Who'd pay a man five thousand dollars, then try to kill him before he'd done his job?"

"And then he murdered Cayuse Bresnahan."

"Yes, Totski spotted Bresnahan before Bresnahan spotted Totski. 'Cayuse Bresnahan' was 'Igor Shawtnik,' really. He was one of two *Mawlniyuh* operatives assigned to this matter. He, too, had checked with Sabatini's, and he'd attempted to arrange protection for Cy Willoughby in Chicago. He failed in that obviously, and Willoughby may have given Ivan Leonid Olga's address, but he was assassinated before he could report to Totski. We had a standoff there."

"'*We?*' '*One of two Mawlniyuh operatives assigned to this matter?*' Who was the other?"

Natasha Gorky sipped vodka, making no reply.

Lockington spun on his barstool. "God *damn* it, Natasha, *level* with me just *once*, will you? You were on *two* payrolls— you were working for the CIA *and Mawlniyuh*, weren't you?"

She hesitated. Then she said, "Back in June, that was my *real* deal with the KGB—return to Youngstown, find Alexi Fedorovich and try to protect him from *Krahsny Lentuh*— this in return for a clean bill of health. I accepted, Lacey— I accepted for my own happiness! Does that make me a whore?"

"The KGB knew that Fedorovich was going to head for Youngstown, that early in the game?"

"It was a foregone conclusion in Moscow *and* at Langley— the general would be coming home."

"*Mawlniyuh* has that kind of authority—it can cook up a swap like that on its own?"

"Absolutely! *Mawlniyuh is* the KGB, it's the *backbone* of the organization!"

"Okay, but why protect Fedorovich, a traitor by Moscow standards?"

"A traitor under Stalin and Khrushchev and Malenkov and Brezhnev and Andropov, yes, but the *Gorbachev* Kremlin doesn't want to make waves. The assassination of Alexi Fedorovich on American soil would create negative impressions. General Fedorovich has seen his day, he's an old man, useless now to the Soviet military, dangerous to no one. The scenario offered in *The Wheels of Treachery* is purely hypothetical, he's done no irreparable damage, and considering the fact that détente's at high tide, that Russia is shedding a dictatorial doctrine, about to become this planet's largest democracy, the Kremlin is willing to leave well enough alone."

"Russia—a *democracy?*"

"That's the way the wind blows."

After a snort of cognac, and another, Lockington said, "So *now* what?"

Natasha said nothing at all.

"That doesn't answer my question."

Natasha repeated her silence.

That was how Lockington learned that more was coming.

70

THE BASEMENT SILENCE WAS AWESOME—it could have been sliced for sandwiches. Then Natasha said, "Lacey, there's one more thing."

"What pure delights this life would bring, if there wasn't *always* 'one more thing'."

Natasha squinted at him. "*Where* in the *hell* did you get *that*?"

"Socrates."

"Socrates didn't write washroom jingles."

"Then it may have been Plato or Aristophanes."

"Neither did they."

"Tell me about the one more thing."

"Yes, well, you see, Lacey, no KGB agents have ever worked under their own names. For instance, Gordon Kilbuck, alias Georgi Totski, was really Nikanov Chusawf, and Cayuse Bresnahan alias Igor Shawtnik, was really Joseph Dawzhy." Her voice was small and shrinking.

Lockington said, "And your real name isn't Gorky—it's Dostoevsky."

"No, it's Fedorovich."

Lockington cleared his throat to say something and he'd have said it, if he could have thought of it.

Natasha's pale blue eyes were brimming with tears. "Gen. Alexi Fedorovich is my father." Her voice broke. "I'm his second child, his second daughter—I haven't seen him since my mother's funeral seven years ago—it was raining on that morning—"

Lockington shrugged a silent shrug, unable to reach her.

Natasha said, "He was trying to establish contact with me through our old wheels code—I knew that he'd been born here—he always spoke so affectionately of Youngstown—he said that he hoped to return some day. He assumed that I knew he would."

"And *that's* why we're in Youngstown."

"Well, Lacey, what would *you* have done?"

"I'd have come to Youngstown."

Natasha's eyes were bright. She said, "The house next door—it's been vacant—the CIA will buy it tomorrow."

"For your father."

"Yes, it wants me to look after him."

Lockington said, "All right, we'll look after him."

Natasha grabbed Lockington's shoulders. "He won't be a burden, Lacey, *honest*! He's financially well-off, he's the independent type—my father leans on *no* one!"

Lockington said, "He was *born* in Youngstown, he *liked* Youngstown, but he came back to 'do right by Nell'."

"Nell?"

"You know her as 'Olga Karelinko'."

"Yes—I see. They hadn't forgotten each other—they've lost their daughter and their granddaughter, but they're so *happy* together! Oh, Lacey, it's *beautiful*!"

"Sure is—bring on the string section, swell to crescendo, fade to—"

Natasha was slipping from her barstool. "Would you like to go to bed?"

"Your ESP is functioning just dandy."

"The court's verdict?"

"Case dismissed—the judge pleads insanity."

71 THE LATE OCTOBER NIGHT was crisp and starstrewn. Natasha had gone next door to give Olga a hand with whatever it was that women need a hand with. Lockington sat on the bench at the rear of the property, the forest at his back, smoking, watching the old man come down the slope, silhouetted against the white of the house. He slid over, making room on the bench, and General Fedorovich sat beside him. Lockington said, "Good evening, sir."

Fedorovich's gnarled hand descended upon Lockington's left shoulder. "Beautiful night, Mr. Lockington."

"Yes, a fine night, sir."

Fedorovich accepted a cigarette and Lockington held a match for them. Fedorovich said, "You've been kind to my daughter, Mr. Lockington. I thank you for that."

"Being kind to your daughter isn't difficult, sir."

"She's a fine girl."

"The very finest, sir."

They didn't speak for a minute or so. Then Fedorovich said, "Mr. Lockington, can you understand why a man would travel halfway around the world to reach Youngstown, Ohio?"

"Yes, sir, I believe I can."

Their second silence outlasted their first. Fedorovich's head was tilted back. He was gazing at stars. After a while he said,

> "When all the world is old, lad,
> And all the trees are brown,
> And all the sport is stale, lad,
> And all the wheels run down . . ."

Lockington said, "Creep home and take your place there . . ."
Fedorovich said, "The spent and maimed among . . ."

Lockington said, "God grant you find one face there..."

Fedorovich said, "You loved when all was young."

There was a third silence before Fedorovich said, "I've been fortunate, Mr. Lockington—I've managed to *do* that."

"Yes, sir, I know that you have."

The general was studying Lockington. "I'm surprised that you know Charles Kingsley's poem."

"Not all of it, sir—I just happened to hear a few lines recently."

"I memorized it when I attended Princeton Junior High School. Then I learned that Charles Kingsley is well received in the Soviet Union. He was a radical Socialist, y'know."

"Yes, so I've heard, sir. That may have been responsible for his Russian popularity."

From the rear of the house next door, a woman's voice floated on the still night air. "Al—Al, are you out there?"

Fedorovich called, "Yes, Olga."

"Are you wearing a sweater, Al?"

"No, Olga."

"Come into the house this very *moment*! It's *cold* tonight!"

Fedorovich got up from the bench. He said, "Good night, Mr. Lockington."

"Good night, sir." Lockington watched the old man go. He smiled. Al. The Lion of Stalingrad.

Natasha was standing at the top of the slope, looking down at Lockington. She said, "You, too."